THE DERBYSHIRE DETECTIVE

PETER YATES

First published in Great Britain in 2026 by Spiral Books
an imprint of Spiral Publishing Ltd

1 3 5 7 9 10 8 6 4 2

Spiral Publishing, 38 Pulla Hill Drive,
Storrington, West Sussex RH20 3LS
Edited by Martin Cooper

email: jonathan@spiralpublishing.com
www.spiral-books.com

ISBN 978-1-0685670-9-4

British Library Cataloguing in Publication Data.
A catalogue record for this book is available from the British Library.

Printed and bound in England by 4edge Limited,
22 Eldon Way Industrial Estate, Hockley, Essex SS5 4AD

BUXTON POLICE STATION HIERARCHY

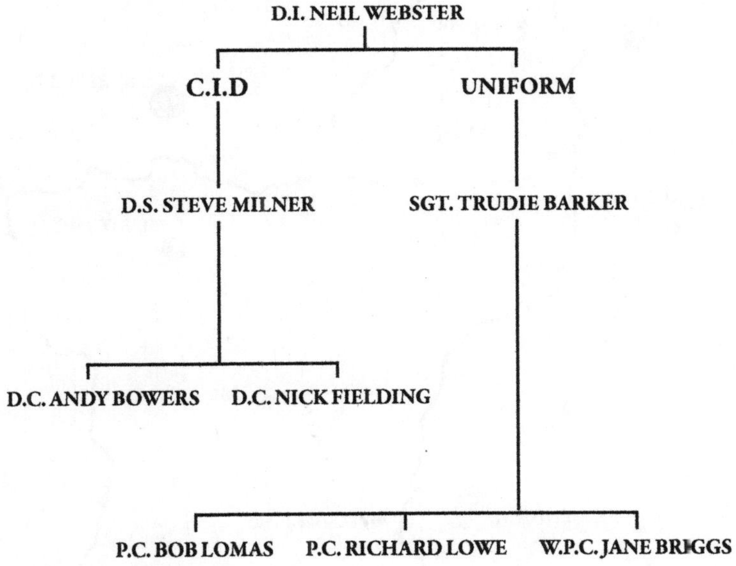

DERBYSHIRE

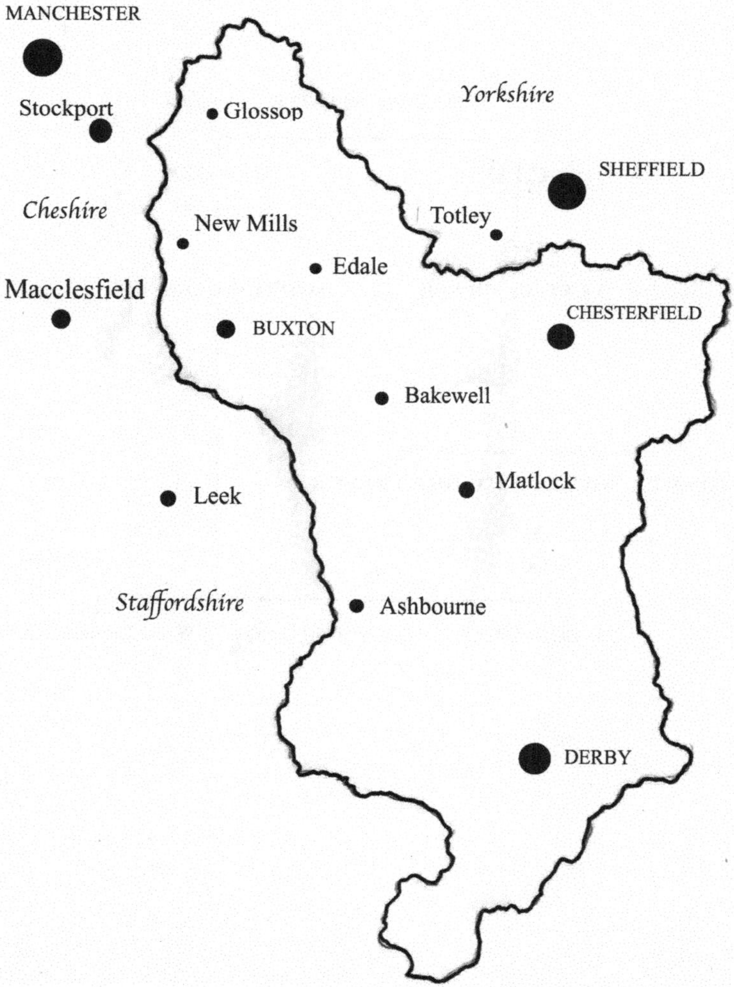
MANCHESTER
Stockport
Glossop
Yorkshire
SHEFFIELD
Cheshire
New Mills
Totley
Edale
Macclesfield
BUXTON
CHESTERFIELD
Bakewell
Matlock
Leek
Staffordshire
Ashbourne
DERBY

CHAPTER ONE

It was a rotten day – blustery, wet and cold. The virtually deserted streets that Monday morning in early April bore testimony to it. A deep Atlantic depression that had swept in over the weekend had battered the north of the country catching many people out, especially the forecasters.

A little way from the town centre was the police station and even *it* seemed to have the hatches battened down. Tucked inside, out of the elements, PC Bob Lomas was settling in at the front desk with his first cuppa of the day and casting his eye over a headline in the morning paper heralding a successful satellite launch, an event that is hardly newsworthy these days but this was 1965 when the space race was just beginning and things like that were big news. He knew it would only be a matter of time before something came along to interrupt his enjoyment and the ringing of the front desk phone was it. He put his cup down and picked up the receiver.

"Buxton police station," he said cheerily.

"Can you help me please?" replied the caller, who was clearly anxious.

"Well I'll certainly try," Bob answered. "What name is it?"

"Mrs Evelyn Rhodes."

"And what seems to be the problem, Mrs Rhodes?"

"It's my daughter. She went hiking with some friends this weekend and they were supposed to be back last night, but there's been no sign of them. I've checked with the other families and they've not heard anything either." Bob glanced at the rain hitting the window of the front office.

"Right, Mrs Rhodes – and what's your daughter's name?"

"Denise." The immediacy of her reply highlighted just how het up she was. "They're all 16 and in the same class at school. I really am getting very worried. I'm sure she would have contacted us if she wasn't going to be back."

"Where were they going?" Bob enquired.

"Edale. We live near New Mills and they caught the train on Saturday morning but I don't know what exactly they'd got planned. I know they're teenagers but Denise isn't stupid and they've camped up there together a few times before."

Bob was starting to feel a twinge of concern but at this stage he felt that reassurance was the order of the day. "Well with the weather how it's been the past 24 hours, Mrs Rhodes, they've most likely found somewhere to shelter and not been able to get to a phone."

That was certainly his hope but he wasn't going to leave things at that. "What I'll do is give them a call over there now and see what I can find out. I'll ring you back as soon as I can."

"You will, won't you?"

Bob had teenage children of his own and knew exactly how she must be feeling. "Yep, just give me half an hour or so."

He took her number, put the receiver down and started thumbing through a directory on the desk. He soon found what he was looking for: Edale youth hostel and the local mountain rescue. About 15 minutes later, he dialled Mrs Rhodes' number again. She picked up after just one ring.

"Hello?"

"It's Constable Lomas here. Is that Mrs Rhodes?" began Bob, but the conversation was suddenly interrupted from her end. There was clearly a commotion going on and he jerked the phone away from his ear. "Hello... Mrs Rhodes?" After a few seconds he heard her voice again.

"I'm *so* sorry about that." Her tone had changed to one of relief. "She's just walked through the door. Would you mind if I see to her? Thank you so much for ringing back."

Bob didn't mind one little bit. In his time in the force he'd had the unenviable task of breaking bad news to a family who'd lost a loved one to the hills. He was only too aware that The Peak on a fine summer's day looked incapable of inflicting harm on anybody but he knew it could change character in the blink of an eye when bad weather moved in. But today was not one of those days and he had no need to detain Mrs Rhodes any longer.

"No problem," he replied. "I'm just pleased she's safe. Bye Mrs Rhodes."

His body language as he put the phone down was noticed by Detective Inspector Neil Webster, who had just entered the front office. "You look very chipper, Bob," he said in his flat Mancunian accent. "It is Monday you know!"

"Yeah... I *am* actually sir. No apologies for that. Someone's day has just got a whole lot better."

The DI decided that a bit of good news was worth sharing. "Come on then, don't keep it to yourself. We get enough of the other."

It only took a few minutes for Bob to explain and on the face of it that was case closed. At least that's what he thought.

Neil Webster was mid-forties, with a worn and worldly look about him; not in a scruffy way but one that suggested he'd been at the sharp end of policing for a long time. A small scar below his left eye did nothing to detract from that. It was a permanent reminder of his time on the Manchester force and latterly being caught in the middle of a gang turf war. He'd been lucky to escape with his life but it had taken him right to the edge –

physically and mentally. A month in hospital and another two on sick leave had concentrated his mind as never before during which time he'd concluded that his wife and family had been put through enough. His boss agreed but also knew that the force would be losing a good man if Neil went. He also knew that retirement this early would drive his DI round the bend and probably his wife Anne as well. Being a copper was in Neil's blood so a sideways move had been engineered to the relatively quiet waters of Buxton. Word on the grapevine was that a fresh face there might be timely.

For their part, Neil and Anne had always found Buxton a bit of an enigma, the sort of place you switch on *and* off, one that stays in suspended animation from the moment you finish a visit to the time you return. Perhaps that was its USP, an ability to help you dip into the past and envisage the heyday of the Victorian era: therapeutic spa waters, majestic buildings and gentility. The gentility might have diminished but the buildings were still there: the Crescent, the Devonshire Dome and the Palace Hotel. While the opera house wasn't strictly Victorian it was still full of character. Anne loved visiting the countryside but she didn't want to live there. She preferred to see human beings rather than sheep when she stepped out of her front door in the morning but the woolly creatures weren't far away should she need a quick fix. Hence they plumped for a house just north of the town centre rather than in one of the Peakland villages. It was no more than a few minutes' walk from the beautiful Pavilion Gardens and convenient enough for the necessities of life.

Having time to ask Bob about the phone call on a Monday morning encapsulated the new situation Neil found himself in. The level and type of crime he was now dealing with was a world away from that which he'd been exposed to in Manchester. But that's what this move was all about wasn't it, to get away from those extremes. The worst the weekend had brought was a bit of trouble between rival supporters after Saturday's football match, Buxton against Goole Town. Apparently some Buxtonites had taunted a group of Goole fans with a bit of anatomical humour which had not been well received, their team having just been thrashed on the pitch. Neil and Bob found the whole thing quite amusing – not so Sergeant Trudie Barker after she asked them what the joviality was all about.

"No danger of you two growing up then?" she chided.

"Nope, absolutely not," retorted Neil, who always tried to see the lighter side of life. Sometimes humour was the only way to get through the stressful moments of being on duty. He was also very much a team player, although fully aware not to let his subordinates overstep the mark.

Trudie was an interesting character, not a party pooper at all, but she'd had to battle hard to reach the rank of sergeant, female versions being a rarity in the Sixties. But she'd earned it having served as a WPC with distinction in Leek, where she'd demonstrated a unique brand of resourcefulness and pragmatism, something Neil had already noted. She loved the job and was extremely determined, although the latter sometimes showed up as being a bit abrasive.

"Come on Sarge," cajoled Bob in her direction. "It's worth a giggle."

"I'd be giggling more if the two we arrested hadn't thrown up in the cells. Honestly, men!"

"Yes... but what would you do without us?" Bob added as she headed towards the door.

"I don't know," she retorted without missing a step, "but I'm sure I'll think of something... eventually!" And she was gone.

The two men returned to discussing what else had come in, Bob handing Neil a report on a road accident that had happened on the Derbyshire side of the Cat and Fiddle on Sunday evening.

"Looks like the guy overcooked it on one of the bends in the weather and took out some stock wire on the other side. No one else was involved, not even a sheep. The farmer's been in touch though – he'll be feeling an insurance claim coming on: 'Ay lad, it might have only demolished a yard or two but it'll need a whole new section.'"

Neil laughed at his colleague's impersonation.

"I'm not joking," continued Bob. "They don't miss a trick."

"Bit cynical that, isn't it?"

"You'll learn. Anyway, cynicism goes with the job doesn't it? Or did they all love their mothers and go to church on a Sunday in Manchester?"

Neil paused momentarily on that thought. "If only. Trust me, Bob, I can out-cynic you any day of the week." He didn't dwell on that for long. "Okay... so... anything else new I should know about?"

"No. I think that's it."

"Right, thanks." With that, Bob gathered up his file and headed out of the DI's office and back to the front desk. Neil, for his part, would have given an awful lot to have had days like this once in a while back in Manchester, although he was beginning to wonder whether you could have too much of a good thing. Anyway, it was back to looking at a case that had been brought hurriedly to his full attention at the end of the previous week concerning farm thefts in the area. It had been on the go for some time but suddenly became a priority when one of the local farmers disturbed intruders in the middle of the night and let off his 12-bore. Whether this was connected to the ongoing case was unclear but it had certainly concentrated minds. The investigation so far had produced few leads but it was clear to Neil that whoever was behind the thefts was pretty organised: one, for nicking the gear in the first place and two, for spiriting it away to heaven knows where. The more he read, the more he sensed a lack of urgency about the whole thing. Well there was some urgency now. He certainly didn't want frustrated farmers taking matters into their own hands and having his powers-that-be wondering how he'd managed to turn this previously peaceful patch into the Wild West in only two months.

During those two months he had gone softly softly as he eased himself back into the job and got to know his new colleagues. But he was now feeling pretty good both physically and mentally, sufficiently so to make his presence felt a bit more. This sudden turn of events with the farm cases suggested the time was right. For the moment, though, he put that file to one side and opened another folder. This time it was domestic abuse, a crime that had no preference for city or rural idyll. The arresting officer was a comparatively inexperienced WPC and Neil wanted to be there when it came to court later in the week, so he needed to familiarise himself with the case. He'd just started going through the notes when there was another knock on his door.

"Come in." It was Trudie.

"Sorry to trouble you sir," she said on entering. "Have you got a minute?" She was holding something in her hand.

"Yes, of course." But her arrival made his mind jump back to the farm case. "Actually Trudie, just before you tell me what you've *come* to tell me, I've been looking at this incident with the shotgun last week and whether it might be linked to these other farm jobs." He gestured to the open file. "According to *that*, we've not exactly been putting our back into it have we? Although I admit that it must be like looking for a needle in a haystack, if you'll pardon the pun, trying to find nicked gear in the hills round here." He looked up at her again. "Any thoughts?" His question took her by surprise but she actually had plenty of thoughts on the matter.

Sergeant Barker had warmed to Neil from the moment he took up his new post. Like most of the station she was aware of what had happened to him in Manchester and wanted to help him adjust to his new situation in any way she could. As a uniformed officer there had been few opportunities – CID was a bit precious about its territory – but now she spotted her opening.

"You needn't tell me about needles in haystacks, sir. We had the Staffordshire Moorlands to contend with when I was in Leek. You don't have to drive far before you feel as though you're in the middle of nowhere."

She'd been a WPC in the old silk town ever since she joined the force and couldn't have been happier when she was transferred to Buxton after her promotion. The two areas had a lot in common and it was her experience at the former that made her think she could bring something to this investigation. Even so, she felt she had to tread carefully, at least initially.

"Err..."

"Come on Trudie, spit it out." Neil took the direct approach because he knew that's how *she* was. Well, usually.

"Okay then. Quite simply, in my view, they're not looking in the right places. I was involved with a case a bit like this once before in my old job. It was a while ago, a few years before I came here."

"And?" pressed Neil.

"Well I don't think there's much hope of finding the stolen gear anywhere within at least ten miles, maybe more. Whoever's involved would probably want to get it out of the county for a start. That's what happened in the case I'm on about. But eventually we did find their hiding place – believe it or not just a few miles south of here, a clapped-out farm in the back of beyond. We were actually tipped off by someone from Bakewell market." She now had Neil's full attention.

"So you think we should search further afield?"

"Absolutely."

"But won't that just give us even more haystacks?"

"Maybe. But it's better than being in the wrong field to start with!" Neil failed to restrain a giggle. "Go on..."

"What I'm really saying, sir, is that if you want to check out a field you don't know, get help from people who do. You could do worse than speak to my old sarge at Leek, Alan Wright. Find out who's got their ear to the ground on the Moorlands patch these days. Same for Cheshire, but I don't have any contacts there."

"Well I have," Neil replied. "Joint operations in the money belt, Wilmslow and Macclesfield way. Posh crime, Trudie. Trust me, there's a few dodgy fortunes over there."

Flicking through the file, the investigation so far looked haphazard to Neil but the chat with his sergeant was bringing things into focus. He sat back in his chair. "Okay, thanks Trudie. I'll bear what you've said in mind." He suddenly remembered that she originally came in to ask *him* something. "Sorry. What was it you wanted?"

"To give you this, sir." She placed a gold-coloured, bangle cum bracelet on his desk. Neil picked it up and looked at his wrist as if assessing its suitability.

"Well I'm touched, Trudie, but I don't think it's really me." She broke into a smile as Neil put the bracelet back on the desk.

"No, it's actually connected with the call that Bob had about the missing girls earlier this morning?"

"Is everything all right?"

"Oh yes... yes, there's no problem, but Mrs Rhodes, the mother, came in just now." She pointed at the bracelet. "She brought in *that*. Apparently her daughter found it somewhere up on the tops before they lost their bearings in the atrocious weather." Neil looked at her in a "what are you bothering me with this for" sort of way.

"Well log it in lost property. You never know, someone might come and claim it." He made to get back to his file but Trudie hadn't finished.

"Yes, I will sir... but would you have another look at it please."

"Okay," he replied guardedly, picking it up and examining it more closely.

"Is it gold?"

"I honestly don't know. I suppose it could be... but check the inside – the writing. That's what I'm more interested in."

Neil tilted it to one side for a better view, squinting as he did. "It's pretty badly worn." He read the letters out slowly as he deciphered each one. "B A R B A R A." He looked up at Trudie again. "So it belonged to someone called Barbara. What's your point?"

"I might be up the wrong tree altogether but apparently five years or so ago there was a missing persons case on the go here. Well on the *stop*, really, because they'd got nowhere and were in the process of shelving the investigation." She paused. "Actually, can we get Bob in, sir? He was here when it happened."

Neil's interest had gone up a notch. "I take it the woman's name was Barbara?"

Trudie nodded.

He picked up the phone. "Can you ask Bob to come in?" Within a minute, Bob had joined them. "Okay, sit down, both of you." They duly obliged. "Right Bob, Trudie's given me a bit of background about a missing person from a few years back. She says you remember it."

"Yes I do, sir. Her name was Barbara Butler. It's one of those names that sticks."

Neil's demeanour changed yet again. "Where will the file be now?"

"I'll have to check. I know it had them all baffled but they were definitely interested in the husband at the time. The view was eventually taken that it was probably her own choice to disappear. Nothing new about that I suppose and no body was ever found."

Neil looked long and hard at the bracelet. For the first time since he'd been in his new job he remembered the feeling he used to get back in the big city, the one that told him when there was more to something than met the eye. They looked at each other without speaking, until Neil broke the silence. "Okay you two, find me that file. And bag that carefully," he added, pointing to the bracelet.

*****

CHAPTER TWO

One of the pluses of Neil's appointment in Buxton was that he could walk to work if he wanted to in the morning. It only took 20 minutes to cut through Pavilion Gardens and across town to reach the police station. More often than not he'd go in the car but to have the choice was a novelty. He wouldn't have contemplated such a thing when he lived in Manchester, mainly because his home was three miles from the police station but the inner city was never a relaxed place, even first thing in the morning.

"Anything interesting on the horizon today?" his wife Anne enquired as he got ready to set off.

"Hmmm, I'm not sure." That sounded enigmatic, she thought. Neil had a rule to talk only in generalities to his family about cases but what he'd just said was true this time – he really *didn't* know, well not exactly anyway. "I think I might do some exploring."

"Oh yes?" said his wife inquisitively. "Bit of caving?" Anne was never short of a quip, a trait that had proved invaluable during her marriage to a man whose job tended to lack humorous occasions.

"No no, nothing underground," replied Neil. "Well not in the speleological sense of the word anyway." He shot her a smile, happy with a rather witty response for that early in the day.

The two officers who'd originally been assigned to the farm thefts were Detective Sergeant Steve Milner, very experienced but who had probably climbed as far up the career ladder as he was going to, and Detective Constable Andy Bowers, who'd made the move from uniform in Chesterfield two years earlier. Shortly before Neil took up his new post he and the retiring DI at Buxton had got together for a drink and, unsurprisingly, there was some chat about the pros and cons of the various officers at the station. The man Neil was replacing had the demeanour of someone who was clearly looking forward to his retirement after more than 35 years in the job and who wasn't about to put the boot in to any of his colleagues, so his comments were on the bland side, although enough to give Neil the general lay of the land personnel wise.

Apart from Trudie and Bob, there were two other uniformed officers, both young constables: Richard Lowe and Jane Briggs. The other officer in CID was another relative youngster, Detective Constable Nick Fielding. The conversation with the retiring DI was useful but Neil liked to form his own opinions about people rather than take his cue from someone else and, in the weeks he'd been at Buxton station, those opinions were starting to take shape.

He did take the car that morning because the exploring he'd mentioned to Anne was definitely going to require four wheels. Once at the station he spent a fair bit of time looking at the case notes and statements relating to the farm thefts: who had been questioned, where they lived, especially the farmer who'd fired the gun.

Over the years he'd spent many a happy hour with his family on a summer Sunday afternoon tootling around the area but this could not have been more different – it was serious business viewed through serious eyes – and as he pored over the station ordnance survey map he began to realise just how many little byways there were that he never knew existed, weaving their way among the hills.

At about 12.30 he made his way to the staff canteen where he soon got chatting to Mary, one of the two ladies who dished up the more than acceptable meals.

"What are you up to today then, Mr Webster?" she asked as she ladled a portion of steaming cheese and potato pie on to his plate.

"Actually, Mary, I'm off up into the wilds this afternoon."

"Oh, yes? Well in that case you'll need stoking up. Here, have another one of these." Before he had a chance to reply, another dollop of pie had been dispensed. "There, that should give you a bit of insulation." He didn't really want the extra portion but nevertheless he smiled and thanked her. She was a thoroughly good sort was Mary and she *did* have a point: it was still blowy out there and up on the tops that would be magnified threefold. Half an hour later, not having partaken of pudding but armed with his map, he made his way to the front office. Trudie was there and they had a quick chat before he set off on a route that would potentially enable him to kill two birds with one stone – hopefully not one of the low-flying grouse that frequented the moors.

While Neil had been examining the case file he'd looked to see if he could detect any sort of pattern: timing wise, geographically, anything that would help provide more direction to their enquiries. Plenty of statements had been taken and case numbers issued against items that had been stolen but it just wasn't gelling. Eventually he arrived at Lower Booth Farm, where the incident with the shotgun had taken place. The landscape all around looked hard and bleak: largely empty fields of stubbly grass etched by miles of drystone walls interspersed with the odd bunch of trees doggedly standing their ground against the elements. Small stone barns were dotted here and there, affording isolated pockets of shelter, while the occasional herd of cows gathered around a hay feeder, up to their ankles in mud. It was a tough life up there, difficult for farmers to scratch a living, and it wasn't hard to see why a sufficiently incensed one might be tempted to take matters into their own hands when faced with someone who would steal rather than do an honest day's work.

The farmhouse and outbuildings were accessed from the road by a concrete track, worn thin and rutted in places, no doubt by the trundlings of many a tractor and trailer over the years. Evidence of repairs to its surface were clear to see but the springs on Neil's Vauxhall Victor were still given a good test as it slowly bumped its way up to the yard, which turned out to be in surprisingly good order. He parked up and walked across to the house, knocking on what looked like the door to the kitchen. Barking erupted from inside, followed by the loud voice of someone trying to quell the racket.

"Oi! Be quiet!" Neil could make out the sound of a dog being manhandled. "Get in there..." The barking suddenly became far less audible. "Won't be a minute." Seconds later the latch went on the door, opening to reveal an out of breath Mrs Mellor. "Sorry about that. It was Tegg. We've got him inside 'cause he's got a bad foot. Caught it on some barbed wire we think and we can't have him running around out there. It's like losing an arm with him out of action. Anyway... yes... what is it you want?' Neil introduced himself but before he had time to continue she started up again.

"Oh, another one of you is it? We've already had two... only this morning!" That didn't come as a surprise to Neil.

"Don't worry Mrs Mellor, it's just that we're doing everything we can to catch the people responsible for the thefts going on in the area." Her response proved that she wasn't quite as bothered as he thought.

"And I suppose it's pure coincidence that all of a sudden there's more policemen round here than cows and sheep after

John let off his gun the other night. Woke you all up did it?" She'd hit the bullseye, and it put Neil on the back foot. Before he had a chance to respond she stepped past him and shouted across the yard. "It's another one from the police, John!" Her husband had been round the back of the main barn and heard a car arrive so he'd come to see who it was.

"Can't move for you lot today," he said as he came within talking range.

"Yes, it probably does seem a bit like that. I'm Detective Inspector Webster."

"You needn't go through all that again," interjected Mrs Mellor.

"Oh aye?" queried her husband, wondering why he was getting a second visit from the law in one day and *this* time from a senior officer. There was a note of frustration in his tone. "Do *you* want to look at my gun licence as well?" That wasn't a priority for Neil that morning and neither should it have been for the other officers he thought.

"No, that's okay Mr Mellor," he responded. "But what I *would* like is to take a look at where things happened."

The farmer sighed. "I already showed it to the other two – but I suppose I can." He turned to lead the way. "I'll get some work done one of these days." The DI gave Mrs Mellor a courtesy thank you and set off after the farmer, taking in everything he could about the place as he went along.

"Bit muddy where we're going," said Mr Mellor. "All this rain we've had. Watch your step." Neil took his advice.

"Did the storm do any damage?" he enquired.

"Well, nothing more than we're used to when we get a bit of a blow. All part and parcel of it up here. We can deal with that. It's them buggers that come thieving cause more trouble."

"I can imagine," replied Neil thoughtfully as he hopped on any grassy bits he could find. They finally stopped at a big stone building with a double door.

"This is where I store most things and it's where they were when I disturbed them. Far enough away from the house not to be heard. Least that's what they thought. Mind you it was Tegg as actually let on. He's got a particular loud sort of whine when he's not happy. It's that what I heard and why they didn't know I was up." He pointed to a spot they'd passed on the way from the house. "I stood over by there, just round that corner of the other barn, and I could see their torches. But I've told all this to those other two."

Neil could understand his irritation at having to go through this again. "Yes, I know. The thing is Mr Mellor, I'm new to this area but I *am* in charge of this investigation. I thought I'd get a better picture of what we're dealing with if I came and got my own hands dirty." He looked down at his shoes. "Well, my feet anyway."

The farmer gave the glimmer of a smile. "Where you from then?"

"Manchester."

"Hmmm. Don't suppose there's much call for wellies there. Best get yourself a pair lad if you're planning on stopping."

With some cordiality established, Neil was soon back to business. "When we came out to you last Thursday night, after you reported the incident, you told the officer that you fired your gun into the air to scare whoever it was off. Is that right?"

"Aye. I wasn't going to tangle with 'em. I just wanted them gone so I thought I'd give 'em a fright." A slightly bigger grin appeared. "It shifted them all right."

Neil had a pretty good nose for whether someone was being economical with the facts and he had a feeling this might be one such case. He decided to dig a bit more. "So tell me again exactly where you were."

"Just round the corner of the other barn like I said."

Neil set off to the spot. "And this is where you fired your gun?" he shouted back.

"Yes."

"Which way?"

The farmer pointed into the air. "Up there, over the roof."

Neil returned. "What about the vehicle they used?"

"It's like I said to your sergeant, it was a big van. Maybe a Bedford. That shape anyway."

"And what happened, straight after you'd fired?"

"They scarpered!"

"Yes, I know that, but think really hard. What actually happened in this process of scarpering? Any little thing you can remember."

The farmer puffed out his cheeks. This chap was being far more thorough than the other two. "Well, I could hear voices, the engine starting up and revving, and then one began shouting... as it was pulling off. Whoever it was, I think he might have been trying to climb in the back as it got moving. I could tell the door was flapping about and I think it caught on something judging by the language."

"You sure he got in?"

"I think he must a done. I heard the door slam a few yards on."

Neil looked around. "And it drove off alongside the barn here?" With that he approached the wall of the building and made his way painstakingly along in the direction the vehicle had gone. After going three or four yards he came to another, much smaller wooden door. Outside was a milk churn stand. A mark on the wood caught his eye. "Is that new?"

The farmer came over to look. "Huh. The van door."

Neil started examining the *little* barn door. He paused about halfway down and pointed at a pock-marked area. "What d'you think caused that?"

The farmer shot him a look from under his cap. Neil stood up. "Look, Mr Mellor. I'm not interested in what *you* may or may not have done in the heat of the moment, I just want to catch the toe-rags that tried to nick your stuff, *for which I need your full co-operation*." The intent of those last few words did its job. The farmer took a deep breath.

"Okay, I did let another one off, but only low down so as not to hurt anyone. Oh, and by the way... it's John."

Neil took a moment. "Right then, John. Well you managed to damage your own property, what about the van?"

The farmer knew there was now no point in holding anything back. "Well, yes. I probably did hit the van – at the back and perhaps a bit of the side – while it was going past that door."

Neil's expression changed. "While someone was trying to get *in*?"

"I don't know!" The farmer was clearly unsettled about where this was going.

Neil weighed things up. "Well at least we now have two lines of enquiry. We'll check the local hospitals to see if they've had anyone come in with some unexplained lead shot embedded about their person. Perverse this isn't it? If you didn't hit him, we wouldn't have that lead. And the other lead's this paint." He tapped the green scuff mark. "Have you got something sharp and I'll shave a bit off to take with me. Let the experts have a look. It may help pin the make of the van down."

Without having to think twice, John produced a penknife from his pocket – a basic requirement for all hill farmers along with binder twine and wellies. "This do?"

"Just the job," replied Neil, who proceeded to cut a thin slice of wood off the stand with enough of the paint stain for a proper analysis to be made. He held up the offcut. "I think with this and knowing the vehicle's got a damaged door and *possibly* been on the wrong end of a shotgun, we've got something to go on. You've been very helpful Mr Mellor... sorry, John."

"I just hope I'm not helping myself to some trouble," the farmer replied, looking less than happy.

"Hopefully not… but I have to do my job. Where I focus my enquiries though is up to me. Let's leave it there shall we."

John stared at Neil. "You know what's really got me about this?" His expression was a mixture of anger and sadness. "It's my own fault in a way. I had an old cashbox in the barn. I just used it for bits and bobs that meant a bit o summat. There was a photograph of Tegg's mother in it, Beth." His face reflected fond thoughts. "Best dog I ever had. Bet they were disappointed when they found no money in it. I can replace diesel and feed, Mr Webster, but I can't replace *that*!"

The pair of them made their way back to the farmhouse, where Mrs Mellor was looking out of the kitchen window. She opened the door as they approached.

"Go and put the kettle on Jean," said her husband.

Neil checked his watch. It was nearly 2.30pm. "That's very kind of you," he interjected. "Maybe another time. It's just that I've got a lot to get through this afternoon."

"Bit different from those other two," blurted Jean. "I thought they'd never go." That really wasn't what Neil wanted to hear, *at all…*

CHAPTER THREE

Back in Buxton, recently appointed WPC Jane Briggs had spent most of the day in the town dealing with the continuing aftermath of the weekend storm. She was particularly checking on one or two areas that had experienced flooding. Fortunately this was a rare occurrence in Buxton but the sheer volume of rain that had barrelled down off the moors in such a short time had become too much for some of the watercourses below to handle. One or two roads in the lower part of the town had been closed but water levels were now dropping and things were slowly returning to normal, although some cleaning up was still going on. The high winds had caused a variety of untethered objects to find themselves in places they shouldn't be but there was no spate of looting. The only criminal incident appeared to have been at the Robert Stevenson Secondary Modern, where opportunist vandals had forced their way through a damaged fence and broken into a sports equipment storage shed in the playground. The school had reported it to the police and Sergeant Barker had asked Jane to call in and check out exactly what had happened. Once at the school, Constable Briggs made her way to the head's office, knocked on the door and waited for it to be answered. While she did so she found herself casting her mind back to the last visit she'd made to the headmistress's office at *her* old school.

Jane had been a bright pupil but she was headstrong too, often overstepping the mark, not maliciously but more out of bravado. She was also a very pretty girl – fair hair, blue eyes – and was nicknamed the "blonde bombshell" in the men's staffroom. Overall, she was quite a handful.

The best head teachers need a variety of skills, including a bit of psychology, and Jane's headmistress was particularly adept in that department. She generally knew which buttons to press to get the best out those who passed through her doors and Jane vividly remembered the last conversation she had with her.

"Jane," Mrs Pierson said as she peered over her glasses in an owl-like manner. "You have been sent to see me twice this term because you clearly think school rules don't apply to you." Jane was about to reply when Mrs Pierson raised an intimidating finger. "Be quiet!" It had the desired effect. "Now then," she continued, "you've made it no secret that you want to have a career in the police force, which is commendable – not many your age have such a clear idea of what they want to do – but frankly I don't think you're up to it."

Jane remembered how shocked she was by this pronouncement. The headmistress carried on. "A police officer's role is to make sure that we follow the law of the land, the rules of society if you like. They are there so that we can all live in a civilised manner. The rules of *this school* are there to keep similar order, for which *I* am the chief police officer. As you clearly don't understand the concept, I suggest that you look for a different career. That's it." With that, she returned to the papers on her desk and gestured for Jane to leave the room.

That encounter had left a lasting mark on Jane but her daydream was interrupted as the door was opened by the school secretary, Mrs Sheldon, who had called the police station to report the incident.

"Oh hello. Come in will you." The secretary gave a deep sigh as a prelude to what she said next. "It's *such* a nuisance all this. I'm sorry we had to call you out."

"No, that's what we're here for," replied Jane, now firmly back in the present.

"Anyway, if you'd like to take a seat I'll tell Mr Cousins you've arrived." Jane duly sat down on a spare chair while the secretary exited through another door. It wasn't long before she returned. "He won't be a minute."

Moments later an imposing figure entered. Mr Cousins was fiftyish; a bit thin on top but tall and with a military bearing. He certainly looked as though he might have been in the armed forces at some time. Perhaps that was an asset in his job.

"Hello!" he announced with gusto. Jane immediately got to her feet and found her hand being shaken before she knew it. "I'm Alan Cousins and you are?"

"Constable Briggs," she replied equally cheerily.

"Pleased to meet you Constable Briggs, sadly though, *not* in the most ideal of circumstances." Then, in a manner suggesting he'd come up with a particularly good idea, Mr Cousins gestured towards the door. "Shall we go to the scene of the crime?" He definitely had a bit of theatre in him, perhaps something else in his armoury that might help to quell stroppy teenagers.

Classes were in session so the playground was deserted as they headed across to the "scene of the crime". The nearer they got, the more Mr Cousins's countenance began to change. His initial bonhomie seemed to be ebbing away. By the time they reached the damaged building, with its splintered door hanging by a single hinge, he had become a picture of frustration. The gusty wind messed with the few strands of hair left on his head, adding a bleakness to proceedings. He delved into a pocket of his heavy sports jacket and produced a piece of paper, which he proffered to Jane.

"Here's a list of the items that have been taken." Jane took the paper from him and cast her eye down it. He knew what she was thinking. "I know it doesn't look a lot but the Mitre footballs on there were brand new, the best you can get. We've got a really good school team at the moment. That's why we bought them and that's what's so annoying about all this." He almost spat his next words out. "You try your best," he said, gesturing towards the shed, "then *this* happens. Grubby stealing – and it's just made us one more job." Jane really felt for him.

As well as the list, he gave Jane a name: Terry McDonald. "Tez" to his friends, or "accomplices" as Mr Cousins called them. He was convinced that this boy was somehow involved but had no evidence to back his hunch. McDonald had been a difficult pupil and the school wasn't sorry to see the back of him but, even so, Alan Cousins felt that they'd failed him. The lad was actually quite able and they'd tried everything in the book to keep him on the straight and narrow. Therefore, it was as much with disappointment as anger that he continued to look at the ransacked shed.

Jane closed her notebook. "Thank you, Mr Cousins. We'll keep an eye out for what's been stolen and another one on young Mr McDonald."

"Yes, I'd appreciate that. Thank you. Anyway, if you'll excuse me I must get back to the office." As he was about to set off they were joined by the school caretaker with his tool kit ready to start repairs now the police interview was over.

"It's all yours Ken," said Mr Cousins, giving him a pat on the shoulder as he passed him.

Jane turned once more to the damaged shed. "It really is mindless isn't it," she uttered to no one in particular. The caretaker rubbed his chin ruefully. They were contrasting figures: Jane, fresh out of police training, looking forward to dealing with society's problem people and Ken, who was probably approaching retirement, world weary having seen it all – schoolwise, pupil-wise, teacher-wise *and* parent-wise.

"Better get used to it, luv." And with that, he bent down and started picking up splinters of wood.

The address she'd been given for Terry McDonald was on the Moor Side council estate and, as she emerged from the school, she looked at her watch. "No time like the present," she thought. It was a bit of a walk from the school but officers on the beat took such things in their stride, so to speak. It was about 20 minutes before she reached the outlying houses of the 1950s development, the layout of which she was familiar with. On this breezy but now bright day the place didn't look too bad. The majority of council tenants took reasonable care of their properties, but you could spot the ones that didn't – and they tended to be those occupied by the more troublesome families. Jane looked at her notebook again: 28 Maskell Road. She knew roughly where it was. As she approached the property she could hear kids shouting somewhere round the back. She thought she caught sight of someone through the front window but decided to take her time, walking down the little jitty that ran along the side of the house and its back garden. It was a shortcut linking Maskell Road to the next street and saved a good five minutes compared with the long way round. As she made her way down the jitty, the shouts and some choice language were interrupted by an intermittent banging on the wooden fence that separated the gardens from the cut-through. One of the pluses of 1950s-built council houses was that many had big back gardens, long and thin and often butting on to the end of an adjoining garden on the next road. They were certainly large enough for youngsters to have a decent game of football. It soon became clear that a kickabout was exactly what was taking place.

At 5ft 6in and with her cap removed she was invisible to the participants on the other side of the 6ft wooden fence. She stopped and waited in the hope that she might hear something in the excitement of the game that might prove useful but all she got was a succession of colourful variants on "pass it", "greedy" and "goal!" amid the banging when the ball hit the fence. Suddenly there was another outbreak of bad language as a ball soared over the fence and into the jitty a few feet from where Jane was standing. Her surprise was doubled by a gate in the fence suddenly opening. She had no idea the gate was there but she was soon standing face to face with a 17-year-old lad who had gone in pursuit of the ball only to find a policewoman in front of him. Jane put her cap back on and picked up the football. The maker's name was emblazoned on the surface: Mitre. There was no need to check her notebook.

"Terry McDonald, I presume?" The lad was clearly rattled and took a second to reply.

"What of it?" came his eventual response. Two other lads, maybe slightly older, appeared in the gate hole.

"What yer doin', Tez?" one of them shouted, but as soon as they spotted the policewoman they just legged it. It gave Terry time to gather himself.

"You can't prove owt." It was an unsolicited confession of guilt but in itself of no legal use. "Someone just give it me," he added, now gaining in confidence.

Jane examined the beautifully stitched leather sphere she was holding, the brand name proud and clear. It was the sort of object any football-loving boy of the Sixties would consider the best Christmas present ever. But this wasn't Christmas, and there was no pleasure in this encounter whatsoever. "Come on, where did you really get it?"

"I found it," he answered dismissively.

Jane flicked the ball a few inches into the air, equally dismissively. "Okay, which is it? You were given it or you found it?"

The lad realised he was in danger of incriminating himself. "I don't have to say anything."

"Right then. Are either of your parents in?"

"No! Dad's not here and Mum's gone out."

Jane gave him a hard stare. "Well there's someone in there, I've just seen them. Look, we can try and sort this out here. If not, you'll have to come down to the station."

At that moment a shout came from the direction of the back door of the house. "Where *are* you Terry?" He hesitated.

"Aren't you going to answer?" prodded Jane. He didn't, so she moved to the gate entrance and shouted back. "He's here!" She watched as a woman, probably in her forties and wearing a kitchen apron, came bustling down the garden towards them.

"What's going on?' she exclaimed, clearly alarmed at seeing a police officer. She looked at her son. "Well?"

He remained silent. The woman's heart was sinking by the second. "Oh Terry, what have you done?"

"Mrs McDonald?' enquired Jane.

The woman took a deep breath to steady herself. "Yes."

"We're making enquiries about a break-in at the school. I'm Constable Briggs and I'd like to speak to you and Terry if you don't mind. Could we go inside please?"

Mrs McDonald looked daggers at her son, then back at Jane. "Yes... yes... I suppose so."

"You go with your mum, Terry," said Jane, who duly followed them inside. As she looked around she was surprised to find the interior in better shape than she expected. "A little lesson there," she thought: don't make assumptions. It was something she knew she had to work on. The back garden was a lost cause – the football was king there – but she'd noticed that the front garden was quite tidy. As she followed them in she spotted a picture of George Best on the kitchen wall and a red-and-white scarf hanging round the bottom stair post. No guesses which football team they supported. They entered the front room. Even though Terry's mother was clearly stressed, it didn't stop her asking Jane if she'd like a cup of tea. There was no argument from PC Briggs. While Mrs McDonald was busy brewing up in the kitchen, an interesting conversation broke out in the front room.

"I bet it was old Cousins sent you here wasn't it?" began Terry. "All the time I was there he never liked me."

"Well I've known you at least ten minutes and I already don't like you."

Terry didn't expect a sharp response like that but he was also taking on board just how pretty his adversary was, making it a bit difficult for him to remain totally objectionable. "Huh. So, what's it like being a copper?"

Jane thought for a moment but saw no reason not to take the question seriously. "It's what you make it. You get to meet nice people like your mum but you have to be disciplined and tough as well." She aimed a half laugh at Terry. "*You* wouldn't get past basic training." This was that edge in Jane that her teacher had noticed and she enjoyed getting an immediate reaction from Terry.

"Hey!" he retorted angrily.

"There you go! So what are you going to do big man? Tell your mummy?"

At that moment "mummy" arrived with three cups of tea on a tray. She passed them around then sat down where she could see Jane and her son. Her face hardened and she glowered at Terry. "It's those footballs isn't it." She gritted her teeth. "You idiot!"

"Mum!" Terry exclaimed. Mrs McDonald took a swallow of tea then closed her eyes and rubbed her forehead as she weighed up what to say next.

The fact the poor woman looked very troubled wasn't lost on Jane. "Look Mrs McDonald, Terry's in a spot here but he's not exactly top of Scotland Yard's 'most wanted.'"

"What d'you mean?"

Jane's priority was to get the matter cleared up with as little fuss as possible but, that said, if Terry was involved, something of which she was pretty certain, he couldn't be allowed to just get away with it – and then there was Mrs McDonald. Jane decided to dig some more. "Is there a Mr McDonald?" she asked openly.

"That's none of her business, Mum," fired Terry defensively.

"Just be quiet Terry will you." He scowled as he sat back with his arms folded. Mrs McDonald took yet another deep breath. "My husband is in prison. He's got two years left of a three-year sentence for a robbery in Manchester. You'll no doubt have it on your records somewhere."

Her sense of shame was difficult to hide and she bit her lip for a split second before continuing. "We were a bit short of money and he reckoned some friends of his had a 'business deal' that would ease things for us." She screwed her face up. "The stupid, stupid man! Business deal my ar... sorry. Some friends, eh? They were just wrong'uns and not very bright either. And since then I've told Terry to watch the company *he* keeps." She threw a withering look in his direction. "But you haven't... have you?" She eyed Jane again. "It's that Lewis Bates and his mates. They swagger about as if they own the estate. If Brian was here he'd see him off."

She looked hard at Jane. "Honestly, my husband's a good man. I don't know what he was thinking. Anyway, I have to work every hour God sends now." She glanced in her son's direction. "And I can't keep an eye on *him* all the time." She stopped for another sip of tea. Jane did likewise, all the time weighing up how best to deal with the situation now that she was getting a better idea of the background. Lewis Bates and his gang were known to her but it was the first time she'd come into contact with them.

"Right, Terry," she announced. "Just in case you're in any doubt, that football you've come into possession of is stolen property. It belongs to the school up the road and if it can be proved that you were involved in the break-in that took place, you are in serious trouble. At best you'll have a criminal conviction against your name, with all the repercussions that will have for your job prospects. At worst you'll face a spell in borstal. Have you got a job?"

The colour was draining from Mrs McDonald's face but, out of the blue, Terry burst into tears. His mum went to him and he dissolved into her arms, staying there for a full minute. Eventually she turned to Jane in anguish. "Can't you do anything?"

This wasn't an easy situation for an inexperienced WPC but she remembered it being drummed into her at police training college to take a step back when things got stressful in "family" situations so that's what she decided to do – well sideways anyway.

"That's going to depend very much on your son." She took the last sip of her tea and put the cup down. "I'd like a word with you on your own before I go if that's okay?"

Mrs McDonald extricated herself from her son. "Come on Terry, pull yourself together. I'm sure Constable Briggs will do her best."

Jane got up. She'd had another idea. "Would you excuse me for a moment, Mrs McDonald?" She nipped out into the hall but was soon back carrying the football scarf she'd seen hanging at the bottom of the stairs. "Keen supporter are you Terry?" The lad nodded. She held the scarf up. "Would you be upset if someone nicked this? I know they're not cheap."

"Course I would."

"Well then, stop feeling sorry for yourself and spare a thought for whoever it is that's had their stuff stolen." She handed the scarf to Terry. "Okay, Mrs McDonald. If you'd like to see me out, I'll have that word and I'll need to take the football with me."

They made their way into the kitchen, Mrs McDonald closing

the door behind them. "D'you want to sit down, constable?" she asked, looking completely wrung out.

"No, this won't take long." Jane gave her a sympathetic smile. "I really will do my best to help. I know it doesn't seem much, just a few footballs, but it's not as simple as that. The headmaster is really upset about the break-in and he's almost certain to press charges."

Mrs McDonald clutched the back of her head and sighed before replying. "I can't exactly blame him. Terry wasn't the easiest and it looks like it's come back to bite him."

"Yes, I think you're right. But if Lewis Bates was the ringleader in all this, it will certainly help Terry if he gives us the full story."

"You mean tell on the others?"

"Well, yes."

Mrs McDonald shook her head. "I don't know if he dare. Lewis Bates is horrible and a lot more streetwise than my lad. That was him playing in the back just now. I bet if you went round his place you wouldn't find any footballs. Trust my son to get caught with the evidence." She gave another deep sigh before continuing. "Well for what it's worth, he lives on Hesketh Avenue, the next road." She pointed generally in the direction. "Number 16. It's not far from where that wife-beater lives."

Unbeknown to Mrs McDonald, Jane knew exactly where the "wife-beater" lived. "Okay, leave it with me," she said. "I'll make my report and I promise I'll get back to you as soon as I can. Oh... yes... just one other thing – how old is Terry?"

"He's 17."

"Well if you don't mind my asking, why hasn't he got a job?"

"Actually he has. He starts next week – apprentice at the local garage. Heaven knows we need some more money coming in – but now this! What do they say? It never rains..."

As Jane left the house her mind was locked on how she could help the McDonalds without breaking any rules herself.

CHAPTER FOUR

The morning after his visit to Lower Booth Farm, Neil arrived at his office to find the Barbara Butler file on his desk. His first instinct was to take a look but, having picked it up, he put it to one side again realising that marshalling the notes he'd made at the farm needed to take priority. He'd actually quite enjoyed his meeting with the Mellors – what a pair of characters – but those same notes also included another call he'd made on his way back home to Buxton, at the Old Grouse Inn, about a mile from the outskirts of the town.

It was an old gritstone property with a stone-tiled roof, typical of many buildings in that neck of the woods. Neil wondered if it had perhaps been farm cottages in the past. Now there was a pub sign hanging over the door picturing a startled-looking red grouse – not a surprising expression he thought if you were being shot at for four months of the year. He drove slowly past the front until he came to a car park at the side. It was virtually empty. He locked his car and headed towards the entrance, passing a small beer garden where a few picnic benches were stationed, more in hope than expectation at this time of the year. He stopped to take in the location, picturing it on a lovely summer's day. The pub was in a shallow valley with a small stream running along on the opposite side of the road and a footpath on the other side of that. It wasn't far from the town but was a good spot from which to start a serious country walk. According to his map, it was also the nearest pub to Lower Booth Farm.

Entering the pub lounge there wasn't a customer to be seen, which suited his purposes just fine. There was a woman behind the bar though, busy readying things for the evening's business. Neil approached and was met with a cheery smile.

"What can I get you luv?"

He glanced at his watch. "I'll just have a half of bitter thanks."

"Coming up." She pulled the pump handle as though she'd done it a thousand times before, which she probably had. After the final drop of liquid settled into the glass she set it down on the counter. "That'll be one and five please."

Neil felt in his pocket and handed over a two shilling piece. The till rang up and he duly received seven pence change. "Thanks." He wandered over to a small table and settled down to check something in his notebook. He soon returned to the bar with what was left of his drink. The woman stopped what she was doing. He glanced around the room and smiled approvingly. "It's really nice in here." He pointed to an open fire glowing in the grate. "You can't beat that – very welcoming."

"Well we do try," she replied with a smile.

"Let me introduce myself. I'm DI Neil Webster and I've just taken over at Buxton police station." He held out his hand which was duly shaken, though tentatively.

She clearly wasn't sure what a DI was so Neil put his drink down and produced his warrant card. She perused it then turned and shouted through a doorway directly behind her. "Can you come, Jim?" She turned back to Neil. "He'll not be a minute."

There was an awkward silence until "Jim" emerged from somewhere in the back. The woman showed her husband the ID. He studied it then fixed his eyes warily on Neil, handing it back before moving alongside his wife. "What can I do for you?" he asked.

Neil didn't expect to be received with open arms but the publican's tone was decidedly cool. Nevertheless he pressed on. "Apologies for calling in unannounced but I was in the area and hoped I might catch you while it was quiet." The couple glanced at one another. "It's Sandra and Jim isn't it? Hargreaves?" They looked at each other again. Neil flashed a hint of a smile. "I'm not Sherlock. Your names are over the door." His quip seemed to lighten things. "And as I just mentioned to Mrs Hargreaves..."

"Sandra," she interjected.

"Yes... Sandra. I'm new to Buxton and I'm just trying to get familiar with my patch."

"Oh yes?" replied Jim economically.

Neil had another go. "I found working closely with the community in my last job really useful and I'd like to do the same here, hopefully for *all* our benefits."

Jim and Sandra exchanged another look. The moment hung until the landlord eventually extended his hand, which Neil happily shook. Finally they were up and running but despite the struggle Neil couldn't help being tickled by the communication method used between the Hargreaves, which required no words. It was either an incredibly advanced technique or just two people who knew each other inside out.

As Neil processed his notes from the previous afternoon, he knew he'd not been entirely honest when he'd introduced himself at the Old Grouse Inn. Yes, he was genuinely interested in how the place had come into their hands, its progress etc, but what he *really* wanted was to know about their clientele. Were they visitors from town fancying countryside surroundings, regulars, weekend walkers, perhaps even a farmer or two? As it happened it proved to be all of those but, while on the subject of farmers, he'd taken the opportunity to mention the case he was investigating and to ask Sandra and Jim to let him know if they heard anything that might be useful. They didn't seem to have a problem with that but he kept wondering why they'd been so defensive when he had introduced himself.

"Look inspector," Jim had eventually replied, "it's been very nice meeting you but we really don't want to go there. All I'll say is... you might want to look a bit closer to home." And that was it!

They'd bade him an amicable enough farewell but Neil wondered what they could have meant by "look a bit closer to home". Devoid of an answer, he decided to tuck the question away for now and return to the Barbara Butler file and her disappearance. The information on the header included the name of the chief investigating officer: DS Milner.

On reading through the file, it appeared that the first notification to the police of her possibly being missing came from the husband, Malcolm Butler, which was hardly surprising. In his statement he said that his wife had arranged to spend a few days with her sister over in Totley, near Sheffield, something she did regularly. She had taken a morning train with one change at New Mills but she'd never arrived at her destination. It took Neil about half an hour to go through the whole file and Malcolm Butler had indeed come in for close scrutiny, but there was nothing to suggest foul play and crucially, *no body*. And there hung the question: was the discovery of the bracelet sufficient grounds for revisiting the case or should he let sleeping dogs lie? He left his desk and made his way through to the CID main office, where Steve Milner and Andy Bowers were sitting at their desks.

"How are you doing, lads?" he asked cordially as he entered the room.

Steve put the cigarette down he was smoking and scratched his head. "Well we paid some more visits up around Lower Booth Farm yesterday and we'll be talking to farm suppliers in the area today, *again*, to see if they've had any whispers."

That answer wasn't good enough for Neil any more and his reply showed it. "Look, we really need to get on top of this Steve so let's go and have a chat in my office and see exactly where we are." Milner took another leisurely sip of his tea – one too many for his boss. "NOW!" snapped Neil. "Bring your drink with you." He left the door open behind him as he headed back to his office.

Milner made a face towards Andy before getting up and setting off, mug in hand. "Sit down, Steve," said Neil when he arrived. His detective sergeant duly pulled up a chair and settled in. The DI wasted no time. "So, what *did* you turn up yesterday?" He posed the question in the knowledge that no one else in the station knew that he'd visited John Mellor's farm himself the previous afternoon. During the next ten minutes he listened to a mixture of whys, wherefores and conjecture, the only hard fact being that the farmer's gun licence was up to date. By now Neil had heard enough and he opened a drawer from which he extracted the piece of the green wooden fragment he'd taken from the farm. He placed it on the desk.

Milner looked puzzled. "What's that?"

"It's paint from the vehicle that was involved in the incident at Lower Booth Farm the other night."

Milner twitched involuntarily. "How did you find that?"

"*Because I went and looked, Steve.*" He gave his sergeant a second or two to take that in. "So now you *do* have something to go on."

Milner attempted to respond but Neil didn't give him the chance. He'd heard enough excuses. "It was a large van," he continued, "probably a Bedford, and I need the colour checked with the trade to confirm it. If it is, let's have eyes on roads everywhere on our patch looking out for it."

Milner groaned. "There's an awful lot of green Bedfords sir."

"Yes, but not with a dent in the left back door." Milner's eyes widened. Neil pressed on. "I want you to put Andy on this because I need *your* help with something else." This was a first move by the DI to put some daylight between those two.

Milner wondered what was coming next in this conversation of nasty surprises. "What's that, sir?"

"A couple of things actually. The first one's probably something and nothing, but tell me anyway. Have you ever had any dealings with Jim and Sandra Hargreaves at the Old Grouse pub? I called in there yesterday and, when I introduced myself, you could have cut the atmosphere with a knife. So is there something I should know?"

Milner relaxed back into his chair. "Huh, *them!* They're lucky they still have a licence."

"Really? Why's that?"

"Well we had a tip off that some dodgy stuff was passing through there: drugs, stolen property."

"And was it?"

"Well we never caught them at it but, as they say, there's no smoke without fire. Anyway it must have put the frighteners on them 'cause we've not heard anything to that effect since."

Neil's immediate thought was that his judgment of character must be slipping if Jim and Sandra Hargreaves had been involved in anything like that.

"What was the other thing, sir?" enquired Milner.

Neil pushed the Butler file across his desk. "Barbara Butler."

It only took a second or two for the name to register with Milner. "You mean the missing woman from a few years ago?"

"Yep." Neil tapped the file. "You were the principal investigating officer weren't you Steve."

Milner sat up again, now in no doubt that he was getting a bit of a grilling. "Yes I was – and I still think there was something suspicious about the whole thing, especially that husband of hers."

"Copper's nose eh, Steve?"

"Too right, but we could never quite pin him down. He definitely had an odd relationship with his sister-in-law. Now she *was* a piece of work! And there was this other woman – Celia I think her name was." He shook his head as he recollected the interviews. "There was definitely some weird stuff going on. Anyway, we kept the case semi-open expecting his missus to turn up eventually, alive *or* dead, but she never did. He nodded towards the file. "Has something happened?"

Webster's tone with his detective sergeant had become more measured. "The simple answer is, *I don't know*." Neil went on to explain the background to the bracelet being handed in, at the end of which he sat there clearly weighing things up. He looked at Milner, eyebrows raised. "Do *you* think she might be up there on the moors?"

Feeling less on the defensive now, Steve sat up straight as he considered the question. He recalled the amount of time he'd invested in the initial investigation as evidenced by the thickness of the file. To him it had always felt like unfinished business, hence his next question. "D'you want me to see if the Rhodes girl could take us to where it was found... the bracelet?" At the same time, his expression reflected the possible difficulties of such a task. "Never been up there myself but I believe it's pretty wild."

Neil ruminated on the idea for a few moments. "Look, Steve, see if you can arrange to visit the family after school today. I'd come with you but I'm going to be tied up. Bob's got their contact details – but tread lightly, okay?"

"Fair enough, sir. I'll see what I can do." He rose and headed for the door.

Webster called after him. "And tell Andy to get his finger out with that paint job!"

Once Milner had gone, Neil wandered through to the front office. PC Lomas was on duty.

"Is Trudie around, Bob?"

"She's upstairs on her break sir."

"All right, thanks." He headed off to the canteen where he found her with a cup of tea and a biscuit. "Sorry to interrupt your elevenses Trudie but I wanted to ask a favour."

"What's that sir?"

"Well I've just put a bit of a rocket up Laurel and Hardy down there so hopefully they'll be out actually fighting crime for the rest of the day." Trudie couldn't help but laugh. "So, as they're not here and I've got to get ready for that court case tomorrow, would you have time to ring round hospitals in the area to see if they've had anyone needing lead shot removed from their person in recent days."

That brought a halt to Trudie's biscuit eating. "Well that's something I don't get asked every day!"

"No, I'm sure you don't." He leant forward a little. "And can we keep this between ourselves please?"

"Can I ask why?"

Neil filled her in on his visit to Lower Booth Farm but, more to the point, the need to try to keep the full details of John Mellor's gun-toting activities under wraps. He knew he could trust his sergeant's discretion. "It's about the only solid lead we've got at the moment," he concluded. "That and the Bedford van." She didn't need to be asked twice about checking the hospitals.

Neil headed back to his office, this time to reacquaint himself with a domestic violence incident that Jane Briggs and Bob had attended two months previously and the subject of Thursday's court case. The defendant, Eric Smith, had been remanded in custody and the preliminary hearing was taking place in Chesterfield. The DI wanted to be there because, even though Jane had participated in court proceedings before, those cases had been pretty mundane. This one wasn't and Neil wanted to make sure her gung ho approach to things didn't get the better of her in what was a thoroughly unpleasant affair. It wasn't your average domestic violence case: the principal plaintiff was not Smith's wife, Angela, it was the woman who lived next door, Rosemary Wild, who was not inappropriately named.

It had all kicked off one Friday afternoon after Smith had returned from a session at the pub where he'd had an altercation. He was well known to the police for having a short fuse and using his fists after a drink or four, but he had a nasty habit of not leaving it there and taking it out on his wife when he got home. The police had been called out on more than one occasion, usually by the neighbour, but as in many cases like this the wife in question had refused to press charges. But this was different. Apart from being her neighbour, Rosemary Wild was Angela Smith's best friend and hated what she was being put through by her thug of a husband.

The families occupied respective ends of a semi-detached and on that Friday afternoon in January it hadn't been long before Rosemary heard raised voices through the wall. Eric began shouting and, in anticipation of what was coming, Rosemary shot off to the telephone box at the bottom of the road to ring 999. But when she returned home the racket next door had reached levels she'd not heard before and she was scared that this time Angela was going to get too much of a pummelling. Her own husband was out and it would be a few minutes until the police arrived, so in a rush of blood she'd shot round and banged on her neighbour's front door like crazy. She heard Angela scream and couldn't stop herself from bursting in to try to help her friend. Eric had his wife pinned to the wall with fists raised and Rosemary threw herself at him in an attempt to get him off. Smith flailed out and Rosemary was the recipient of a sickening blow to the head. Mercifully for his wife, her friend's falling to the floor stopped him in his tracks.

He realised he was now in big trouble and started to panic. When two police officers arrived a minute or two later the scene was mayhem. One of those officers was Jane, who was accompanying beefy Bob Lomas. The latter dealt unceremoniously with the semi-paralytic Smith and had him in handcuffs before he knew it. Jane took one look at poor Rosemary and got on her radio to summon an ambulance.

She then stood squarely in front of Smith. "You pig!" she shouted at him from point blank range.

"Jane!" snapped Bob.

She got the message and returned to the moaning woman on the floor. Angela knelt down as well, mortified that her friend had taken a beating on her account. It was a thoroughly distressing scene. Jane had also called for back up to deal with Smith and it arrived at the same time as the ambulance. She accompanied both women to the hospital while Smith was manhandled into one of the cars by the other three officers who weren't in the least concerned if he banged his head in the process.

During the three months since the incident the two women had recovered, at least physically, from their ordeal and would be in court as joint plaintiffs and witnesses. For Angela, seeing what her husband had done to her friend that Friday afternoon had been the final straw so, in the end, *both* women had pressed charges. The testimonies of the arresting officers were there to back them up so it looked to be an open and shut case. But Neil didn't want to take any chances. He'd seen strange things happen in court over the years and, in particular, he didn't want his most inexperienced officer losing her cool, however much she might despise the defendant. He wanted the brute sent down!

In the Sixties, women constables weren't considered equals by their male colleagues and were often stuck with carrying out menial duties. Steve Milner had done nothing to discourage that view among his CID colleagues but the younger guys had trouble holding that line when it came to Jane Briggs – because they really fancied her. It didn't help that she loved to turn herself out immaculately, from white-topped, air hostess-style cap, perfectly knotted tie and belted tunic, right down to her black seam-backed stockings. They particularly liked watching her riding her bike on patrol with one hand while she tried to stop her skirt billowing up with the other. But Neil was all for equality. In his eyes it was ability to do the job that counted and, in Trudie and Jane, he had two very talented female officers. He was determined to give them every opportunity to flourish.

More generally, the strengths and weaknesses of his team were beginning to distill in Neil's mind. In uniform he had Bob, an unambitious but hugely experienced and solid copper who, day by day, was passing on the benefits of that experience to PCs Briggs and Lowe. The latter had been in the force three years but was definitely looking to climb the ladder. He was gaining confidence, enough to rib his mentor from time to time, but Bob was more than able to put him back in his box when required. Richard Lowe was probably the uniformed officer Neil had least dealings with but the young lad was also under the watchful eye of Trudie. She knew Richard wanted to get on but was going to make sure he worked hard for it just as she herself had had to do – and that meant *really* hard. And then there was Jane, such a live wire, potentially capable of going far in the job but just as liable to crash and burn from a great height. She was a real challenge for Trudie but her sergeant so wanted to see another female officer buck the system that she was perhaps guilty of giving her a bit more latitude than she gave Richard when maybe the opposite was required. As for Trudie herself, Neil thought she was a great copper and he was determined to put her talents to much wider use at the first opportunity. He knew it was *not* going to be easy but the little task he'd given her with the hospitals that afternoon was his first, albeit quiet attempt to start that ball rolling. All in all he felt pretty comfortable with the way uniform were performing. He certainly didn't think the same of CID.

Even though DI Webster had been transferred to Buxton from the Manchester force for his own well-being, Derbyshire Constabulary couldn't wait to get their hands on him and for the incumbent to retire. For his part, Neil hadn't gone into the job blind. He knew there were issues in CID but wanted to get his own take on things before making changes. The previous DI obviously had more of an eye on his retirement than he had on Steve Milner, who in turn was passing on his sloppy habits to Andy Bowers. But there was another detective constable in there, Nick Fielding, a bit younger than Andy and definitely more cerebral than the other two – very much a "do it by the book" merchant. To Milner and Bowers, Nick wasn't "one of the boys" so was kept at arm's length when it came to what you might call the more "interesting" cases. Just *how* interesting Neil was beginning to wonder. His encounter with Jim and Sandra Hargreaves at the Old Grouse Inn did nothing to ease those concerns.

On more than one occasion Trudie had mentioned what she saw as an under-used asset at their disposal in the form of rural constables, which had really struck a chord with Neil. In the Sixties, the role of the village bobby was changing. Originally on call 24/7 from their own police houses, they were switching to eight-hour shifts covering each other on their respective adjoining patches as required. The new arrangement was assisted by the introduction of motorcycles to cope with the extra miles; modest machines but a massive step up from the traditional pedal bike. It was with this rural resource in mind that Neil paid Trudie his second visit of the day, this time in her own little office where she was sat at her desk busy making hospital investigation phone calls. He popped his head round the door. "How are you getting on?"

She looked up. "Nothing yet sir, but I'll keep trying."

"Okay. There's something else I'd like you to do once you've finished that hospital job." He gave her a knowing smile. "That is when you've got a few minutes."

She didn't look too pleased but Neil was learning fast what made Trudie tick and carried on. "Can you organise a briefing for all officers on our patch out there," he pointed generally to the world outside, "and get them in here one morning so we can start dealing with this farm job properly."

Sergeant Barker was unable to conceal a smile.

Neil continued. "You see... I *was* listening. The thing is, I thought I ought to get my local ducks in a row on intelligence-gathering first before I asked for help from further afield. And I want you to involve Nick Fielding in this. I'd like to see what he can do with a bit more freedom."

Sergeant Barker's expression suggested she had no problem with that at all. But Neil hadn't finished. "Use Andy Bowers as well. He can do it alongside his Bedford van enquiries. I want that lad kept busy and away from Steve Milner as much as possible."

Now that *did* make Trudie think twice. "I doubt the DS is going to be very happy about that sir," she commented.

"Well keeping the DS happy isn't high on my list of priorities at the moment. Getting some action out of our two young detective constables is! Don't worry, I'll tell him what we're doing."

That seemed to satisfy her. "Anything else sir while I'm at it?" she enquired. The question came with a sideways look.

"Well... now you mention it,' he responded before stopping

and smiling. "No... just kidding. But you do know what they say: if you want a job doing well, give it to a busy person." It was the sort of comment that heads off a grumble from the recipient – which it did. With that he upped sticks and headed briskly back to his own office.

Sergeant Barker sat back in her chair mulling over the conversation. "This really is a new broom," she thought to herself with a look of approval.

CHAPTER FIVE

Thursday arrived, the day of the preliminary court hearing for the Eric Smith domestic violence case. It was taking place in Chesterfield starting at ten o'clock. The turbulent weather of the previous weekend had been replaced by glorious spring sunshine as DI Webster's roomy Vauxhall Victor wended its way through the stunning South Peak countryside with Constables Lomas and Briggs, the two arresting officers, also on board. On the face of it, proceedings in court ought to be straightforward, with the testimonies from the neighbour and Smith's wife being pretty damning. Add to that those of the police who attended and an expected guilty plea from the defendant himself, what could go wrong? During the journey, however, Neil warned his passengers about being too confident and particularly Jane about keeping her personal feelings in check. In the end he needn't have worried and at 11.15am Eric Smith was being led away from the courtroom to begin his prison sentence.

"Two years!" crowed Bob with a clenched fist as they exited the court building into the fresh air. It would have been three but, as often happened when a defendant pleaded guilty at a preliminary hearing, it was reduced by a third. Bob tapped Jane playfully on her head. "Well done. You managed to keep a lid on it then!"

"I don't know what you mean?" she protested with feigned innocence. Bob was a practised leg-puller and this was the banter of two workmates who had become good friends, although he stood out of shin-kicking range just in case.

"Well if you hadn't made *that* one stick," intervened Neil, trying to get their feet back on the ground, "there would have been serious questions asked."

On their way back in the car, Neil decided to take a detour and it wasn't long before they were descending the hill into the picturesque riverside market town of Bakewell.

"If you don't mind my saying so sir," said Bob, "this is a bit of a long way round isn't it?"

"I don't mind at all Bob. I told Sergeant Barker we'd be back probably by two o'clock but, as we've just put a thoroughly nasty piece of work away in double quick time, how does a bite to eat and a walk down by the river sound? An antidote to the likes of Eric Smith."

"It sounds excellent," replied Bob, who never needed asking twice if food was involved.

"What about you Jane?" enquired Neil.

"I think that's a great idea," she responded. "It'll help get that horrible man out of my mind."

"Anywhere you'd recommend Bob?" asked the DI.

"Well there's one or two places I know, and then there's the hotel by the roundabout. My wife and I come here quite often."

"In that case I'll park up and we'll follow you. Hey, we could have a Bakewell tart, or should I say *pudding*? When in Rome as they say..." There were no objections and it wasn't long before they found just the place, no more than a stone's throw from the town centre. All three of them ordered the same.

While on their brief sabbatical, the only reference they made to work was the Terry McDonald case. Jane, along with her fellow officers at the station, really sympathised with the mother's situation and to some degree that of the son, who was stuck between a rock and a hard place – either risking being beaten up if he informed on the real culprit or carrying the can himself if he kept his mouth shut, with all the consequences that would have for him. The Lewis Bates's of the world had no conscience.

But Neil wasn't having any of this shop talk and, as they sat at their table with the sun streaming in through the window, he nipped things in the bud. "Hey… come on you two. I didn't bring you here to discuss work. Save it for back at the station."

There were no arguments. Mind you, he was aided and abetted by the arrival of three plates of fish and chips, the perfect distraction. In fact they did touch on the job on the odd occasion but very much on the lighter side of things and by the time they set off back to the car they were in the best of spirits. That's how Neil wanted it: work hard but don't be afraid to play a bit as well. When they finally did get back to the station, their happy mood was still intact and noticeable.

"I didn't know court was so much fun," commented Trudie.

"We're just flushed with success, sarge. That's all," replied Bob with a wide grin.

"Hmmm, well perhaps you'd like to flush yourself back to the front desk so I can get on with some of my own stuff."

She threw an accusing glance in Neil's direction, which he studiously avoided. Top of *his* agenda was to see how Steve Milner had done on his visit to the Rhodes family. He switched from relaxed "Bakewell" mode to deadly serious DI mode as he entered the smokey atmosphere of the CID office. Milner was on the phone but that didn't stop Neil grabbing a chair and plonking himself down on the opposite side of his detective sergeant's desk. The hint to cut the call short could not have been clearer and Milner took it.

"So, how did you get on at the Rhodes's?" Neil asked.

Steve tapped cigarette ash into the glass ashtray on his desk. "Well the mum and the daughter were both there but it wasn't the easiest trying to explain why we wanted to know where the bracelet was found. Like you said, I couldn't push too hard. Anyway, they're going to talk it over with the dad and let us know. The parents are clearly very protective of the girl and I think they might feel it's all a bit much for her. Personally, I think she's up for it. She's not exactly a shrinking violet."

That brought a smile to Neil's face. "How have you left things then?"

Milner rubbed his chin. "I think we should just give them a bit of time. Let's face it, a few days won't make any difference with this one will it?"

"No, that's true," agreed Neil. "Okay Steve, but have a look at the file again just to refresh yourself. Oh yes, and make some enquiries with the nearest search-and-rescue team will you about their availability. Just in case we need them."

Neil got to his feet but he was clearly far from relaxed. "D'you know Steve, I'm beginning to wonder if this is a can of worms we're going to regret opening. I know you've got a gut feeling about the husband but I reckon there's some murkier waters here. That sister for a start, Alison Edwards, the one you interviewed."

"Yeah, she was a piece of work all right," agreed Milner. His expression suggested the same. "Anyway, I'll keep you posted sir."

"Yes, please do."

With that, the DI left the CID room and made his way to the front desk where Bob was in situ. "Can you tell the switchboard not to put any calls through to me for the next half hour Bob."

"Will do, sir."

"Thanks." It was short and sweet but Neil had a couple of pressing phone calls of his own to make, top of the list being one he didn't want anyone else to know about – to Strangeways prison in Manchester.

Another call he made during that half hour was to Macclesfield police station. He waited while they tried to locate his opposite number there, Detective Inspector Phil Morris. Eventually they did.

"Phil... it's Neil Webster here," he announced once he'd heard DI Morris's voice on the other end.

"Well, well, well," came an almost disbelieving reply. "Finally escaped the trenches have you?"

"Oh, you heard? Yeah, the only trenches I'm in these days Phil are farmland furrows. Anyway, how's things over that side of Cat and Fiddle?"

"Pretty humdrum really. Never as exciting as it is for you city boys."

"*Was* Phil, *was*," responded Neil, "and, believe me, there is such a thing as too much excitement."

"Yes, so I understand. You're okay now I hope. Anyway, to what do I owe the pleasure?"

"Well I could do with having a chat with you about a case I'm currently dealing with. Any chance you could spare me some time tomorrow?"

"Are you coming over here then?" asked Phil. There was a moment's silence at the other end before Neil replied.

"Tell you what, Phil. I've discovered a nice little pub just out of Buxton – the Old Grouse Inn – where we could get a bite to eat at the same time. My shout."

"Oh well, in that case I'll clear my diary. I do know the place."

"Excellent! Well if you can manage to get yourself over the hills for twelve o'clock I'll meet you there. It'll be good to see you again."

"Yes, you too."

Hanging up, Neil pressed the button for one of the internal extensions. "Have you got a few minutes?" Neil asked when Trudie picked up.

"Yes sir."

"Right, stay put and I'll pop through." In less than a minute he was standing in front of her.

"That was quick," she remarked.

"Well I wanted to know how we're getting on with organising that briefing for our boys out in the sticks."

Trudie had a natural affinity with rural bobbies, and any hint of them being taken less than seriously wasn't going to go down well with her.

"Just waiting for the carrier pigeons to get back sir," she replied with a meaningful smile.

"Yes, okay sergeant," Neil replied, getting the message.

"It's going to be next Tuesday morning actually, and I think we'll be having a good turnout by the looks of it." She enjoyed telling him that, and it did take him by surprise

"Well that's great. We'd better alert Mary in the canteen then – send them back into the hills on a full stomach. Can I leave that to you?"

"Yes – that'll definitely keep them happy. I'll ask her to make enough for the stage-coach driver as well."

Neil thoroughly enjoyed this sort of repartee and the joust wasn't over yet.

"Now look here Sergeant Barker," he responded, "until this outburst of cheek I was going to offer you a nice trip out next week to Leek. I'm arranging to meet your old boss, Alan Wright, *as you suggested*, but if you're not interested..."

"Oh well, in that case..." She proceeded to perform a mouth-zipping gesture.

"Good," said Neil. "Now then, what's Nick Fielding doing to help you with all this?"

"Well at this moment he should be sorting out some transport for the day."

"And Andy Bowers?"

"He's gone to a motor paint place I think."

Neil couldn't disguise a look of quiet satisfaction. Trudie smiled. "You're enjoying this aren't you sir?"

"Yeah... I suppose I am," Neil confessed.

"Well to be honest," she added, "I can't ever remember the station having so much buzz."

She was interrupted by the phone ringing. Neil made to leave as she picked up the receiver but Trudie motioned for him to stay. The call was from one of the local hospitals. "And when was this?" Trudie started writing on her notepad. "Do you have a name and address?" She continued to take notes as the person on the other end gave details. After a short while, Trudie said: "Yes, I'm not surprised he didn't talk a lot but thanks for getting back to me. You've been a great help."

Putting the receiver down she turned to Neil with a pleased look on her face. "That was the cottage hospital in Matlock. I don't gamble, sir, but if I did I'd put money on this being our man." Neil quickly pulled up a chair as Trudie continued. "I honestly thought I'd drawn a blank with the hospitals. I mean it's six days since the incident and you'd have thought if anyone had been shot they'd have needed attention sooner than that."

"Depends how bad it was," Neil replied. "My guess is they probably tried to deal with it themselves but it was starting to turn nasty. When did he go in?"

"About two hours ago."

Neil considered things for a moment before nodding towards Trudie's notepad. "Have you got a name and address?"

"Well... sort of," she replied cautiously. Neil leant over and she pushed the pad over to him. He read out loud what she'd written.

"John Jones." It prompted a despondent shrug. "Could have been worse I suppose. He might have used *Smith*." He didn't bother looking at the address. "Still, I suppose we'd better check it out."

But Trudie didn't look despondent at all.

"Okay... what am I missing?" enquired Neil.

"Well someone down in Matlock must have had their buttons sown on. They were so suspicious, one of them followed him out to the car park and took his number plate."

Neil's countenance changed completely. "Well how about that!"

When Neil got back to his office it dawned on him that it had only been a few days ago that he'd been thinking how quiet things were... but now, suddenly, everything was happening. And it wasn't long before things ramped up further. There was a tap on the door and Steve Milner entered.

"Yes, what is it Steve?"

"We've had the okay from the Rhodes family sir. The mother rang just now."

Yet another positive development, Neil thought. "Excellent. Well done, Steve."

"But there is a proviso," Milner added. "The father insists on accompanying his daughter. He'll take time off work if necessary. Oh yes, and one of the other friends has agreed to come as well." Neil nodded in approval but then leant back in his chair with his hands clasped behind his head looking pensive.

"What's up, sir?"

"Well, it's like I said before, Steve, part of me still thinks this could be a fool's errand. We're talking about mile after mile of windswept moorland up there."

Milner clearly wasn't seeing it the same way. "Well it might not be as bad as you think."

"And why's that?"

"Denise, the daughter, told me that when she found the bracelet the weather was still pretty good. It was before the storm arrived and she was certain that she'd recognise at least the general area."

Before Neil had a chance to respond, his sergeant had something further to add. "I also managed to get hold of a guy at High Peak Mountain Rescue who said he'd be more than happy to help us in a preliminary search."

That pretty much made Neil's mind up. It sounded as though finding the initial location where the bracelet was found could be conducted with minimal use of police time and resources. Either the girls could take them there or they couldn't.

"Right Steve," he eventually announced. "How's your hiking these days?"

Much as Milner wanted to chase this case along, he wasn't exactly built for moorland trekking, even along a well-trodden path. Neil didn't prolong his discomfort. "Don't worry, *I'll* go, but I want WPC Briggs along to accompany those girls."

"D'you think that's a good idea, sir?"

"I do! She can expend some of her excess enthusiasm." Milner had no option but to go along with it, albeit with a shrug.

Neil felt it was time to wrap things up. "Right then. I'll clear it with Sergeant Barker regarding WPC Briggs. You organise the rest and keep me posted. Okay?"

"Yes sir."

Another thought popped into Neil's head. "Just one more thing, Steve. In case we do find something up there, check out exactly where Malcolm Butler is these days will you."

Neil thought Milner would like that idea. He was right. But no sooner had his detective sergeant made his exit than the DI had another visitor. "Yep!" called Neil when the knock on the door came.

This time it was Andy Bowers, clearly bearing information. "That paint sample, sir. I've shown it to a number of vehicle paint shops and they all reckon that it's from a Bedford CA van."

Neil thrummed his fingers on the top of his desk while he deliberated what to do next. From here on, he wanted to keep

Steve Milner as far away from the farm theft investigation as he could. The reactivated Butler investigation had played right into his hands on that score. It was now time for him to go to work on Bowers. "Right Andy," he began. "I want you to tell me everything you know about these thefts that *isn't* in the file."

Bowers hesitated. Neil looked heavenward in annoyance. "Shut the door."

Andy obeyed and the DI pointed to a spare chair. "Now sit down there and *stop messing me about*!"

Bowers was rattled. He was a youthful-looking lad with a gingerish mop and a pale face that easily flushed... and it was certainly flushing now.

"*Well*?" Neil pressed. He knew how to be intimidating when he wanted to be and this was such an occasion.

Andy pushed his hand through his hair nervously. "Just that you've been up to John Mellor's place, sir, and got this..." He held up the stained wood. "So we know what sort of vehicle to look for."

"That all?"

"Yes sir."

"Nothing about any damage to it?"

Bowers looked genuinely surprised. "No sir. He's always told me not to ask questions and just to leave things to him. It seemed to be his way of operating and finding stuff out."

Neil inwardly despaired. "You sure he didn't mention any damage, Andy? Because if I find you're holding out on me, I'll have you back in uniform so fast it'll make your nose bleed."

"It's the honest truth sir," blurted Bowers.

Neil throttled back. "Well I'll enlighten you then. That splinter of green you're holding came from John Mellor's milk stand. The back door of the van hit it. So now you know what we're looking for... *don't you Andy*?"

'Yes sir. A green Bedford CA van with damage to the back door."

"Correct. Now listen. If you haven't heard, we're having a briefing here, probably Tuesday morning, which will include trying to locate this van. Unless you hear differently, *from me,* I want you there. Trudie is in charge so you speak to her. Leave Steve to me." He looked Andy in the eye. "Understand?"

"Yes sir," replied a chastened Bowers.

"Okay, that's it. Now off you go."

Andy couldn't leave the room quickly enough. He'd never seen this side of Neil Webster before and any illusions that the new DI might be an easy ride had gone right out of the window. He also realised that the wheels were in grave danger of falling off the cosy relationship he had with his immediate boss. Suddenly he felt very uncomfortable, very uncomfortable indeed.

That afternoon, Jane had arranged to see the headmaster again at the Robert Stevenson school regarding the break-in. She and PC Richard Lowe had visited Lewis Bates's house and, as Mrs McDonald had expected, they had found no evidence of the stolen items. But the two mothers could not have been more different. Both Mr *and* Mrs Bates were at home, Lewis as well, and Jane could understand exactly why their son had turned out as he had. The place was a tip – she could have imagined the word "feckless" having been invented especially for them. Needless to say Lewis denied any knowledge of the break-in or association with the football in Terry's possession.

"Well why did you run away the moment you saw me that afternoon then?" Jane had asked him.

"Because I don't like coppers," replied Lewis sneeringly before momentarily changing his tone. "But I might make an exception for you." Jane took a deep breath. Then, as if the Bates's weren't objectionable enough, they had the gall to point the finger at Terry.

"We've told Lewis he shouldn't associate with that McDonald

lad. He's a bad influence on him," bleated Mrs Bates. What a test of self control this was for PC Briggs. Richard Lowe knew she was ticking and was relieved to see her take another deep breath. It worked and the officers eventually left the house without incident.

"I thought you were going to blow a gasket in there," he remarked as they walked down the path and back on to the street.

"Well I felt like it. The creep!"

It infuriated Jane to think that a potentially decent lad like Terry could have his life blighted by a bunch of ne'er do wells like the Bates's. It was with that in mind that she found herself sitting opposite Mr Cousins in his office at the school that afternoon hoping that the sight of the Mitre football she'd brought along would put him in a forgiving mood.

Once more he was ebullient and charming. "Well that's one back at least," he said with a beam as he surveyed the ball. He looked up at her enquiringly. "Terry McDonald?"

With great reluctance, she replied: "Yes, that *is* where I found it Mr Cousins."

"No sign of the other stuff I suppose?"

"Not so far I'm afraid."

The headmaster sat back looking resigned to the situation as it stood. "So, what do I do to press charges?" he asked.

Jane had hoped he might have mellowed since their last meeting but it seemed quite the opposite and this was probably her only opportunity to try to change his mind. "The thing is, Mr Cousins. We're pretty certain it wasn't Terry who broke in."

"But I bet he was involved wasn't he?" Cousins was giving no quarter. "Do you know who the others were?"

"I think so but we can't prove it and Terry's too scared to name them."

Cousins looked as though he was about to explode with

frustration but took a deep breath. "What are you asking me to do, constable?"

"Well would you just hold off making a formal complaint for the moment while we make further enquiries? He's starting his first job next week."

The head sat there silently, his facial expression a clear indicator of what his brain was wrestling with. It was with a huge sigh that he gave way. "All right, but that boy can't keep thinking he can get away with things. I'll give you one month but that's it!" He looked at the Mitre then back at Jane. "Can I have my ball back please?"

Jane had warmed to Mr Cousins so it was with the utmost reluctance that she had to decline his request.

"Evidence?" he enquired.

"Evidence," she confirmed.

He scratched the back of his head disparagingly. "Not my day is it?"

"Well you see plenty of days like that in my job, Mr Cousins."

He managed to raise a faint smile. "You sometimes wonder why we do it, don't you? Try to do the best for people, that is."

Jane pondered the question for a second. "Because it's what we *do* Mr Cousins, isn't it." She was winning.

"Ah... an old head on young shoulders." He looked wistful. "I'm just an old head on *old* shoulders."

She took on board the sentiment. "Oh I think there's plenty of life in you yet, Mr Cousins."

He absorbed the kindness of the remark and smiled. "I see they have charm lessons at police training these days."

Jane laughed. "Trust me, I can be incredibly *un*charming when I want to."

"I don't believe it for a moment," he countered. "Anyway, must get on. Got a parents' evening tonight. No peace for the wicked as they say." With that he got up.

Jane did likewise, thanked him and made her exit from the office with the football tucked underneath her arm. What neither of them knew was that a twist in events was going to turn the Terry McDonald case upside down.

CHAPTER SIX

By Friday morning, Trudie had received from the DVLC details of the owner of the vehicle that had been in the hospital car park at Matlock. It belonged to Eddie Slater, who ran a business, if you could call it that, a few miles outside the town. It would be difficult to categorise what sort of business it was but it had several unroadworthy-looking vehicles in the yard and other "junk". There was a small house and a big shed, where one could imagine repair work would be carried out. Unsurprisingly, he was already on their radar at Matlock station and they took no persuading to watch his movements, at least for a few days, and report back.

Mid-morning found Neil in the canteen chatting to Mary about the number of dinners she'd have to prepare for the briefing next Tuesday.

"Don't you worry, Mr Webster," she assured him. "There'll be three of us in and we'll be ready for them. It'll be toad in the hole with roly-poly pudding and custard for afters."

Neil laughed. "It's a good job they're not on their bikes, Mary. They'd never make it back into the hills."

"What d'you mean? It'll be light as a feather."

"No I didn't mean it that way. They'll probably just eat too much."

"Oh, that's all right then. Are you in for lunch today?"

"No, I'm meeting an old colleague of mine for a bite at the Old Grouse Inn."

Mary rolled her eyes.

"What? Is the food there not good enough or something?" Neil asked.

She leant over to him, making sure no one was in earshot. "I don't know about the food but something funny went on up there a while back." She leant closer. "I'm not sure exactly what it was but I know Steve Milner got a bit flustered."

No sooner had she said the words than who should come through the door but the man himself. Mary dived back towards whatever she was cooking. As Milner approached she gave him the most unconvincing of smiles. "All right, Mr Milner?"

He gave her a circumspect look in return. "Yes thank you, Mary," he replied before turning to Neil. He seemed keen to talk to the DI and it soon became clear why.

"How are you fixed to go up Kinder tomorrow sir?" There was a definite hint of pleasure in the question.

"Tomorrow!"

"Yes sir. The Rhodes family wants to get the whole thing out of the way as soon as possible... and the forecast's good."

Neil wasn't supposed to be on duty that weekend and his wife more than likely had something planned. Sudden calls to action had been commonplace in Manchester but that was supposed to be a thing of the past. She'd no doubt understand, but that didn't mean she was going to be happy about it.

"Okay Steve. Where are we meeting?"

"The youth hostel in Edale. Ten o'clock. The chap from the local mountain rescue will meet you there. His name's Brian Parker."

"Have you spoken to Constable Briggs?"

"No sir. I thought you'd like to do that as you were keen to have her along."

That mildly irritated Neil but he let it go. "All right. Leave it with me and I'll have a word with her."

Mission accomplished, Milner went on his way. He was practically whistling.

Mary waited until he'd gone. "He looked happy!"

"Yes, he would do," Neil replied darkly. "Now then Mary, what were you just saying... about the Old Grouse?"

"Oh yes, that." She peered to see if the coast was clear again. It was. "Well," she began. "It did have a bit of a bad reputation. It's where... I don't know... *less desirables* frequented." Pointing towards the canteen door, she whispered: "But *he* used to go there, or so I heard on the grapevine."

Something splattered behind her on the cooker. "Just a minute. I'll have to go and turn that down." She was soon back. "Now where was I? Oh yes. Apparently he claimed it was a good place to *find things out.* But then the landlord suddenly got the boot by the brewery – I don't know what he was up to but I think he'd been turning a blind eye to goings on. Anyway, they'd had enough and put it up for sale."

"And then the Hargreaves took over?"

"Exactly, and they weren't happy with what was going on... at all. They came in here – you see they didn't *know* Mr Milner was a policeman. It was young Mr Bowers who saw them but Mr Milner soon took over and it all went quiet again. I wouldn't normally have paid attention but I heard grumblings. *A bit too close* was the word."

The door of the canteen suddenly opened. Mary's eyes glanced in its direction. "Oooh, I better get on."

Neil thanked her as she turned back to her stove.

He set off, coffee in hand, back to his office wondering what other pearls of information she might have under her apron. She hadn't told him anything specific but he presumed that Milner must have done something to discourage the Hargreaves from taking things any further. It crossed his mind to broach the subject with them when he met his counterpart from

Macclesfield for lunch there. Something for him to dwell on. He picked up the phone and buzzed the front desk.

"Constable Briggs around?" he enquired. After a few seconds he got an answer in the affirmative. "Ask her to pop into my office will you." He only had time for a couple of sips of his coffee before she arrived.

"You wanted me, sir?"

"Yes, sit down will you."

Jane could see he didn't look too happy and thought she was going to get a ticking off for something. She was wrong.

"Fancy some overtime constable?" the DI asked.

She didn't expect *that* but was quietly relieved. "Oh... er... yes sir. Of course."

"Have you got any walking boots?"

She looked baffled. "I'm sure I could find something."

"Good, because you'll need them for some detective work I've got planned for tomorrow."

WPC Briggs was a real-life jack-in-a-box and by the time she'd left his office Neil knew the task that lay ahead of them on Saturday would be a lot less dull with her on board.

The clock had ticked round to 11.30am, time for Neil to shut up shop and head off to his car. On the way out he checked in with Trudie to let her know where he was going and for roughly how long. When he eventually arrived in the pub car park, Phil was there waiting. He'd made good time coming over from Macclesfield, a journey he'd made numerous times. Like most locals he knew the short cut that took out the endless long bends – an absolute godsend if you were in a hurry – but it also allowed motorists to get a great view of Tegg's Nose, the quirky promontory that stood out among the otherwise featureless moorland in the area.

Even though the weather was an improvement from Neil's first visit to the Old Grouse Inn, the pub's fire had been lit. They sat down at a table close to it and engaged in general chit-chat while perusing the menu. Sandra Hargreaves made her way over. She didn't recognise Neil until she got quite close but her welcome was definitely a degree warmer than when they first met.

"Oh hello. I didn't expect to see you again quite so soon."

"Well I am a man of my word, and I did say I'd be in for a meal some time – so here I am." He nodded towards his colleague. "Phil's a mate of mine. A softie from Cheshire."

"Watch it!" his friend rebuked.

Sandra warmed up another degree. "So, can I get you anything to drink?"

"Just a jug of water please," replied Phil, with one eye still on the menu, but we'll definitely have some food. I'll go for... the gammon and chips." He looked over to Neil. "What are you having?"

His colleague had already made his mind up. "Easy – sausage and mash."

They handed the menu back to Sandra. She soon returned from the bar with their water. "The food won't be long."

"That's fine, no rush," replied Neil as they settled in.

Phil decided to open proceedings proper. "Right, putting my stimulating company to one side, tell me a bit more about why you wanted to meet up?"

Neil pulled his seat closer to the table. "Okay, well as I mentioned on the phone it's this case I've got that goes back to before I came to Buxton: the theft of farm gear. The thing is, the number of incidents has been increasing and one of our local farmers recently decided to take matters into his own hands."

"Ouch!" said Phil.

"Well it was definitely an *ouch* for someone," Neil replied, "but in a cock-eyed way it was good news for us because it has provided our first solid lead."

"Oh yes?"

"Yes. The injured party appears to have turned up at hospital in Matlock needing attention and we think we might know how to find him." Phil was showing more and more interest. Neil continued. "So that's one thing but my sergeant also has a theory that the gang's operation extends a lot wider than just our patch. As you're my next-door neighbour, I wondered if you'd heard any whispers."

Their conversation was interrupted by the arrival of the meals. "There we are," said Sandra, placing the plates down. "Would you like any sauce?"

The policemen looked at one another. "No, I think we're okay thank you," replied Neil.

Sandra duly left them in peace to survey their fare.

"Well this looks all right," Phil said, eyeing a prime piece of gammon topped with a pineapple ring and some seriously chunky chips with peas.

Neil surveyed his own meal. "I used to love this when I was a kid. I'd get the mashed potatoes into a ring with the sausages and gravy trapped in the middle, but you had to make sure there were no leaks."

"Well don't let me stop you," Phil replied. "There's no law against it. Well, not yet anyway."

Twenty minutes later there were two clean plates and the detectives got back down to business but, considering how much he'd enjoyed his meal, Phil didn't look too happy.

"Is that sergeant of yours psychic?" he enquired.

"Well she's pretty sharp but I don't think she's got any mystical powers," Neil replied with a laugh. "Though I wouldn't be surprised if she's working on it. Not a lot gets past *her*!"

"Oh, she's a she is she?" responded his colleague, clearly surprised by the gender. "*Very* progressive."

Neil wasn't sure whether he could detect a condescending tone or not. "Yes, and she's damn good at her job," he shot back.

"So don't *you* start. I have enough trouble back at my place."

"Hey, steady on. I'm completely with you. She could be a Martian for all I care. All I was going to say was that, since your phone call yesterday, we've had a report from one of our lads about something gone missing from a farm near Wilbercluff – a sort of hedge cutter that works off a tractor."

"You mean that place spelt 'Wild-boar-clough' near Macclesfield Forest?"

"Yes, but it is pronounced *Wilbercluff*."

"Oh well, if you say so," Neil replied acceptingly.

Phil continued. "Anyway, the farmer reckons he had visitors last Monday when he and his missus were away at Chelford market."

Sandra rolled up to see if they'd finished. "Nice to see two empty plates," she said.

"Yes. It was lovely thanks," replied Neil. Phil nodded his approval.

"Would you like a sweet?"

"Not for me,' replied Phil.

"No, I'm fine too, thanks," added Neil.

"Any coffees?" They both happily agreed. "Pity that Sergeant Milner hasn't got your manners," she remarked nonchalantly as she departed. That threw Neil. What was it with Milner that had upset the Hargreaves so much?

Phil noticed his concern. "Problem?" he enquired.

"Yeah. I think so. I just don't know how big."

Sandra brought the coffees and returned to the kitchen. The detectives returned to Phil's account of what appeared to be the first case of agricultural skulduggery on his side of the Cat and Fiddle. Their conversation was interrupted as the large clock that sat on the mantelpiece over the fire struck the hour. It was one o'clock. Phil looked at his watch as if to check it was right.

"You okay for time?" Neil enquired.

"Yeah, I'm fine."

"Tell you what then. I want to call on someone not far from here. Got a bit of news for them. Fancy joining me?"

"Depends what it is?"

"All right. I'll just settle up and tell you more when we get outside."

Amid the pleasantries while paying the bill, Neil whispered to Sandra: "You know where I am if you and Jim ever want a chat." Sandra flashed him a smile as she gave him his change. This time Neil felt that the message had fallen on more receptive ground. Ten minutes later, his Vauxhall Victor was rumbling its way up the track to Lower Booth Farm followed by Phil in his Rover 90.

So far, Neil had kept the matter of John Mellor's pot-shot between himself and Trudie, but he knew he could trust Phil and had explained in the pub car park the background to this farm visit. Phil was an excellent bloke to bounce things off and, because he now had some "skin in the game", it was even more relevant. They parked up in the yard. Neil had hardly stepped out on to the concrete before someone emerged from the kitchen doorway – Mrs Mellor.

"Hello?" she called sharply, making a beeline for the cars. She didn't take kindly to strangers turning up unannounced but she realised as she drew closer that one of them wasn't a *complete* stranger. "Oh, you're that police chap aren't you?"

Phil stood by his car with an amused look on his face.

"We wondered who it was," she continued.

Neil approached with an apologetic smile. "I'm sorry to call out of the blue Mrs Mellor, but I was in the area and wanted to update you on things." Neil's charm disarmed her but it was clear that if an unwelcome visitor needed to be repelled, Jean Mellor was up to the task.

Neil turned towards Phil. "This is a colleague of mine from Macclesfield."

"Oh yes? What's he doing? Having a day out?" This time it was Neil's turn to stifle a laugh. "Anyway, you'd better come in and have that cup of tea you turned down last time. Come on." Neil nodded to Phil to follow them into the kitchen.

"Sorry it's a bit of a mess," said Mrs Mellor. "We've only just finished dinner. I'll just shout John then get this table cleared." She walked to the hall door and called through: "John. Come in the kitchen will you!" She returned and started moving some pots to the sink. "He'll be along in a minute."

"Well don't do it on our account, Mrs Mellor."

"*Jean!*" she insisted.

Her husband appeared at the door. "Oh, it's you again." It sounded blunt but it wasn't meant like that – it was just the Mellor way.

"Sit yourselves down," said Jean. "Anywhere you can find."

As in so many old farmhouses, the kitchen was large; the "nerve-centre" of the farm where most activity in the house took place. There was a huge table at its heart with all sorts piled on it, including a wash basket, sewing machine and a pile of newspapers, but there was still plenty of room to host a meal. There was a big settee against one wall and at the far end a large fireplace. In front of that, suspended from the ceiling, was a clothes dryer, about six feet long with five wooden rails to hang items on and a rope on a pulley to let it up and down tethered to a hook on the wall. Old-fashioned it may have been but very effective. Neil and Phil chose to sit on the settee but there was little support left in the cushions, causing the pair of them to sink a lot lower than they expected. Not exactly the dynamic face of local law enforcement!

"Got some news then, have you?" John asked.

"Well, a bit..." Neil knew he needed to preface what he was about to say. "Just so you know, there's only *me*, one other officer and Phil here that know what really happened the other night and I'll do my best to make sure it stays that way."

The farmer gave a minimal nod of approval.

"But like I said to you, it did give us a lead and I think we might be on to who it was that paid you that visit."

Now that's what John Mellor wanted to hear. To him, it wasn't just about getting his property returned, although that would be nice. He wanted to see the thieves behind bars. He was prepared to accept some minor punishment himself as long as justice was served. Just then the Mellors' farm dog wandered into the kitchen, sniffed the air and made straight for Phil, giving his ankles a serious vacuuming with his nose.

"Leave him alone, Tegg!" called Jean sharply. But the dog was deaf to her command.

"Don't worry about him," Phil said. "He can probably smell *my* dog. "You're a nice feller, aren't you Tegg?" He gave the dog a fulsome rub on the head.

"What sort have *you* got?" asked Jean.

"A working cocker," Phil replied, pointing to his head. "Can't you see by the grey hairs?"

Mrs Mellor grinned. "Bit lively is it?"

"Yes, you could say that. We're still trying to find the 'off' switch." He looked down at Tegg again and patted him. "But we love her really." The dog continued to sniff. "That's some nose he's got on him."

John broke into a half smile. "Aye, that's why we called him Tegg – because of his nose."

That tickled Phil. "Ha... that's brilliant," he replied, looking over to Neil, who had a blank expression on his face. "I'll explain to you later."

Neil decided that was enough "doggy" talk for now. "So the reason Phil's with me today is because we're getting our heads together about these farm thefts. He's just had what looks like one at Wild-boar-clough."

John looked baffled. "D'you mean Wilbercluff?"

CHAPTER SEVEN

The following Saturday morning at about ten o'clock, two vehicles pulled into the car park at Edale youth hostel within five minutes of each other. One of them was DI Webster's, with Jane Briggs as his passenger. The other car belonged to Simon Rhodes, the father of Denise, the girl who'd found the bracelet. She was accompanied by her friend, Janice. The weather was as Steve Milner had predicted, fine if a bit nippy. Once everyone had got out, there was some handshaking as introductions were made, then some hand *rubbing* reflecting the cold temperature. Anoraks were the order of the day at this time in the morning. Everyone carried a rucksack but none compared to the one on the back of the seasoned-looking hiker type who was approaching them across the car park. He clearly meant business. "Is anyone here Detective Inspector Webster?" he enquired as he came to a standstill.

"That's me," replied Neil.

"Morning. I'm Brian Parker, from High Peak Mountain Rescue."

Neil shook Brian's hand before introducing everyone else.

"I do quite a bit up here at weekends," said Brian, gesturing towards the YHA building. "It feels like home from home sometimes."

"It's very good of you to help us out Brian."

"I'm more than happy to. Your sergeant – *Milner* is it? –

explained the situation. So, how would you like to do this?"

Denise's father, Simon, was the first to respond. "Is there any reason why we shouldn't just follow exactly the same route as the girls did?" There was a consensus of approval to his suggestion. The girls were clearly excited about the prospect of playing a central role in a police investigation.

Denise was the more confident of the two and couldn't wait to offer her input. "Shall I tell you which way we went?" she began. "Starting from here?"

Neil couldn't think of any reason why not. "Everyone okay with that?" He and Simon exchanged a smile, while everyone else nodded in agreement. "Over to you then, Denise."

She needed no further encouragement. "Well we got off at the station at the bottom of the village," she said, pointing in the general direction, "and then we walked up the lane to where the main track starts." The path she was referring to was soon to become known as the Pennine Way. "It's opposite the pub. The Old Nag's Head, I think it is. And basically we just stuck to that. It was only when we got on to the tops that we wandered around a bit." Her dad winced. He'd specifically asked her to keep to the track if they went up Kinder, aware of how tricky things could be up there.

"And was it somewhere round that area that you found the bracelet?" asked Neil.

She nodded. "Yes, it is. Well, sort of." She looked sheepish and tried to move the conversation on quickly. "It's actually really interesting up there. A bit spooky. Lots of weird-shaped rocks. I didn't think it would do any harm just to explore a little bit." She glanced at her father, knowing what he was thinking. "Honestly, Dad. I didn't take any chances." She hoped her public semi-apology might avert a ticking off later.

Jane had been listening intently and Denise's description had intrigued her. She was looking forward to visiting this mysterious world, while Denise sounded like a fun person to be with. Having said that, WPC Briggs knew she'd have to behave herself bearing in mind the circumstances.

The party set off along the trail and Neil soon found himself chatting away to Brian about this and that, including the subject of teenage girls. He'd dealt with plenty of them one way or another during the course of his job and also had one of his own – Rachel.

His daughter didn't live at home any more, having been at university for well over a year now, but he remembered just what a handful she'd been at Denise's age, especially when she was with her friends. By all accounts she was having a whale of a time up in Lancaster. He'd no objection to that; he just hoped she was learning something at the same time. In truth he was in no doubt that she was, and happy to concede that his daughter had inherited her mother's academic brain rather than his own. He was also more than happy to make the counter argument that the possessor of a bachelor of arts degree was well down the list of usefulness should your toilet be blocked or you were trying to get the better of the criminally inclined. With his own experience in mind, he was keeping a close eye on the two live-wire 16-year-olds. That said, he thought it would be an interesting test for Constable Briggs. Her task on this day had been made quite clear to her; stick close to the two girls and keep them focused.

Neil also had a son, Paul, three years older than his sister. Unlike her, Paul's inclinations were far more on the practical side. He didn't mind getting his hands dirty and, at the age of 23, was making his way at an engineering company in Stockport, where he shared digs in the town with one of his co-workers. For Neil and his wife Anne, not having the kids around had taken a lot of getting used to. Sometimes the house *did* seem a bit empty, but whenever they were down about it, which wasn't often, they consoled themselves with the fact that both their children appeared to be making good starts to their independent lives.

The party made its way up the lower valley where the trail was wide and not at all steep, enabling a brisk pace. That all changed when they reached the little packhorse bridge which crossed the river at the foot of the steep incline known as Jacob's Ladder. The location was one that demanded walkers stop and take in the sparkling little waterfalls and tranquil pools before they tackled the steep and rugged terrain that lay ahead.

During this break from walking, Brian Parker gathered everyone around for a brief pep talk. "Okay," he began. "Denise and Janice already know what the next section is like but for those who don't, it's pretty steep, but it eventually brings us out on to the plateau at the top. Anyway, just mind how you go."

They set off again, with Denise and Janice leading the way. Jane wanted to have a word with Neil, who was following with Brian and Simon. Until now she had conducted herself impeccably – walking, talking and laughing with the youngsters – but Neil was acutely aware that she sometimes struggled to keep her effervescent personality in check. He was never quite sure what was going on in that brain of hers. Now here she was with a mischievous look on her face. "Can I help you, constable?" he enquired.

"Yes. It's just that Brian said it gets pretty steep up here and the girls say so as well."

"And?"

"Well, if you need any help sir, just let me know – that's all." She had trouble keeping a straight face.

So did Neil but he gritted his teeth, refusing to rise to the bait. "That's very kind of you but I think I can just about manage, thank you."

Simon and Brian couldn't disguise their smirks but Neil wasn't going to let her get away scot free and called after her as she set off back to the girls. "Did I tell you I was putting you on nights next week, Constable Briggs?"

"Sorry sir... I didn't quite catch that," came the distant reply accompanied by a cheeky grin. She'd had the last word.

The good-natured tone of the expedition continued as they began their ascent but conversation waned as the amount of huffing and puffing increased. Neil was competitive by nature and even though Jane was more than 20 years his junior, he had no intention of letting young Miss Briggs get the better of him. He liked to keep as fit as possible – swimming regularly and playing a bit of golf – so at least he was in with a fighting chance.

It was now 11.30am, with the sun well above the hilltops, but it was still on the nippy side, mainly because they were getting close to 2,000 feet above sea level. But no one in the group was feeling the cold as they ploughed on up Jacob's Ladder. The girls had opened up a gap on the men, regularly sneaking a crafty peek behind them, but their pursuers, under Brian's supervision, were maintaining a steady pace and imperceptibly inching their way closer. But there was a balancing act to be had and even though an unspoken contest was undeniably taking place, safety was still paramount. The three men knew it and Jane did too. Denise and Janice were soon struggling to keep up with her pace so it wasn't long before she called a halt for a drink and a sit down. The men were now right behind them.

"Honours even I think," said Neil as they rested.

"Yes, you're doing very well sir," Jane replied. There was a hint of condescension but he let it pass... just. With batteries recharged they set off again. The next stopping point, right at the top of the climb, was Edale Cross, a medieval stone relic and for many hikers a more general resting place after completing the climb. Unsurprisingly, they were not alone when they reached the spot.

As instructed at the briefing, Neil's group kept any conversation with others to generalities and the usual chat between walkers who crossed paths broke out – the weather, where they were from, a good place to get a bite to eat locally and so on – but you could bet your bottom dollar that no one else up there was involved in a missing persons investigation. However, during the break a seriousness began to descend over the party. They were close to the surreal world of the plateau and things felt *very* different.

As soon as they had the spot to themselves, Neil called them together. "Denise, we're really in your and Janice's hands now. Where next?"

"It's up here," replied Denise without hesitation, pointing ahead of them. "That's right, isn't it Janice?"

"Yes, but it's still a long way." She didn't sound too thrilled about the fact. "We were up here about an hour and then the weather started to go funny."

"Okay then," said Brian, taking over. "You two girls continue up front with Constable Briggs and get your bearings as you go along." He checked his watch. "We've made good time up to here, so there's no rush." The group donned their backpacks and resumed the trek.

Neither Neil nor Simon Rhodes had been up Kinder Scout before and, as they walked along, Denise's dad looked ill at ease. Brian noticed. "You okay, Simon?" he enquired.

The reply contained both a touch of recrimination *and* guilt. "Had I known what a desolate place this was, I would never have let Denise come up here in the first place." He looked around bleakly. "All these boulders and bogs. We asked her not to take any risks and the area looks full of them."

Brian understood how he felt. Heaven knows, if anyone knew the dangers of walking the High Peak he did, but he thought a word or two in support of Denise wouldn't be out of place.

"I do get that, Simon. I've got three kids of my own, but sometimes you just have to trust them. Actually, I think Denise deserves a lot of credit. She and her friends did the right things in difficult conditions when that storm arrived and because of that they were okay."

Simon realised he hadn't looked at it that way and that Brian had a point... a very good one. He and his wife had been so concerned about their daughter they'd overlooked how sensible she'd ultimately been. He shook his head and smiled almost apologetically. "Ha! Well that's told *me*, hasn't it?"

Brian hadn't meant it as a ticking off, more a pat on the back for Simon's daughter. He hoped he'd not rocked the boat but as they walked on Simon's demeanour took a definite turn for the better. He was soon chatting away as the three men walked together. "If it can be wild up here in April," he said, "heaven knows what it must be like in the depths of winter."

"I've no intention of finding out," Neil replied. "What I do know is that they bring juvenile delinquents up here as punishment."

"What, in winter?" Simon asked disbelievingly.

"Yeah."

"I bet they think twice before reoffending."

"Oh, they do," assured Neil.

The conversation was interrupted as the girls ground to a halt ahead.

"Hmmm, looks like something's happening," said Brian. Their group rapidly caught up.

Over the last 100 yards or so, the two schoolgirls had been getting increasingly confident in their recollection of where they were. It was time for another discussion. Denise did the honours. "Janice and I think this is the spot where we stopped. It is, isn't it Janice?"

"Yes, I'm sure it is," Janice replied, pointing to something in the distance. "It was that funny boulder thing over there. I went to have a look at it. Liz stayed here on the path but when I came back I could see you Denise... well just your head anyway... right over there." She pointed to the spot she meant. It was in a totally different direction.

Elizabeth Thorpe (Liz to her friends) had been the third girl in the party of campers but she'd had more than enough of Kinder Scout and wanted no part of today's search. Minds were now being concentrated.

"If it's okay with you Simon," said Brian, "I'll go with Denise and see if she can point out roughly the spot. I'll leave a marker and we'll come straight back. For the moment I'd prefer the rest of you to stay put." Simon and Neil bowed to Brian's experience.

"You okay with that, Denise?" Brian asked.

"Yes, I'm ready."

"Just be careful," called her father as Denise and Brian set off.

"Don't worry, Dad. I will."

Waiting behind gave the rest of the group an opportunity to take in more of the unique landscape that surrounded them. Janice had seen it all before but to Neil, Simon and Jane it was a whole new experience. They could see why regular visitors to the plateau described it as "unworldly".

Brian and Denise returned 20 minutes later. As they set foot on the main track again they took a few seconds to get used to its even surface, a sharp contrast to the stones and boggy hollows of the the terrain they'd just been dealing with.

"Okay," said Brian. "It is tricky down there but if *you* could join me, DI Webster, I think we should take a look together."

Neil agreed straight away. There was no way he was leaving without checking the scene personally. He turned to the others. "Right, I don't want anyone else going down there apart from me and Brian. You'll just have to be patient, I'm afraid, but we'll get back as soon as we can."

He turned to Brian. "After you then." As they set off there was the vaguest sign of a path, which was presumably what had enticed Denise to go exploring in the first place. It was most likely the work of sheep that were now back on the moors after spending the winter down in the valley. Eventually the two men reached Brian's marker. As Neil took in the surroundings, he wondered how on earth the bracelet could have got there. At this stage he could think of only two plausible scenarios. Then again, an even more unlikely third *did* pop into his head.

It was really quiet apart from the sound of the wind blowing through the rough moorland vegetation and Neil jumped when a sheep suddenly shot out in front of him as if from nowhere. As he made his way slowly forward, a scoured-out hollow revealed itself; the sort that becomes etched into peaty moors as the elements carve their way under the roots of vegetation. It was the perfect place for sheep to shelter when things got tough.

He realised he needed Brian's help and beckoned him over. They both stood looking at the hollow. "What d'you think about this?" he asked.

"It's a scrape," replied Brian. You'll find them everywhere up here. I slept in one once when I did my survival training."

Neil looked shocked. "Really?"

"I *was* under canvas as well. The trouble is the ground can collapse at any time and peat is heavy stuff." He looked out across the bleak landscape. "The elements work relentlessly up here, carving away. Some of the animals do a bit as well." He turned his gaze back to the scrape and looked at it inquisitively. "D'you think something could have happened here?"

Neil craned his neck, not sure what he was looking for. It was just a moorland feature like hundreds of others in the vicinity. He rubbed the back of his neck in thought. "Who knows. It's certainly not like any other potential crime scene I've been to, if that's what it is. Anyway, now I've had a look, like I said, I'm prepared to get a dog up here and give that a go, but if that doesn't produce anything I'm not sure what else we can do." That nagging thought popped into his head again about the wisdom of the whole thing. He turned quietly to Brian. "At the end of the day, if young Miss Rhodes hadn't accidentally spotted the bracelet, the file would have remained in its cupboard and we'd have all been none the wiser."

CHAPTER EIGHT

That same Saturday evening, Anne Webster was pleasantly surprised to see her husband's car pull into the driveway much earlier than she'd expected. Neil had been quite right about her being less than pleased about his having to work that day so this was a nice, if limited, surprise.

"How did it go?" she enquired once he'd set foot in the hall.

"Well it was certainly different."

"Are you hungry?"

"Ravenous. It seems like a long time since I ate those sandwiches you packed for me." His expression suggested he had more to say about culinary matters. "So, to make amends for messing up our Saturday, I thought you might like to go out for dinner."

"Really?" she replied, looking surprised. "I'm amazed you've got the energy."

"I've certainly got enough to walk into town and try that new Italian place you keep mentioning and to share a bottle of wine. But could I have a quick cuppa first? Get rid of the trail dust so to speak." He gave her a smile that he hoped would elicit a positive response to his idea. "So... what do you think?"

Anne returned an even bigger smile. "D'you know, sweetheart. That would be *really* nice." Her smile diminished slightly as she gave his appearance the once-over. "But you'll have to have a bath after that cuppa or we won't be going anywhere!"

"Spoilsport!" he replied.

As Anne headed for the kettle, Neil eased himself on to one of the kitchen chairs. He really *was* tired, but tried not to show it.

"By the way," said Anne. "We've got the pleasure of Paul's company tomorrow."

"Oh yes?" Neil replied. "Sunday dinner for three then is it?"

"Actually it's *four*. He's bringing his girlfriend with him."

They had met one or two of their son's girlfriends in the past but only briefly, so for him to bring one to meet his mum and dad – *officially,* and for dinner too – that was definitely different.

"Apparently he's been going out with her for quite a while," added Anne. "Her name's Charlotte."

"He's kept that a bit quiet hasn't he?" replied Neil.

"*You know Paul...* He's never been one for keeping us informed about his love life."

"That's true."

"But I get the feeling he's quite keen on this one. Anyway, don't go embarrassing him in front of her."

"What me?" her husband replied, as though butter wouldn't melt in his mouth.

"Yes you! They should be here about half past twelve," she added as the kettle began to boil.

The cup of tea hit the spot and the kitchen chair Neil was sitting on was becoming more comfortable by the second. Anne could tell. "Are you sure you're up to going out?"

For a moment he was tempted to change his mind but his conscience prevailed. "A quick bath and I'll be bright as a button."

His wife laughed. "Well you needn't be bright as a button, just don't nod off in the restaurant."

Neil managed to stay awake throughout a thoroughly pleasant meal but as soon as they got home he headed straight for bed and was soon out like a light. Some say that we dream the most when sleeping lightly, so in his comatose state there would be little reverie for DCI Webster *that* night. But even in his wildest dreams he would never have expected what the following day would bring.

Anne was a regular churchgoer. She'd been brought up in a traditional Christian family and had continued attending after she married. Neil accompanied her from time to time. While on the force in Manchester he was exposed to the worst aspects of human behaviour and he found spending an hour with a group of the more godly once in a while was good therapy. On this Sunday morning, though, Anne would definitely be on her own: when she awoke the man beside her was inert.

"See you later," she said quietly before she went on her way. "I'll get back as quickly as I can." She gave him a quick kiss on the forehead and then left him in peace. He acknowledged it with a sleepy smile. But despite her efforts not to disturb him, the spell had been broken and half an hour later he was up and looking around to see what he could do towards the dinner. The answer was *not a lot.* While he'd been dozing, a joint of beef was cooking steadily away and vegetables were in saucepans waiting to be switched on. He smiled benignly as he surveyed it all.

"Well, I suppose I'd better make myself a cup of coffee and some toast then," he said to himself. Spying The Sunday Times on the kitchen table he took the newspaper, coffee and toast into the living room. Passing the dining room he saw the table set for dinner. Suppressing a twinge of guilt, he settled down to read the headlines. Anne was a very organised person and in truth she sometimes found that "help" from her husband wasn't always... *helpful.*

Not long after 11am, Neil heard the door latch go. He put the paper down and made his way out into the hall to see Anne taking her coat off.

"Hello, Rip Van Winkle," she chirped.

"Yes... okay... point taken. Good service?"

"Not bad but to be honest my mind was more on dinner and meeting this girlfriend of Paul's."

"Yes, I'll be interested to see what she's like myself. Anything I can do to help?"

"Not really. I'll put you in charge of the wine." He couldn't go far wrong with that and he soon had a bottle of red set up on a side table together with the glasses.

Half past twelve came and everything was ready to serve, but there was no sign of the visitors. Neil and Anne were left twiddling their thumbs. There was no point in starting anything else so they both sat down, Anne having turned everything low in the kitchen. They were just starting to scratch their heads when they heard car tyres on the gravel driveway. Anne was up like a shot to look out of the window.

"They're here." She set off for the front door, with Neil trailing in her wake. Paul was about to press the bell when the door opened as if by magic to reveal his beaming mother.

"Sorry we're a bit late Mum..."

"Don't worry about that," interjected Anne. "You're here now. Come in." She stepped aside to allow Paul to enter while peering at the young lady who was tentatively following him. "Hello. Do come in," Anne said, the warmth in her voice encouraging the girl to overcome any shyness. Soon all four of them were standing in the hall. Paul stepped to one side so he could introduce his girlfriend.

"This is Charlotte," he announced. Anne and Neil detected a note of pride in his voice.

"Hello, Mrs Webster," said Charlotte in an assured manner, holding out her hand. It took Anne slightly by surprise but she wasted no time in shaking it and returning the greeting.

Neil watched with interest.

"And this is my dad," continued Paul. Neil stepped forward, his hand already poised to shake Charlotte's.

"*What a thoroughly pleasant young lady,*" he thought to himself.

By the time the guests' coats had been taken and Paul had explained why they were late, it was nearly one o'clock and dinner was ready to serve.

"If you'd like to take Charlotte through to the dining room, Paul," said Anne, "we'll bring everything through. Could you give me a hand, Neil."

Within ten minutes everyone was round the table and happily tucking into dinner. If Paul's parents were concerned about conversation being difficult with this new acquaintance, they needn't have been. Charlotte was charming, with good manners, a gentle confidence and a ready sense of humour. Neil and Anne soon understood why their son had taken to her. *They* certainly had and the time seemed to fly as they made their way through the main course.

"That was lovely," said Charlotte as she put her knife and fork together on a clean plate.

"Thank you," replied Anne. "I'm pleased you enjoyed it. Now you two, chat among yourselves while Neil and I clear these dishes away. I've made an apple pie for pudding if that's okay?"

"Oh yes, that's fine," confirmed Charlotte.

Anne and Neil ferried the plates into the kitchen and put them down next to the sink before gazing at each other.

"Well, I don't quite know what to say," said Anne quietly.

"Me neither," replied Neil, looking dumbfounded. "It wasn't the wine, was it?"

"No," insisted his wife. "Definitely not!" They stood for a second or two in silence.

Neil broke the silence. "Hey, come on Anne. They'll wonder what we're doing."

She put her oven gloves on and extracted a beautifully browned apple pie from the oven. "I'll take this through. You bring the dishes."

More wine was dispensed as they worked their way through pudding but Paul took it steady knowing he had to drive later.

"I hope you've noticed how responsible I'm being Dad," he happily pointed out.

"Quite right. You can't be too careful. Those coppers get everywhere these days."

"Yeah, you can't even have Sunday dinner without coming across one." He looked pleased with his joke.

"Don't say that Paul," Charlotte gently chided.

"Quite right," echoed his Dad with a grin.

"Don't take his side," Paul protested to his girlfriend.

"Now, now," interjected Anne. "Come on Paul, you take Charlotte into the living room and I'll make us all some coffee and bring it through." The youngsters rose from the table while Neil and Anne gathered the dishes and took them through to the kitchen. They closed the door behind them.

"Well *this* is a revelation isn't it," brimmed Anne.

"You can say that again!"

"She's charming."

"Yeah, and a bobby dazzler as well."

"Hey!"

"I'm only stating the obvious. The lad's done well." Neil gave his wife a sideways look. "Mind you, I don't think I did so bad."

"Oh give over!"

"I'm serious. Now come here."

"You've had too much wine. Now stop it, they might come in."

Neil let out a pantomime sigh. "You're no fun," he said before giving his wife a crafty grin. "But they'll be gone in a bit."

"Will you behave yourself!" she tutted. "Help me with the coffees."

After half an hour of light-hearted chat about where the couple had met and what Charlotte did for a job, Anne suggested the youngsters have a walk down to Pavilion Gardens while she and Neil cleared up in the kitchen. The gardens were a lovely place to be on such a sunny day.

"Young love, eh?" said Neil as they watched the couple disappear off down the path.

"I bet *she* doesn't live in Stockport."

"What?"

"Charlotte," replied Anne. "That school she went to rings a bell. I'm pretty certain it's Chester way – *and* posh!"

"Well wherever it is, it's done a good job," Neil said. A frown suddenly crossed his face.

"Anything wrong?" asked Anne.

"No, not really. It's just that... well... I can't help thinking he might be punching above his weight. There must be a lot of money in the background somewhere. I wonder what her father does?"

"Well if they keep going out, I'm sure all will be revealed. Anyway, don't be so suspicious."

"I can't help it. I'm a copper."

At four o'clock the sound of happy chatter could be heard outside as the couple walked back up the front path. While they'd been away the washing up had been done and it wasn't long before they were all sitting down for a cup of tea and a final chat.

"I'm dropping Charlotte off at her parents' place in Bramhall on my way back," Paul said as they were finishing their cuppas.

"Bramhall! *Very* nice," said Anne.

"Well I think it's very nice *here*," countered Charlotte.

Anne laughed. "That's good of you to say so."

"Actually I don't spend much time at home now. I work in Manchester and luckily Dad owns some apartments in the city.

It's great not having to commute every day. Luckily I don't have to be in first thing tomorrow, so he'll drop me off when he goes into work."

"Oh he works in Manchester as well does he?" asked Neil casually.

"Yes, he's got a motor dealership there and a small nightclub."

Neil's eyes widened. "Sounds like an entrepreneur."

"Oh, he's definitely *that* all right!" she replied with feeling. Neil took note. Paul checked his watch.

"Come on, Charlotte. We need to get going."

"If you insist," she replied with a hint of reluctance. On the face of it, she did seem to have enjoyed herself. Anne and Neil certainly had.

Once Paul and Charlotte had collected their coats, Paul opened the front door and gave his girlfriend the car keys.

"You hop in and I'll be along in a minute."

"Bye," said Charlotte to his parents as she stepped out. "And thank you so much for lunch."

"Our pleasure," replied Anne. "It's been lovely to meet you."

"That goes for me too," added Neil.

Paul waited until Charlotte was out of earshot before turning to his parents. "Well, what do you think?" He was almost bursting with pride and it was a real pleasure for them to see their son so happy.

Neil replied without hesitation: "All I can say, lad, is you can bring her here anytime. She's smashing. What's her second name by the way?"

"It's Radcliffe."

"Oh right. Well just you look after Miss Radcliffe."

"Oh don't you worry... I will Dad. And thanks for dinner Mum. Anyway, must go."

"Drive carefully," Anne replied.

"I will."

Anne and Neil remained at the front door, smiling as they waved them off, but the moment they'd disappeared, so did Neil's smile. Anne noticed immediately. "What's wrong?"

"Frank bloody Radcliffe! That's what's wrong." He looked to the heavens. "She must be his *daughter*!"

Neil had always kept information about his work on a "need to know" basis as far as his family were concerned. The name Frank Radcliffe meant little to Anne.

"What about him?" she asked.

This was definitely one of those need to know moments. Neil looked deflated and took a second or two to gather himself. "Okay. It goes back to my days at Manchester. I wasn't involved much with his case or, shall I say, *cases*, but others around me were." His face hardened. "Respectable Francis Radcliffe. That's how he likes to portray himself these days. A successful businessman who enjoys demonstrating the fact by spreading his largesse around where it can be seen. And trust me he's got plenty."

"And?" pressed Anne.

"Frank Radcliffe. Respectable?" he said sarcastically. "He's as crooked as the spire on Chesterfield parish church!"

"But how can you be sure it's him?" Anne asked in desperation.

"Because he's got a big car dealership, a dodgy nightclub and some swanky apartments in Manchester, *and* a mansion in Bramhall. That's why I'm sure!"

Anne's jaw dropped. It was a body blow to the pair of them after what had been such a happy afternoon.

Neil gritted his teeth. "How could a piece of work like Radcliffe have produced a daughter like her?"

"Perhaps she takes after her mother?" Anne replied hopefully.

"Well judging from what we've just seen, she certainly doesn't take after her father!"

CHAPTER NINE

In the police station the next morning, after the usual catch up on the weekend's criminal activity and with all thoughts of Sunday's events at home put to one side, Neil headed for the CID office. It seemed a strange place these days. It was already filled with cigarette smoke thanks to Steve Milner. Nick Fielding didn't smoke. It took the DI a while to find Andy Bowers' whereabouts but eventually he did.

"Right, listen up," he announced as he settled them down. "As you probably all now know, the Barbara Butler missing person case from a few years ago is being looked at again. Steve is the lead and I've brought him up to speed this morning after I saw for myself last Saturday where the bracelet was found on the moors near Kinder Scout. Things could go either way with this one. If nothing else is found then it's as you were, but if something suspicious *is* discovered it could involve you all. Anyway, it's over to you Steve." Neil sat down.

"Thanks, sir," acknowledged Milner. "Okay. So we now know where we're looking but, unless we find a body to go with the bracelet, as you've just heard, the case isn't going anywhere. So, we're going to get a small search team with specialist dogs up there to see if they *can* find something. I'll let you know times and dates when I get them. If there is a body, though heaven knows what state it will be in, as DI Webster says, it will be a whole new ball game."

"Any news about the husband?" asked Andy Bowers.

"Well, as it happens, I heard back from the council just before I came in here. They've been checking the county electoral roll and it turns out he's now in Derby."

"Is there anyone else registered at the same address?" enquired Nick Fielding.

"Yes there is," answered Milner. "Celia Knowles" His announcement caused a ripple around the room. "But there's no point in surmising anything further at this stage."

"Steve's right," interjected Webster. "We're not going to put in any man hours unless we've got something solid to go on." He turned to Milner. "Anything else, Steve?"

"No, that's it sir."

"All right then, get back to what you were doing and we'll update you as and when we have more information. Okay – carry on."

Neil turned to Steve. "When we've got a date for the next search just make sure Brian Parker can make it. He knows the area like the back of his hand. It's okay if you stick to the paths but stray off them...!" He was going to leave it at that but then another thought popped into his head. "Whichever date it is, I'd like you on hand here in case there's something to report. After all, it is your case." Milner couldn't very well disagree. "Anyway, I'll leave things with you, Steve, but just keep me posted."

"Okay sir," replied his sergeant.

Meanwhile, up in the canteen, Trudie, Bob and Jane were enjoying their first break, the latter two having just returned from their morning beats. Jane was regaling them with her account of the expedition on Kinder over the weekend. PC Lowe was manning the front desk.

"Rather you than me up there," said Bob to Jane when she'd finished. Not my cup of tea at all." Bob was a big chap – very handy in a situation like the Eric Smith arrest – but ill-suited to hill walking. Nevertheless, he was genuinely interested in the Barbara Butler case but not as keen as Trudie. She was *really* intrigued as to how the bracelet had got where it had.

"I wouldn't have minded going and taking a look," she commented.

"You wouldn't have been allowed to," said Jane.

"Well *you* went."

"Not to the spot. We were told to stay put on the footpath and not to go trampling about. It was just Inspector Webster and the mountain rescue chap that took a closer look."

Trudie didn't look impressed. "Huh, it's a bit late to worry about trampling about. I don't know how many sheep, wayward hikers and goodness knows what else must have *trampled about* around there in the past few years. Denise Rhodes had clearly *trampled about.*"

"A bit tetchy aren't we sarge?" commented Bob.

"Well considering it was you and me Bob that brought the bracelet to their notice in the first place, I thought at least one of us would have been in on that briefing with CID this morning."

"Ohhh... that's it is it? Come on sarge, you know what CID are like when they've actually got something to do. They get all possessive. Anyway, you're always moaning about the cigarette smoke in there."

"That's not the point Bob." Her nose was definitely out of joint.

Jane followed the conversation with her own pennyworth of frustration. "Actually, I thought I might get something out of the DI about the Terry McDonald case but I couldn't. I mentioned it as well when we were in Bakewell that day. It just seems completely wrong, the likes of Lewis Bates getting away scot-free while someone else carries the can. I don't know, Mr Webster just doesn't seem interested."

"That's because he's got bigger fish to fry than trying to collar someone for nicking a few footballs," said Bob.

"Sticking up for your fellow men are you?" jabbed Trudie.

Before he could reply, their attention was drawn to someone coming through the canteen door. "Talk of the devil," muttered Bob quietly.

Neil Webster spotted the three of them straight away and made a beeline for their table. "Ahh, there you are. I've been looking for you pair," he said, directing his words at Trudie and Bob. "D'you mind if I join you?"

There was plenty of room at the table and nobody was going to object so Neil sat down next to his sergeant and began. "I know it was you two who brought this Barbara Butler thing to my attention, so I've come to update you. The CID office is never the most hospitable place for uniform, and you hate the stink of smoke Trudie, so I thought I'd fill you in separately."

Bob managed to stifle a laugh but still emitted a grunt.

"You all right, Bob?" asked Neil.

"Just a bit of indigestion, sir."

Trudie's eyes speared him as Neil continued. "Constable Briggs here has probably told you how we fared on Saturday, so going on from that, a formal search is being organised, with dogs. We'll just have to see what they turn up. Oh yes, and Mr Butler has been tracked down to Derby." Neil tried to think of anything else he might have missed but couldn't. "So, that's about it really." He smiled as he got up. "Right, I'll leave you to your tea and bickies."

Trudie spoke up as he rose to leave. "Oh sir, by the way, I've had a call from Matlock. A DS Redfern, about Eddie Slater. You were in the briefing when he rang. He wants you to ring him back. I've got his number in my office."

"Oh thanks, but finish your break first Trudie and I'll see you when you're ready."

"No, it's okay sir, I'm about done. I'll come down with you now." She got up and duly followed Neil out of the door.

The moment they disappeared, Bob looked at Jane with a big grin.

"Don't you *dare* say anything Bob!" she said.

"Just one word Jane," he replied. "Fickle!"

DI Webster was soon back in his office having got the Matlock phone number he wanted. After a useful conversation with Detective Sergeant Redfern he was soon heading back to the CID room. Only Andy Bowers was still there after the briefing.

"Ahh... Andy. Have you got a minute?" Neil didn't wait for a reply but headed back out into the corridor.

DC Bowers followed to find Neil waiting for him.

"Come on... my office." Once there, Neil closed the door.

"Right, sit down and don't look so worried." Andy immediately felt a bit easier and pulled up a chair. "What are you doing today?" Neil asked.

"I'm preparing some stuff with Nick Fielding and Sergeant Barker for tomorrow's get together with the backwoodsmen."

Neil couldn't resist laughing at the name. "Is that one of Steve Milner's?" he asked, already guessing the answer. "I'd keep that one to yourself if I were you."

"Yes sir."

"Anyway, I'm reassigning you! I want you down at Matlock nick... pronto... to see DS Redfern. We're interested in the movements of a character on their patch called Eddie Slater. They've been keeping an eye on him for us but you're going to take over now. It's in connection with the farm thefts, but for the moment I just want him watched and tailed if necessary. A bit of old fashioned detective work – long hours, very boring, but he's our best lead at the moment."

"Am I looking for anything in particular sir?"

"Well certainly that Bedford van, but other than that nothing specific – mostly where he goes, who he sees and who comes to see him. Take a camera with you, make sure it's working and have your notebook at the ready."

"What about tomorrow morning's briefing?"

"Don't worry about that. I'll square it with Sergeant Barker." He gave DC Bowers a hard look. "You report only to me on this one... got it!" Andy nodded. "Now you get off before Steve Milner has a chance to give you a grilling. Just leave the explanation to me."

"Right sir." He was up and away like lightning, keen to avoid crossing paths with Steve but with a bit of a spring in his step – something he hadn't felt in the job for a long time.

With his office to himself again, Neil picked up the phone to Trudie and asked her to bring him the list of items reported stolen in the farm thefts. While he was waiting, a private call came through, with no name given to reception. It turned out to be from a parole office in Manchester. The caller had some interesting news for him which Neil had just enough time to digest before Trudie appeared at the door.

"There you are sir," she said as she placed the list of stolen items on his desk.

"Thanks."

"Any particular reason you wanted it?" Neil cast his eyes down the list and grinned. "Something funny, sir?"

"Sorry. It's just that I was comparing it with the type of stuff that used to get reported nicked on my old patch – cars, televisions, booze..." He looked at the list again. "And here we've got cow cake, red diesel, sheep dip... The fact is, Trudie, I think I should have looked in far more detail at what's actually on this list. There's only a bit of what you'd call heavy gear, it's nearly all stuff that's physically easy to nick and move on quickly in one form or another... and very profitably no doubt."

Sergeant Barker's expression confirmed that she agreed. Neil continued. "So now I'm wondering, who *are* they moving it on to? If your theory's right about its final destination not being anywhere round here, we definitely need to get some ears listening further afield." That was music to Trudie's own ears. "And on the subject of faraway places," he added, "we'll work on your old boss when we go down to Leek later this week. I'll gee up Phil Morris in Macclesfield again as well. I saw him last Friday."

Neil then brought up the subject of sending Andy Bowers to carry out surveillance on Eddie Slater's place near Matlock, conscious that he'd only just lent the officer to Trudie to help prepare for the farm case briefing the following morning. She didn't mean to laugh when Neil asked whether she could manage without him."

"Oh, I think we'll cope sir." Her quickfire response wasn't lost on the DI. A spell under Sergeant Barker's watchful eye wouldn't do the lad any harm at all he thought to himself.

It certainly didn't look as though Trudie was missing DC Bowers' assistance when the rural officers began arriving the following morning. The occasion smacked of affable but meticulous organisation. Nick Fielding had commandeered anyone with a car to ferry colleagues who didn't have their own transport to the venue. They ended up with 30 officers, the majority looking interested to be there. This was a novelty for a lot of them, although the more seasoned of those among the contingent were sceptical. They'd seen too many "initiatives" succumb to the realities of life and now they had this CID guy from the smoke in charge. What was *he* likely to know about the world outside the big city? They were about to find out.

They didn't have the luxury of a conference room at the

station – the biggest room in the building was the canteen – so after some negotiations with Mary, tables were repositioned and additional chairs squeezed in. It wasn't ideal but even she had to admit it would make the catering side of things easier. Mary might have been a humble dinner lady but her little team more than rose to the occasion and everyone was given a welcoming cup of tea or coffee on arrival. Some of the visitors already knew her and Mary's light-hearted banter ensured a good atmosphere from the word go.

"It's not the Savoy I know," she announced from the counter when everyone had assembled, and I apologise in advance if there's a bit of clattering from behind here later on but it's the price you will have to pay if you want any dinner!"

"Isn't it ready yet Mary?" quipped one old wag.

"No it's not!' she countered. "But when it is, I defy the Savoy to do a better toad in the 'ole than mine – so there!"

That raised a cheer from her audience because that's what it had become – *an audience.*

Neil was observing from the back of the room, enjoying the show, but it was time to get started now. He made his way to the front with Sergeant Barker in close attendance. "Okay everyone," he began. "Thanks for coming today. I'm fairly new to the patch so, for anyone who doesn't know me, I'm Detective Inspector Neil Webster. I hope you're all suitably refreshed but before I say anything else I'd like to thank Mary and her assistants *now* for the work they're putting in today to look after us all."

His words provoked a general chorus of "here here".

"I thought it was a master stroke of Mary's to let it be widely known that her toad in the 'ole would be on the menu – an incentive to keep you awake until lunchtime."

That brought a ripple of laughter but this was really Trudie's show, so he wasted no further time in handing proceedings over to her and joining Nick Fielding at the back of the room.

If there had been any doubt about the event being a success, by the time the aroma of dinner began emanating from behind the counter, those doubts had been dispelled. Putting Trudie in charge of this get together had worked like a dream. It didn't matter that she *was* a woman – she was one of their own and it made it a far friendlier ride for CID's Nick Fielding when she asked him to contribute. Neil didn't speak until he wrapped things up at the end. The three of them received a smattering of applause and this new working relationship was sealed as they joined everyone for the meal. That's where Neil learnt more than anything about the problems the patch had been having with CID, particularly from one or two of the old guard who were too close to retirement to care about a loose word. And that word was usually "Milner".

CHAPTER TEN

As the week went by Trudie found herself busier on the phone than normal. There had been a number of thank yous from bobbies who had thoroughly enjoyed their Tuesday morning out in Buxton. They'd found it constructive from a work point of view but it had also been a great social – a chance to hook up again with colleagues they'd not crossed paths with in years. That aside, bits of information were beginning to filter back. Nothing of great use had turned up until Friday, when one of the officers who had attended the briefing rang up.

"I think I might have spotted that green Bedford van you've been looking for," he said. "I've just filled up with petrol at a garage near Youlgreave and there's one in its repair shop with a clear dent on the nearside back door. I'm still on the forecourt. What d'you want me to do, sarge?"

It was a good question. Trudie knew that at this stage DI Webster preferred just to keep tabs on the movement of any potential gang members in the hope that they'd lead them to others. "Can you get the registration number without alerting anyone?"

"Yeah, I think so. That all?"

"Yes, and then contact me again once you've left... okay?"

"Yep, will do." The bobby put his radio down and drove his car slowly past the repair shop entrance, making a mental note of the number as he did so. He parked up at a turn a few hundred yards further on and jotted the registration down in his notebook before getting on the radio again to Trudie. When she'd finished taking all the details she thanked the officer for having an eagle eye and permitted herself a self-satisfied smile. Perhaps the meeting last Tuesday *was* bearing fruit?

The previous afternoon she and Neil had made the arranged trip back to her old station in Leek to discuss liaising with them about the farm theft cases. It was a journey down memory lane for Trudie and she thoroughly enjoyed meeting up again with some of her former colleagues including her old sergeant, Alan Wright. He'd been her mentor from when she was a wet-behind-the-ears junior constable, encouraging her as much as he could in a very male-dominated environment. No one, apart from Trudie herself, was more happy than he was when she got the sergeant's job in Buxton. As she'd mentioned to Neil, Alan was a fount of practical knowledge and while she and the DI walked back to the car after the meeting, they discussed how much ground they'd covered in the past two weeks.

The chat continued as they negotiated their way out of the town, along the Buxton road, past the twin gritstone outcrops of The Roaches on their left and on to the moors. The colleagues had every right to be satisfied with how things were going but, as the drive went on, Neil became increasingly quiet. Trudie noticed. He was clearly preoccupied with something. "Penny for 'em, sir," she eventually asked.

His reply was simple. "What am I going to do about Steve Milner, Trudie?"

You couldn't blame him for asking the question. A situation like this was so tricky. Was Milner just a long-in-the-tooth police officer who didn't want anything to spoil the cosy number he'd established for himself, or was there more? Neil had come to trust Trudie implicitly and finally felt able to open up.

"D'you want my honest opinion, sir?"

"Of course."

"He's bent!" Well he did ask.

Neil couldn't help laughing. "Okay... but to what degree? Like a bend in the road?"

"Yes – if it was a hairpin!"

Trudie was sharp as a tack – and Neil knew it. He chuckled at the analogy but he also knew from long experience that things in his job were rarely that black and white. He thought it a good moment to remind her of that fact. "The problem is, Trudie, sometimes to get a result we do have to get our hands a bit dirty."

His expression suggested he was thinking back to his Manchester days. She suspected as much and tempered her tone. "I bet it's nice to have left the big city behind."

"That's true enough," concurred Neil. "The thing is, I'm not entirely sure the city's done with me."

Neil said little else during the journey, obviously lost in thought, but with only a few miles left, Trudie wanted to raise another matter – the McDonald case. Neil was well aware that Jane had been moaning about it behind the scenes. "Constable Briggs been in your ear has she sergeant?"

Trudie couldn't very well deny it. "Well yes... she has – but I can see her point sir."

"So can I, but Constable Briggs needs to learn a bit of patience." His tone was definitely testy on this one. "As it happens, I'm more than aware of the McDonald situation and I know *all* about Lewis Bates."

"Oh," replied Trudie. She was a bit surprised but DI Webster's next comment left her in no doubt.

"They're like a festering boil, the Bates family. So I've decided we're not just going to pick and piddle at it – we're going to lance it... once and for all!" He'd said far more than he meant to and regretted letting himself be drawn that much. "Let's leave it at that shall we?"

She got the message loud and clear and quickly moved on to another, not entirely unconnected, subject. "You know my views on how little respect the CID boys in this nick give to uniformed officers, sir? Present company accepted, of course."

"I do."

"Well there they're making one exception."

Neil smiled when he realised where this was going. "Don't tell me... *Constable Briggs*."

"Well detected, sir. Every one of the lads in there fancies her. Turn her loose on them and I bet she could find out all sorts of things if we wanted, and she'd have them at each other's throats before you could say Jack Robinson."

He looked at her with a pained expression. "And I thought *I* could be devious! Please, *please* don't give her any ideas."

"I'm only joking really," Trudie replied, before breaking into a crafty grin. "But it's an interesting thought, isn't it?"

It certainly was. Trudie then proceeded to move things away from police matters. "Have you got anything nice planned for the weekend sir?"

"Yes," he replied without a second thought. "Not going up Kinder Scout like I had to last weekend. What about you?"

Trudie was just as rapid with her response. "Well quite a bit actually. I'm playing tennis on Saturday afternoon, going to the cinema in the evening and on Sunday we're hopefully driving over to the Goyt Valley."

Neil noted the "we". This was the first time they had chatted about their lives outside work. It made an enjoyable change. "I didn't know you played tennis?" replied Neil.

"That's because I've probably never mentioned it."

"So how long have you been doing that?"

Trudie cast her mind back. "Well I used to play when I was

younger back in Leek and when I came up here I thought I'd take it up again so I joined the local club. I'm really pleased I did. It helps keep me fit and there's a nice social side to it as well."

Neil noticed the warmth with which she talked about it and couldn't resist asking another question. "Been playing a bit of mixed doubles have you?"

She looked vaguely offended. "Honestly! You men!"

He'd only said it jokingly but he suddenly realised he'd hit on something. "What is it Shakespeare said? 'The lady doth protest too much, methinks.'"

"I'm not protesting at all!"

"No, of course not," he replied, looking the picture of innocence. "But on Saturday you're playing tennis with him, going to the pictures with him and then strolling in the countryside with him on Sunday."

"All right," she finally conceded. "But it's not easy having a relationship when you're a copper, well not a meaningful one anyway. I tried it more than once in Leek and the job always got in the way. I even tried it with someone from the station thinking it would work because we'd both be on the same wavelength."

"How did that go?"

"A complete disaster! It's one thing talking shop nine till five but you don't want it after you've clocked off as well. It was like a busman's holiday. And you've still got to work with them after you've split up." Trudie suddenly remembered that she was speaking to someone who'd worked in a big city station and probably seen it all. "Sorry about the rant sir."

"Don't apologise... and you're absolutely bang on when it comes to station romances. It's fine when everything's hunky dory but when the wheels fall off..." He shook his head as he recollected such occasions. "It can be a pretty toxic place. I've just been incredibly lucky that Anne knew what the job entailed." He grimaced slightly. "Although she wasn't best pleased about me being called to action in Edale last Saturday without much warning."

"Will you have to go up there again with the next search?"

She didn't get an immediate reply but noticed he was smiling and asked why. His answer was simple. "Because I think it's time the lead officer on this case visited the site. Either he is in charge of the investigation or he isn't and, think about it, the Barbara Butler case is the only thing that he seems prepared to put his back into. And while he's doing that, it might keep his nose out of other things. I particularly want to separate him from young Bowers."

"Is that why you sent Andy Bowers off to play detective down near Matlock?"

"Pretty much, but, you never know, he might actually come up with something."

The thought of DS Milner struggling up Kinder Scout had made Trudie's day. He'd given her a rotten time ever since she'd arrived at Buxton. Firstly because she was a woman doing what he perceived as a man's job and secondly because she was his equal rank-wise but without the years behind her that *he* had. He'd engendered a negative atmosphere towards her in CID from the word go and she'd received scant protection from Neil's predecessor, who had little interest in staff morale as he counted the days to his retirement. The other issue was that Trudie had seen how an effective CID *should* be run, at her previous nick, and unwisely commented to that effect on occasion, which hadn't helped. Milner also knew that she was on to him; partly through the things he did but, more to the point, the things he *didn't* do such as pursue the farm thefts properly. The saving grace for her was that uniform really liked her, mainly because she stood her ground whenever the "detectives" decided to take a liberty at their expense. All in all, the arrival of DI Webster was the answer to her prayers but the sheer frankness of her earlier remark with regard to Milner had still taken him by surprise. It was as though pressure had been building up inside her and finally the dam had burst. Neil decided to delve further. "Have you got anything solid?"

Again, Trudie had a ready answer. "Well no, but I think he knows a lot more about these farm thefts than he's letting on. Before you came he seemed to do nothing but put things in the way of a proper investigation. Frankly, I think we owe John Mellor a thank you for letting off his 12-bore that night."

Neil smiled at the thought of the farmer. "Yes," he replied. "You certainly know where you stand with John."

"Yeah, out of shotgun range!" she joked, prompting Neil to burst out laughing.

"Yes, very good, but I also think Jim and Sandra Hargreaves at the Old Grouse know a lot more than they're letting on. Then again Steve Milner's not stupid, so if we're to get anywhere, we're going to have to get one step ahead of him somehow. The thing is... how do we do it?" The Vauxhall Victor pulled into the police station car park, leaving the question hanging in the air.

On the following Friday afternoon, WPC Jane Briggs made a point of taking in the Moor View council estate on her beat. She was trying to stop herself getting too wound up about the Terry McDonald case but wanted to let his mum know that she hadn't forgotten them. The trouble was, she didn't have any good news. There had been no suggestion from the school that the headmaster was relenting on his decision to press charges and the month's grace he had offered was gradually eating away. Those thoughts as she approached the house were interrupted by an unwelcome shout from behind her.

"Hello gorgeous!" Jane swung round. "Couldn't resist coming to see me again?" Who else but Lewis Bates, accompanied by a couple of his moronic sycophants grinning like Cheshire cats. He pointed to the house. "He's not in you know. He's gone and got a job. Bet it doesn't last long," he added mockingly.

"I'm surprised you know the meaning of the word... *Master Bates.*" Lewis's friends burst into howls of laughter. Her adversary was furious at being ridiculed and pushed towards her. Jane held her ground with a stoney smile. "Why don't you hit me Lewis?" She now pushed towards him. "Go on, I want you to, so I can have you up for assaulting a police officer – and I'll have witnesses." She pointed to a window in a nearby house. Lewis glanced over and saw a twitching curtain. She'd baited him perfectly and he gritted his teeth in anger.

"I'll get you!"

He practically spat the words at her but she wasn't intimidated at all. "Oh no Lewis," she replied coolly, one day somebody's going to get *you*! And I just hope I'm there to see it. Now clear off you excuse for a human being before I do you for harassment!"

Realising he'd lost the battle, Bates stomped off in a fury, his mates not sure what to do with themselves. Jane stood there for a moment and took a deep breath. Despite the outward bravado, she needed to steady herself before she went up to the McDonald's front door and knocked. She also had to negotiate the McDonald's dustbin, which appeared to have been left half on the path, presumably by the dustman earlier in the day.

Constable Briggs knew it was hit and miss that anyone would be at home. Mrs McDonald went out to work and, of course, she hoped that Terry would be at his new job. She didn't have to wait long for an answer.

"Oh hello," said a surprised looking Mrs McDonald when she opened the door. "Do you want to come in?"

"Yes please," Jane replied, noticing that Terry's mum was checking to see whether anyone was loitering in the street. "Everything okay, Mrs McDonald?"

"I was looking to see if that lout was hanging about."

"You mean Lewis Bates?"

"Who else. He's been hassling Terry whenever he can to keep his mouth shut about those footballs. Anyway, come on in. Would you like a cuppa? I've only just got back myself and I was making one."

"Yes, that would be lovely thanks."

Mrs McDonald gestured to the front room. "Go in and have a sit down luv, I'll be back in a minute."

Jane preferred to stand while she peered through the lace curtains, mulling over what it must be like to live on a council estate. Her parents had been "lower middle class with aspirations" and Jane was given every encouragement to better herself. But if you were born on a council estate she wondered, did that wire you into limiting your expectations in life? It was a dreadful thought for her but it in no way made her look down on the likes of the McDonalds. In fact she admired their spirit in battling the odds. Perhaps that's why she wanted to help them.

The arrival of the tea interrupted her thoughts. "Have you got any news?" Mrs McDonald asked Jane when they'd sat down.

"Not really, I'm afraid. I'm still hoping Mr Cousins will have a change of heart but he's shown no signs yet." She took a sip of her tea. "But I'm still working on him. Actually, the main reason I called was to see how the job was going."

"You mean Terry?"

"Yes, this was his first week wasn't it?"

"Well they haven't sacked him yet and I'm sincerely hoping that he'll be back within the hour with his first pay packet."

"That's really good news, Mrs McDonald."

"Call me Marion. You know me well enough now." It was her turn to have a sip of tea. When she put her cup down she continued conspiratorially. "And that's not the only thing."

"Oh yes?" enquired Jane.

"I had a letter from the parole office at the prison."

Constable Briggs was all ears. "And?"

"Well it's a bit odd really. I'm sure my husband has been a model prisoner – he'd do anything to be released early – but I didn't think he was up for a review just yet. It's as though someone with a bit of clout has put a good word in for him or something." She looked nonplussed. "It won't reduce his sentence but he might be out on licence sooner than either of us thought." She laughed. "The thing is, we don't know anyone with any clout."

"That's fantastic, Marion."

"I know." Mrs McDonald could hardly contain her excitement. "But I mustn't get carried away. It's not happened yet."

"Well I'll keep everything crossed for you," said Jane.

Marion looked pensive. "Oh dear. I hope it's not a case of one out and one in – with Terry I mean."

Jane looked at her sympathetically. "Let's hope not."

Jane enjoyed seeing Mrs McDonald with a smile on her face for a change. It was only a little thing but represented in its own small way why she'd joined the police in the first place – to do something that made a difference. Eventually they finished their tea and she stepped out on to the doorstep once more.

Marion noticed the dustbin on the path. "Huh, it looks like the dustman was in a hurry this morning." She pointed at the bin. "That normally lives by the back door. Anyway, I'll move it when you've gone."

Jane glanced up and down the road. "Well it looks like the street is Lewis Bates free at the moment," she observed. "I had an encounter with him out here earlier on."

The very thought of him brought a sour look to Marion's face. "Pity the dustmen didn't pick him up and take him away with the rest of the rubbish."

They both laughed and on that merry note Jane set off to finish the rest of her beat, intrigued about the turn of events at the prison.

Meanwhile at the station, just as Trudie was about to knock off for the weekend, she received a call from the Vehicle Licensing Department in Swansea. The owner of the damaged Bedford van was one Eddie Slater. At the same time she was taking the call Andy Bowers walked into the station having finished his week's stint of surveillance near Matlock. DI Webster had instructed Andy to report his findings directly to him first thing on Monday morning but Trudie saw no reason not to tell him the news about the van.

That done, Bowers headed off home, ready for the weekend and some fun with his mates but, as he neared his front door, his mood darkened as he recognised the car parked outside. The driver's door opened and out stepped Steve Milner looking anything but pleased.

"Hello Andrew," he said coldly. "Been doing anything interesting this week?" Andy started to bluster.

"Look," continued his boss. "How about you and me have a little chat?"

CHAPTER ELEVEN

Neil and Anne's hopes for a quiet weekend went pretty much according to plan. A lie-in on the Saturday morning with a cup of tea and the newspaper followed by a trip to Ashbourne in the afternoon, a town they'd yet to really explore. The couple hadn't exactly been in denial over their son's revelations about the identity of his girlfriend's father but they hadn't discussed it much either. Perhaps it was a spot of "ostrich syndrome" but, as they drove along in the car, Anne touched on the subject again.

"D'you think it'll last?"

"Will what last?" Neil replied dimly.

"Paul and Charlotte of course!"

"Oh them..."

"Yes, them!"

In fact Neil *had* been thinking about it, quite a lot. "Well, I suppose the question is, do we say anything at this stage? Who knows, some rich bloke from her dad's circle of friends might come along in his Jag with a fat wallet, sweep her off her feet and Paul's steady job and little Ford Anglia won't get a look in... or it might just fizzle out."

Anne had been mulling things over too. "Ummm... maybe... but something tells me there's more to Charlotte than that."

In truth, Neil thought the same. "I know *exactly* what you mean Anne," he replied.

They were on the same wavelength now but his wife was

a realist. "It'll be a long time before our son could offer her anything like that." She dwelt on that thought for a moment. "But you'll put up with a lot if you love someone enough – I did." She gave her husband's hand a squeeze.

"Yes – me too," replied Neil as he focused on the road ahead.

Anne snatched her hand from his. "You're not supposed to say that!"

When he arrived at work on Monday morning, DI Webster was feeling bright and breezy and so was Sergeant Barker, both of them having enjoyed their weekends. Trudie was at the front desk with Bob and Richard Lowe when Neil walked through the door. There was a general *good morning sir,* to which he replied in kind. As he passed Trudie he couldn't resist a quick aside. "Game set and *match,* was it sergeant?"

She ignored him but as soon as Neil was out of sight the other two were on her case.

"What was all that about then?" enquired Bob.

"Nothing," answered Trudie, keeping her eyes unnecessarily glued to a piece of paperwork.

"It didn't sound like nothing sarge," followed Richard passively.

Trudie looked awkward. It was like blood in the water to Bob. He looked at Richard. "Is our copper's intuition telling us something, Constable Lowe?"

"I think it is, Constable Lomas."

They both knew they'd struck oil, causing Trudie to blush. "Haven't you two got anything better to do?" she replied tersely, her arms folded.

"No!" came the joint reply, in such perfect harmony that the constables both laughed.

"Come on sarge, the place needs some decent gossip," continued Bob.

Trudie looked pained. "And that's why I'm not saying anything. I don't *want* to be the subject of gossip."

Bob changed tactics and proceeded to put a sympathetic arm round her shoulder. "Tell you what. Just let me and Rich in on it and we'll do our best to keep it quiet."

"Puh!" Trudie retorted, shrugging him off. "I might as well put it in the Advertiser."

Bob tutted. "I don't know. I just thought a quote from the horse's mouth might prevent wild speculation spreading through the station."

Trudie couldn't fold her arms any tighter. Bob and Richard were loving it. Eventually she cracked and threw her hands in the air. "All right! And I'll overlook the *horse's mouth* analogy..." She took a deep breath then made what seemed like a formal announcement. "I'm going out with a very nice chap from the tennis club and that's it. Will that do?"

Bob and Richard nodded to each other. "See, that wasn't so hard sarge," replied Bob with a beam. He turned to his partner in crime. "Right, Rich, who shall we tell first?"

"Oh clear off the pair of you!"

The constables scuttled off, satisfied with their handiwork.

No sooner had they gone than Nick Fielding sidled across from the CID office to the front desk.

"Seen anything of Andy Bowers, sarge?"

"Nope." She looked at her watch and thought for a second. "Hmmm, he is a bit late – and the boss wants to see him this morning." She eyed Nick again. "Everything all right?"

He looked concerned. "Don't know."

"D'you want to come into my office?"

"Yeah, perhaps I'd better." Trudie opened the door behind her and shouted: "Richard... Bob... one of you please!"

Bob popped his head round the door. "Can I be of *service*?" He was beginning to try her patience.

"Not now Bob. Just hold the fort will you."

Trudie and Nick entered her office. He remained standing as she closed the door after them. "Right Nick, what's up?"

He really did look troubled. "It's grim in there sarge." He gestured generally towards the CID office. "I know Andy wasn't in the station for most of last week and Sergeant Milner's gunning for him. I can't put my finger on it but something's far from right." Before Trudie had a chance to respond, her phone rang.

"Hello. Sergeant Barker," she said. "We were just wondering where you were." She listened. "Oh... well... if you're feeling that bad..." She listened again. "All right, I'll tell him. Bye Andy."

She put the phone down and looked at Nick."Well, there's your answer. He says he's gone down with something. He certainly sounded odd. She thrummed the desk with her fingers as she gave the situation further thought. "Okay Nick, leave it with me, you'd better get back – and keep your head down."

"Right sarge. Thanks," he said as he went to open the door.

Trudie was about to do the Monday morning briefing with Neil and now she had an additional and unwelcome item on the agenda – but she was interrupted yet again. This time it was PC Lowe putting his head round the door.

"Phone call for you sarge. It's someone from Leek nick." Trudie plonked her files down again. She was getting nowhere fast. "Okay Richard, put them through."

It was Alan Wright with a bit of interesting information. There'd been a break-in at an animal feed wholesaler's yard between Leek and Ashbourne over the weekend. It was quite a big job as the place had been cleaned out. If it was connected to the other thefts, it marked a significant escalation in the gang's activities and was spreading – yet another issue to put before the DI. She thanked Alan and hot-footed it up the corridor towards

Neil's office to avoid further interruptions only to be practically barged out of the way by a furious Steve Milner coming from the opposite direction.

"Excuse me!" she exclaimed but he was gone. The inspector's office door was still open and she entered looking rattled from her encounter.

Neil noticed immediately and stopped what he was doing. "You all right?" he enquired, looking concerned.

"Well I've just been nearly knocked flying by Steve Milner."

"Oh dear," Neil replied. "Sorry, that was my fault. He'd come in to tell me the possible dates for the dog search but when I broke the news to him that *he* would be going this time instead of me – he was *not* happy. Anyway, that's his problem."

Trudie grimaced. "I'm just glad *I'm* not married to him. It must be awful. I feel really sorry for his wife – she's ever so nice." She took a deep breath. "Anyway... back to business. I'll start with the bad news."

"And that is...?"

"I'm afraid there's no Andy Bowers this morning sir."

"Oh just great!" Neil thumped the desk with frustration and mentally counted to three while he simmered down. "Okay, when we've done will you get me his number. I really need to know if he's come up with anything from last week."

Trudie went through the remainder of things on her list including the call from Leek, her chat with Nick Fielding and the question they'd been increasingly asking themselves: *where was all this farm stuff going?* A hint to the answer would turn up sooner than they thought but it was clear that, one way or another, things were starting to happen, evidenced further by a telephone call made to the station late that morning. The person on the phone was female, would only speak to DI Webster, and refused to give her name to anyone else. When Neil spoke to the woman she asked one question: "Can you come today?" It was a call he'd been hoping to receive and he set off in his car mid-afternoon – but he had another house call to make first.

After pressing the bell to the block of flats a couple of times, the door to the house was eventually opened... by Andy Bowers. He looked terrible. White as a sheet.

"Can I come in?" Neil asked. "I take it you've nothing catching?"

Andy gave the faintest glimmer of a smile but said nothing, stepping aside to let Neil enter the building. His flat was on the ground floor of a big old town house not far from the centre of Buxton. Andy ushered Neil in from the main hallway.

"Let's start with a cuppa shall we Andy," said Neil to open proceedings. He meant business but kept his manner low-key. "I'll go in here shall I?" he asked, pointing to the front room.

"Yeah... okay sir." Andy disappeared into the kitchen and soon returned with a mug in each hand, one with a picture of a guitar-toting Jimi Hendrix, the other with the afro hair-styled Bob Dylan.

Neil looked at them and smiled. "I'm more of an Ella Fitzgerald man myself." They sat in silence, sipping their tea. Finally Neil sat back and said casually: "You're between a rock and a hard place aren't you lad?"

"Huh, you could say that sir."

"All the same, you shouldn't have missed that meeting we were having this morning."

PC Bowers closed his eyes for a couple of seconds. He looked dreadful. Eventually he spoke. "I panicked sir."

Neil knew he had to tread carefully. "All right... well stop panicking and just listen." He gave him a moment. "You okay now?" Andy nodded. "If it makes you feel any better, your immediate boss is panicking as well, otherwise he wouldn't have tried to put the frighteners on you, which I assume is what he's done." Neil took another sup of tea and cast his eyes around the room while he weighed up the situation.

"What's going to happen now sir?" asked Andy. This was a horrible moment in the young officer's life.

Neil's expression eased a little. "Well, quite simply, I'm going to try to clear this mess up. *That's* what's going to happen. And *you're* going to help me." Neil glanced at his watch. "I haven't got time to go through it now but let me have the camera. It'll take a day to get what's on it developed so make the most of tomorrow, go out and get some fresh air into your lungs or something, and I'll see you first thing on Wednesday morning – 9am sharp, okay?"

"Yes sir."

"Now go and get me that camera."

Andy disappeared through the door, returning minutes later with the camera. He handed it to Neil. "There's probably some rubbish on there sir. I did my best but I think someone must have clocked me because, from Wednesday on, the bloke hardly moved."

Neil looked at his watch again. It really was time for him to go. He took the camera and headed for the door. "Oh, by the way," he said. "I've got something that might cheer you up a bit."

"What's that sir?"

"I'm sending Detective Sergeant Milner up Kinder Scout for the day tomorrow with the search party that he's organised." DC Bowers broke into a smile. "You see, Andy. Life's not all bad."

About 20 minutes later, Neil arrived at the Old Grouse Inn. The only vehicles in the car park belonged to the proprietors but the surrounding landscape had improved from his last visit by the presence of lambs dotting the fields. Their insistence on trying to suckle despite their now chunky stature was more of an irritation to their mums than a necessity now that the grass was growing again. Such a positive scene contrasted starkly with the negative side of humanity that Neil's job so often brought him into contact with. The next half hour was going to show both sides.

It was four o'clock and the pub was still closed. As Neil walked past the front window he could see the bar lit up and Mrs Hargreaves busying herself around it. The main door was firmly shut so he gave a modest tap on the window. Spotting Neil, she motioned him towards the hefty oak door. Neil could imagine it being opened slowly on a rain-lashed winter's night with a creaking hinge and the pub sign overhead swinging in the wind *Jamaica Inn* style. Perhaps this was Buxton's version of that den of intrigue, Neil mused. He was brought back to reality by the clacking of the latch and the door opening – with no sign of a squeak. Neil was mildly disappointed. Jim Hargreaves obviously knew where the oil can lived.

"Hello," said Sandra. "Come in."

Neil stepped inside and she shut the outside world away behind him. It fitted the cloak-and-dagger feel of the occasion. "I'll shout Jim," which she duly did. "He'll not be a minute." She scratched her head for a moment. "Thanks for coming... now, let me think... right... follow me." She set off towards a back room with a narrow door and a couple of well-worn steps. "Watch how you go," she said. "They're a nuisance really, especially when you're carrying something, but they add to the character of the place." She pointed to a table in the corner. "Go and have a seat over there. Would you like anything?"

"Nothing alcoholic but I wouldn't mind a cup of coffee," Neil replied.

"I'll get you one and give Jim another shout. I don't know what he's doing." No sooner had she uttered the words than the man himself appeared in the doorway. He stepped back to let his wife return to the bar.

"Hello," he said as he approached. Neil rose and they shook

hands. "Thanks for coming." Jim gestured to Neil's seat. "Make yourself comfortable." As they sat down, Neil scanned the room. A fire had been lit in an old-fashioned, black-leaded fireplace – not on the scale of the one in the lounge but no less welcoming for that. It was puttering away nicely.

"It's really cosy in here, isn't it? Nice and private," Neil said, receiving a wry look from the landlord in return.

"Yes... well... perhaps a bit too private for its own good. You'll know why in a minute." Neil's curiosity was piqued.

Sandra appeared at the doorway and made her way gingerly down the steps carrying a tray. "I didn't know if you took milk and sugar, so I've brought both." She put the tray in the middle of the table and pulled up a chair.

Once Neil had dealt with his coffee, he started the ball rolling. "I take it there's something you want to tell me?"

"Yes," Jim replied. "And like I said, it's why we particularly brought you in *here*. It's to do with Milner. We hadn't seen him for a while, that was until last week – but it wasn't just him. He was with two blokes."

Sandra took up the story. "I better start at the beginning. We first saw them in the pub not long after we took over. I think they had some arrangement with the old landlord. Honestly, anybody would have thought they owned the place. There was a Scottish one – he was particularly horrible – and every time they came in, Milner told us to keep other people out. Well we didn't like it and eventually I told him, quite politely, that if he did want to book the room he could, but he'd have to pay. Well he turned ugly, didn't he Jim? and said if we wanted to keep our licence we should learn to play ball. Anyway, we'd had enough, so Jim threatened to call the police only for Milner to shock us by telling us he *was* the police and he showed us his ID. I mean, we'd no idea. He was acting more like a crook than a bobby."

Jim took over again. "Well we had to do something, didn't we? So we went to the police station to complain – a bit stupid in hindsight – and of course he made sure he dealt with it. He took us into a private room and basically threatened us again about the licence – so you can see why we were so loath to talk to you about it."

"So what's changed?" asked Neil.

"*You!*" Sandra exclaimed. "We'd never have brought it up again unless we thought we could trust someone."

Neil appreciated the implied compliment but they'd only partially answered his question. *Was there something new?* He got his answer immediately.

"Like I said," continued Jim, "we hadn't seen Milner or his mates for a while, thank goodness, but then last Friday they came in again and he didn't look happy at all." Sandra jabbed a finger at the tabletop.

"They were in here," she said. "At this very table. They practically forced us to move someone else out. It was so embarrassing. I kept peeping through the doorway from a distance and I could hear them. The Scottish bloke was actually *threatening* Milner. It was really nasty."

"The language was horrendous," added Jim, "and we'd got customers within earshot."

"So what did you do?" asked Neil.

Sandra was bursting to take over again. "Well it wasn't what *we* did," she began. "We'd got two of our farmer customers in, Bill Ollerenshaw and John Mellor. They like to come in on a Friday for a pint."

This was serious stuff but Jim and Sandra's double-act style of recounting events made it hard for Neil to maintain a straight face. But he pricked his ears up at the mention of John Mellor's name.

"*Well!*" continued Sandra with undisguised glee. "You

wouldn't believe what happened next. John came over and asked what we were going to do about them – in his words, '*these foul-mouthed 'uns in there*'. Anyway, I said it was a bit difficult. Sounds terrible doesn't it? John replied, '*No it isn't*' and he went and stood full square in the doorway up there." She pointed towards the steps... "And off he went! He says, '*Would you mind toning the language down please, there's people out here trying to enjoy a quiet drink.*' We could all hear it. John was about to turn away when the Scottish bloke got up, came to the bottom step and confronted him. He said, '*And would* ***you*** *mind pissing off!*' Well! John turned to Bill Ollerenshaw, casual as you like – he was only sitting a couple of yards away – and said, '*Ay up Bill, I think someone's mouth here needs washin' out with soap and water*'."

Sandra's impression of John tickled Neil. She was clearly a natural mimic. "And I take it John thought him and Bill were the men to do it?"

"You know him then?" asked Jim.

"I most certainly do."

"Well you'll also know what a strapping feller he is... and Bill's no lightweight."

"So what happened?"

Sandra obliged. "Honest... before the bloke knew it John had him by the collar and between him and Bill they dragged him out the front door and were gone for a good two minutes. The other two just scarpered. We went and had a look outside. The Scottish one was floundering about in the stream with his mate trying to drag him out. It was wonderful!" enthused Sandra. "Hey... and when John and Bill came back in they got a round of applause. '*It wa nowt,*' said John, '*compared with dealing with an 'ockered bullock, was it Bill?*'"

Neil couldn't suppress his laughter any longer, slapping the table as he let it out. "Well if I want to see some action on a

Friday night, I certainly know where to come!" he said.

"No thank you!" replied Jim bluntly. "Peace and quiet and to be left alone, that's all *we* want, otherwise we'll start losing business." He did have a point.

"Yes... of course," Neil acknowledged. "I appreciate your filling me in."

Sandra had stopped giggling now and was becoming fidgety. "Are you going to do anything about Milner then?" she asked bluntly.

This was a tricky one for Neil. He fully intended to bring his sergeant to book but at this stage he hadn't got anything sufficiently solid to nail him with – everything was circumstantial. He asked the couple whether they'd seen any money change hands between Milner and the Scotsman. Sandra waffled a bit but despite dying to say *yes*, she couldn't hand on heart do so. Neil also thought he had more chance of catching bigger fish if DS Milner was still swimming free in the pool.

But the couple needed some reassurance, which Neil duly did his best to provide. "Well to start with, your licence is safe. I'll deal with Detective Sergeant Milner soon enough, but not just yet."

Sandra was about to protest but Neil raised his hand gently. "Look, I know it's hard but you'll just have to trust me. There's other things at play here. Just leave it with me. I assure you I *will* get it sorted."

Neil thanked them for the coffee and left. He wanted to squeeze in one more call before he headed home, and it wasn't far away.

Within fifteen minutes, and for the third time in three weeks, he found himself easing his car up the bumpy driveway to Lower Booth Farm. He was getting a bit better at it each time because he was learning where the worst ruts were. As he swung round into the farmyard, he spotted what looked like a fully recovered Tegg. The dog ran up to him the moment he stepped out of the car. Neil gave him a pat. "Hello lad. Bet you're glad to be out and about again."

"Oh aye?" came a call from an open barn door. John Mellor had heard the car. He came into view carrying a lamb. He looked at Neil then down at the cuddly little creature. "It was a late one – a bit on the small side and not doing very well – so we put it in there with one or two other odd bods that needed some help." He pointed to the barn. "Anyway, what brings you here?"

"I'm on the trail of a vigilante."

The farmer rocked back and chortled. "You've heard then?" Neil shook his head. John looked at the lamb in his arms. "Let me put this little feller away."

Neil waited patiently as John re-entered the barn. The surroundings epitomised what a tough life was all about: hard stone buildings, weathered wooden gates, a yard brush that looked as though it had been made for Goliath propped by the barn door and the wind whirling bits of loose straw wherever it wanted around the yard. For a moment Neil forgot about police work.

"Do you like farming?" he asked John on his return. His question clearly surprised the farmer.

"Well it's certainly not for the money, I can tell you that!"

"It's just that it looks such a hard life, John."

"And you've come up here just to tell me that?"

Neil realised his question probably sounded odd. "No, I didn't... sorry."

John grunted. "Well, seeing as you asked. Yes, I do like being a farmer, and yes, it is hard, but you see that little chap I just put in the barn – *that's* why." He looked at Neil. "Do you like being a policeman?"

Neil realised he'd opened a can of worms and John had put

him on the spot. He kept it simple. "Well let's say I don't have many moments like you just showed me."

That was good enough for the farmer who decided to co-operate – in a John Mellor sort of way. "About Friday," he began. "Never mind what *you* want to know, what *I* want to know is what your... whatever his name is... who came up here asking me questions that day, was doing with those two at the pub. They're badduns. And I've seen one of 'em in there before – him who went for a bath. Pity Bill and I didn't have the soap." He couldn't disguise his pleasure at the thought.

Neil secretly sympathised with what John had done on the night of the break-in at his farm *and* how he and his mate had dealt with things at the Old Grouse but he still felt a word was needed. He'd warmed to the guy and didn't want him getting into trouble. "Look John, you can't keep taking matters into your own hands. You've got to leave it to us."

That niggled John no end and he wasn't having it. "Now *you look here.* You've said yourself it was me that gave you your first lead cause I shot at 'em." He was getting wound up now. "And what were Jim and Sandra to do with those blokes – call the police when there was one in there already, and fraternising with the enemy?" He was exasperated. "What in heaven's name is going on with you lot?"

The outburst shook Neil. He felt ashamed. He finally broke the silence. "Any chance I could come and have a look at those lambs, John?"

The farmer had cooled down a few degrees. "Aye. Come on."

After a few minutes observing the little creatures cuddling up around a small heat lamp and John giving them some warm milk from a bottle, the edge had been taken out of the earlier exchange.

"I can see why some people say being around animals eases stress," said Neil. "I could have done with some of this while I was in Manchester."

"A bit rough was it?"

"You could say that," he replied ruefully.

John's own countenance then took a dip. "I was only speaking for miself just now – about being a farmer. A chap not far from here topped himself a few years back. It can get to you if you let it – on your own for long periods with maybe just the dog to talk to, especially if things are going against you. The shotgun can be just a bit too handy."

They both went quiet, but Neil was determined not to leave on such a negative note. "Well just so you know, Derbyshire Constabulary does occasionally have its moments and you'll be pleased to hear we've found that green Bedford van and almost certainly who was driving it the night you had visitors."

"*Now that was more like it*," thought John. "Are you going to tell me where he lives?" he asked Neil with a crafty wink.

"Not in a month of Sundays!"

Anne noticed that Neil was a bit quiet when he finally returned home so, over tea, she decided to delve a bit. "Anything wrong?"

Neil put down his knife and fork. "Well… nothing disastrous." He sighed thoughtfully. "The thing is, Anne, in basic terms, the deal we, the police, have with Joe Public is that, if they conduct themselves in a law abiding manner, we will protect them. That's what they pay us for. It's just that today I was made to feel that we were not fulfilling our side of the bargain and, if I'm being honest, with some justification."

"Oh dear," responded his wife sympathetically.

"I'm not saying that people out here are naive compared with city dwellers but there's… I don't know… a sort of innocence, a vulnerability if you like, which I feel needs protecting."

"And you're not doing it?"

"It certainly doesn't feel like it."

Anne could see it was troubling him. "Well, look – tomorrow's another day," she said. "Enjoy the rest of your tea and then let's get our feet up." It was like pouring soothing oil on troubled waters and experience had made Anne a master.

❋❋❋❋❋

CHAPTER TWELVE

When Tuesday morning dawned the weather was cloudy but at least it was dry, much to Neil's relief. It was the day of the dog search up on Kinder. Whether DS Milner managed to make it to the top was immaterial as far as Neil was concerned. Yes, he wanted his detective sergeant to be closely involved but, more to the point, just plain out of the way. The real expertise in an operation like this lay with the dog handlers and Brian Parker. However, Neil knew it would be early afternoon before the party reached the site and he didn't expect to hear anything of significance until at least then. With that in mind he turned his immediate attention to having the film from Andy Bowers' camera developed and tasked Nick Fielding with getting that done as fast as he could. He also took the opportunity to assure him that Andy was okay. Those two were a long way from being friends but that didn't stop Nick from at least looking out for his work colleague. CID was a far from happy place for anybody at the moment, with Steve Milner seeming to be in a permanently bad mood.

That state of affairs was to be brought into even sharper focus when his wife Janet telephoned Trudie late on Monday and asked if she could have a discreet chat with her as a matter of urgency. Despite Sergeant Barker's antipathy towards Milner, she and his wife had got on really well on the occasions they'd previously met – hence her earlier comment to Neil about how someone as nice as that could have married the man she had.

Janet Milner had been guarded on the phone, so when Trudie arrived at the little cafe where they'd agreed to meet early on the Tuesday morning, she approached the appointment with some trepidation. She was not in uniform. The only other person that she'd informed of this meeting was Neil. All she'd said to Bob Lomas was that she might be in a bit late.

The truth was she didn't want to be meeting Janet at all, at least in these circumstances, but the woman had virtually implored her to. It was a very uncomfortable position to be in. Milner was the villain of the peace and now here *she* was, having a private face to face with his wife. Anyway, she braced herself, switched on a smile and walked over to join Janet, who had arrived early and was sitting in a quiet corner.

She got up as soon as she saw Trudie. "Oh hello. I'm so sorry to be troubling you Trudie."

"No, that's okay. I expect Steve's grumbling about being sent off hiking today," she quipped, trying to set a friendly tone."

Janet smiled faintly. "Oh he's always grumbling about something. Anyway, let me order you a coffee. How would you like it?"

"At this time in the morning, black with no sugar please." Trudie could see that Janet was stressed and, when the coffees duly arrived, her originally intended question "*What can I do for you*?" had become a straightforward "*What's wrong*?"

After taking a deep breath, Janet began. "It's Steve. I think he's in some sort of trouble. I've tried to get it out of him but he just clams up every time I ask. He came in on Friday night looking terrible. He went straight upstairs and shut the bedroom door." Her face contorted. "D'you know... I think I actually heard him crying."

She had to stop for a moment. Trudie gave her arm a gentle squeeze while Janet regained her composure. Eventually she continued.

"It's been building for weeks and, as if that wasn't bad enough, while we were out last Saturday someone came and smashed all the windows in our greenhouse. It was horrible – yet Steve would hardly talk about it. He just tried to blame some kids in the area. The thing is, I feel like I'm being disloyal coming here behind his back but I'm at my wits end Trudie, and I'm worried sick about him."

Sergeant Barker was well and truly on the spot. How could she reassure the poor woman when she knew what the situation was with Steve at work. Still, she did her best to try to calm her.

"It's the job I'm afraid, Janet. It gets to us all at some time or another. We have to deal with a lot of rough characters out there and I think Steve's got it pretty full on at the moment. If it's any consolation, I do know that the new boss is more than aware of the situation and if anyone knows about the pressures, he does. Inspector Webster probably thought despatching Steve to Edale would help take his mind off other things and, after all, your husband's the lead man on the case."

Talk about walking a tricky line! But Trudie hadn't done badly and Janet didn't seem quite so stressed. "Thanks. I know it's difficult to talk about police stuff with, well, outsiders."

"In that case," Trudie replied, "don't let's talk about it any more. Hey! I wonder how he's enjoying the great outdoors?"

Janet grimaced. "I daren't tell you what he said!"

Trudie laughed and the two of them engaged in further small talk before they went their separate ways.

But what was Detective Inspector Webster going to make of it all, she wondered? She intended to tell him about the conversation as soon as she could but no sooner had she donned her uniform at the station and entered her office than a call came in from Derby nick. What they had to tell her seemed as though it could be the first solid clue as to who the recipients were of the stolen farm gear.

Neil had been engaged on the phone when the call came in, hence it had been put through to Sergeant Barker. Entering DI Webster's office, Trudie had to decide what piece of new information to tell him first. She plumped for Janet.

"As if the situation isn't complicated enough, Trudie!" he replied with a huge sigh. Trudie then went on to brief him about the information she had just received from Derby.

So far there had been no leads as to where the stolen farm stuff was ending up, but reports had started to trickle in from the wider agricultural community in the south of the county about a new direct supplier who was undercutting the prices of established merchants. The products, particularly animal food, medication, fertilisers and red diesel, all appeared to look professionally presented with a perfectly believable, if unfamiliar, brand name. Your average frugal farmer was unlikely to shout it from the rooftops when they were on to a good thing but grassroots police work by the rural bobbies was clearly starting to pay off.

That put Neil in a better mood and prompted him to tell Trudie about his meeting with Jim and Sandra Hargreaves. She laughed when she heard about John and Bill Ollerenshaw's part in things. "No wonder Steve Milner's stressed out," she noted. "Hey! Perhaps we should make John a special constable?"

"I don't think so," replied Neil.

"We could fit him up with a mask and cape."

"Like *FARMERMAN* you mean?" added Neil. And that was it. It took a while for them to return to seriousness again but, when normal service finally resumed, Neil mentioned that he'd also been to see Andy Bowers... at his home.

"When was this?" she replied with surprise.

"Yesterday afternoon. He's not ill, but he's certainly in a bit of a state. I want to see what's on those photos he took. If we *have* got enough to arrest Eddie Slater for harbouring stolen goods, you never know, it might start him thinking where his own best interests lie."

Neil sat back in his chair. "D'you know what, I'm wasting valuable time here waiting for a call from Steve Milner up on Kinder Scout that might not even come. I'll just nab a quick bite to eat from the canteen and, if it's okay with Derby nick, I'm going to shoot off and see exactly what's happening down there." His mind flipped momentarily back to Kinder. "If there *is* any news from the search, just get someone to contact me will you."

Trudie happily agreed and gathered up her notes. "Probably see you tomorrow then sir."

"Yep." And with that she returned to her own office.

After a couple of phone calls – one to Derby and another to Matlock police station – Neil made his way up the stairs to the canteen. "That smells really good Mary," he commented as he approached the counter.

The dinner lady remained unmoved. "Flannel won't get you anywhere I'm afraid, Mr Webster." She looked over her glasses at him. "Perfection cannot be rushed."

Spotting a baking tray in one of the ovens, Neil pointed to it. "What's in that?" He had his suspicions. It *was* Tuesday.

"Sausages, but the potatoes aren't ready yet."

"Are they done? The sausages?"

"As a matter of fact they are, I'm just keeping them warm – *until the potatoes are cooked.*"

Neil assumed a look of great disappointment. Mary responded... grudgingly. "I suppose, at a push, because it's you, I could do you a sausage sandwich." Her expression remained pained. "And I suppose you'll be wanting a cup of tea with that?"

"You read my mind, Mary. You're a treasure!" She gave him a sideways look in return.

Suitably fuelled after his banger butty, DI Webster set off down the A6. This time he paid little mind to the beautiful scenery along the Wye Valley, including the entrance to Haddon Hall – that medieval gem he and Anne had on their list of places to visit as soon as they got the chance. Gnawing away at him was the behaviour of his detective sergeant. He was beginning to wonder if, apart from what they already suspected about his dealings with the criminal fraternity, there was something else going on, something so troubling that his wife had felt the need to confide in Trudie about it.

As he drove through Darley Dale, the outline of Riber Castle perched high on the hill in front of him announced that he was nearing Matlock. Once in the town, he parked up and made his way to the police station where Detective Sergeant Mick Redfern was there to greet him. Over a coffee, they agreed that the time was now right to bring Eddie Slater in for questioning, search his premises and get hold of that Bedford van. Knowing that the Matlock lads had been looking for an opportunity to collar Slater, Neil was happy to let them get on with it. After all, it was squarely on their patch.

Meeting over, Neil was off to Derby where, again, minds were as one. The priority was to track down some of these delivery lorries and see what info they could squeeze out of the drivers. Apart from that, it was just a case of keeping everyone in the loop. But before he left Derby police station, he put in a call back to Buxton to see whether there was any news from the search.

Bob took the call. "Nothing doing, I'm afraid sir," he reported.

"Didn't they find *anything*?" persisted Neil.

"Well they hardly got started."

"What!"

"Low cloud apparently. According to Brian Parker it was like pea soup up there so he had no option but to abandon it for the day."

"Just great!" bemoaned Neil.

"Sorry sir."

"It's not *your* fault Bob." Neil thought for a second. "When you say *abandon it for the day…?*"

"I was just about to say sir. They're staying over in Edale for the night and going up again tomorrow bright and early. Apparently the weather forecast's better. I presume that's all right?"

"It'll have to be but there'll certainly be some raised eyebrows at Division when the bill comes in. I just hope we'll have something to show for it."

Neil signed off and an hour later he was back in Buxton, rolling into his driveway. It had been a full-on day and he was really tired so, after he'd given Anne a peck on the cheek, he flopped into his armchair.

"Oh dear... you look whacked!" she said. "Shall I get you a drink?" Those last few words were commonplace in the Webster household in Manchester but it was the first time she'd used them in a job-related context since they'd moved to Buxton.

"Yes, a glass of beer would be nice, thanks."

She could tell her husband was really bothered about something and, when she returned with his drink, she sat down opposite him. "Bad day?"

"Complicated," Neil replied, bending his rule again about discussing work matters at home, but it was an occasion when he thought Anne's input might help. He took a serious glug of beer.

Half an hour later and, after a lot of soul-searching, Neil had come to a decision. His wife's thoughtful contribution had been priceless.

"Can *I* say something now?" she enquired.

Her husband got the message. "Yes, sorry sweetheart."

"That's okay... but I bet what I'm going to tell *you* will take your mind off what you've just been telling *me*." There was a twinkle in her eye.

"What d'you mean?"

"Well... guess who *I* had a phone call from today?"

Neil frowned. "I have no idea."

Anne couldn't wait to tell him. "Our son's girlfriend!"

She was right, that had really got her husband's attention. "You mean Charlotte?"

"No, it's another one. Her name's Esmeralda. Of course I mean Charlotte! She's invited us to a do that her parents are throwing." Neil's face was a study. It oozed suspicion. "Don't look like that!"

"What do you expect? It's Frank Radcliffe we're talking about here."

"Well just hear me out."

Neil sat stoney faced as Anne continued. "Apparently our son was supposed to have mentioned it but clearly forgot... although that's not really the point. Charlotte said that she and her parents thought it would be a nice opportunity to meet one another if we would like to come."

"No I would not!" retorted Neil without hesitation. "This is typical of Radcliffe. No doubt he wants to flaunt his *Mr Successful* and supposedly *legitimate* image at his potential son-in-law's parents. We'll I'm not having him flaunt it at me!"

Anne counted silently to ten then looked enquiringly at him. "Quite finished?"

"I don't know... probably!"

"Right, well listen to *me* now. Do you seriously think that Charlotte's father hasn't already checked *you* out?" Neil was clearly irritated by this astute observation. "And what sort of reaction do you think *he* had when he found out who his potential son-in-law's father was, with all the lowdown *you've* got on him?" That silenced Neil well and truly, but his wife hadn't finished. "Furthermore, if you think this invitation is Frank's doing then you're more naive than I thought. It'll be his wife and Charlotte's idea. He probably wants *you* there like a hole in the head!"

That definitely cheered Neil up. "Oh well," he said after due consideration. "If we've got to meet them, I suppose doing it among a lot of other people might make it less awkward."

Anne smiled inwardly at her husband's apparent change of heart. No one was better at the art of reverse psychology than she was – and he hadn't felt a thing. She was also right about another thing: Charlotte's invitation *had* taken her husband's mind off his difficult day at work.

CHAPTER THIRTEEN

As expected, Andy Bowers *did* turn in on the Wednesday morning and he didn't have to wait long until he and Nick Fielding received a visit from Neil in the CID office.

"Morning, Andy. Pleased to see you back." The DI didn't wait for an acknowledgment, turning his attention to DC Fielding. "Right, Nick. What's the state of play with those photos?"

"I was just about to check sir."

"Well between the pair of you, get hold of them as soon as you can, will you. Go and pick them up if necessary and, if they start messing you about, tell *me*."

The two officers knew the boss meant business and didn't hang around. Neil left the office but, once in the corridor, he could make out a conversation taking place just out of his view at the front desk. It stopped him in his tracks. He listened intently and smiled. "*Yes!*" he said to himself with quiet satisfaction as he returned to his office.

He didn't expect to be undisturbed for long and, sure enough, after a couple of minutes there came a knock at the door.

"Come in."

It was Bob Lomas, looking baffled. "Sorry to interrupt sir but I thought you ought to know, we've got Lewis Bates out front... with his mother. He says he wants to admit to nicking that sports stuff from the Robert Stevenson school. It looks like someone's worked him over."

DI Webster looked unmoved. "Really? Can't someone else deal with it?" he asked in a dismissive tone.

"Well I just thought you might be interested, Jane Briggs having been in your ear about it and all that."

Neil sighed. "Okay Bob. Sit them down. I'll be there as soon as I can."

PC Lomas was just about to leave when Neil stopped him. "You don't happen to know where Constable Briggs *is*, do you?"

"Yes, she's just nipped upstairs sir."

"Okay... thanks."

As soon as Bob was out of sight, Neil made his way up to the canteen and, sure enough, there was Jane coming out, drink in hand. "Best leave that here constable," he said. "We've got Lewis Bates and his mother at the front desk."

"You mean they're here?"

"Yes, that's exactly what I mean. Come on, we've got some work to do."

He set off back down the stairs and waited for her at the bottom. "Now who knows what they want," he continued, "but Bob says it looks as if Bates has been in the wars. I think this might be interesting. Would you like to sit in?" She didn't need asking twice. "Right, I'll go and get them. You can follow me in, okay?"

"Yes sir."

Neil paused for a second. "While we're in there, just keep it buttoned unless I tell you otherwise. Is that clear?"

Jane didn't answer.

"*Is that clear Constable Briggs!*"

"Yes sir."

Bob's description of Bates's condition had been an understatement. The boy had two black eyes and a swollen bottom lip, while his nose definitely looked out of shape. "Dear, oh dear. What have *you* been up to, young man?" enquired Neil as he approached them.

Mrs Bates looked as though she was about to say something sharp.

"Shut up Mum," snapped her son before she could get a word out, wincing and touching his lip after his efforts.

"Well, if you'd like to follow me." Neil shepherded them into the interview room, Lewis walking slowly and awkwardly. Neil went out of his way to help him sit down. "Careful now." The lad winced again as he settled into the chair. PC Briggs sat down next to her boss opposite Mrs Bates. She was taken aback by the state of Lewis but stuck to instructions and kept quiet.

"So then... what happened?" asked DI Webster.

"Nothing!" Lewis replied, though his diction was impaired by his fat lip. "I just want to make a statement."

Neil tapped at the desk while he considered how to respond. He looked quizzically at Lewis. "And this is about the theft at the school, is that right?"

"Yes, it was me and nothing to do with Terry McDonald."

At this point the DI sat back. "Okay. Stop there," he said, holding up his hand to emphasise the point. Mother and son looked at him blankly. "We need to do this properly," he continued. "If you're going to make a statement, by law at this stage we have to formally caution you."

He turned to Jane. "Constable Briggs, would you do the honours please."

Jane duly obliged, somehow managing to conceal the increasing pleasure she was taking from all this. With that done, Neil sat back and began the questioning. It didn't take long until he had a short but concise written statement from Bates admitting to the break-in at the secondary school, exonerating Terry McDonald and agreeing to repay the school for the stolen equipment. Mrs Bates remained silent throughout the interview but glowered irritably, clearly bottling up some bile. The moment formalities were over, she and her son couldn't get out of there fast enough, and Neil was more than happy to oblige. Looking out of the window, he could see mother and son exchanging harsh words in the car park. It was most satisfying.

When he returned to the interview room, Jane was agog at what had just happened. "I can't believe that," she gasped. "I just can't believe it."

"Yep, this job will never cease to surprise you Jane." He didn't call her by her first name very often but the occasion warranted a bit of familiarity.

She still couldn't take it on board. "But what could have made him come in here and confess?"

"Well my guess is he was probably getting a bit too big for his boots and trod on someone's toes in the criminal world – someone with *bigger* boots – and they've taught him a lesson."

"Yes, but wasn't a beating enough? Why did he come in here and do what he just did?"

It was a perfectly reasonable question to which Neil appeared to have a perfectly reasonable answer. "When you've been in this game as long as I have Jane, you'll know that the bad guys can sometimes move in mysterious ways, especially if they want to make a point. Honour among thieves if you like."

"Such as?"

"Well for instance, in this case, it was maybe someone with a bit of muscle who didn't like the idea of schoolkids being deprived of their footballs. A big soccer fan perhaps. You'd be surprised how word can get around. Anyway, a win is a win and we move on." He smiled at Jane. "But don't let me stop you breaking the good news to the McDonalds. That brought an extra big smile back his way, one that brightened up even the dowdy old interview room.

In the corridor on his way out he nearly bumped into Andy Bowers, who was clutching an envelope in his right hand. "Is that what I think it is Andy?"

"Yes sir."

"Right, well while Steve Milner's up Kinder Scout, let me have those. I'll see you in my office in ten minutes and bring Nick Fielding with you."

"Right sir."

Neil checked his watch. It was 10.30 – time was slipping through his fingers. He returned to his office as quickly as he could and began working his way through the photos. One made him stop and think. He placed it in his desk drawer. He'd just closed it when a knock came at the door.

"Come in."

The two CID officers entered. "Okay... sit yourselves down." They pulled up a couple of chairs and Neil placed the photos on the desk. "Right Andy," he began. "Take me through these – one at a time."

The first couple were of no consequence but the third was a of a Land Rover with a large, covered trailer.

"When was that taken?" Neil asked.

"Early evening on the Monday. It was really difficult. I wasn't near enough to see any detail otherwise I would have been spotted. All I could make out was that they spent about half an hour loading stuff into the trailer from an outbuilding. When the Land Rover left, I decided to follow it. I had to keep a long way back and I thought I was bound to lose it – on a couple of occasions I nearly did. I'm not kidding sir, I thought he was going on forever. I mean, we were the other side of Rudyard Lake. Anyway, he eventually turned off up a steep little lane – more of a track really – and to be honest I wasn't sure what to do. If I'd have followed in the car I'd have looked too obvious, so I decided to park up. If I lost him, I lost him, but I'd at least remember the location. I walked along the road a bit then started over the fields and up the hill in the general direction the Land Rover was heading. When I reached the top and looked down I could make out some stone buildings. I think it might have been an old farm but it looked pretty derelict."

Andy picked up the next photograph. "This one's the best I could do. You can see the trailer parked up and some other vehicles, including those two." He tapped on the picture on what appeared to be a couple of medium-sized lorries.

Up to that point Neil had been happy to let Andy give his account without interruption but the discovery of the lorries was of particular interest to him. He scrutinised the photo closely. "Couldn't you get any nearer?"

"Well it was getting a bit dark but there were some lights so I had a go at working my way closer – and that's when I heard them."

"Heard what?"

"Dogs! At least two of them. They went absolutely mental. I think they'd have ripped me apart if they'd caught me. I could hear voices, too, so I didn't hang about."

The remaining photographs didn't reveal much but, as they turned the last one over, Andy looked perturbed.

"What's up?" Neil asked.

"I'm *sure* there was another one... outside a pub. It was early doors on the Tuesday: a back-street place up near Glossop, the Quarryman's Arms."

"Glossop!" repeated Neil with surprise.

"I know. Talk about see the world!" replied Andy, who was running through all the photos again, looking for the missing one.

Neil intervened. "Don't waste any more time on that now. I want Trudie to join us. Could you see if she's free Nick? But give us five minutes first, will you?"

"Yes, okay sir."

Neil waited until Nick had closed the door behind him. "Well done Sherlock."

Andy looked surprised at the comment. Webster continued: "You were definitely clocked somewhere lad... maybe that Tuesday in Glossop." Neil opened his drawer and took out the missing photo. "But you'd already taken this."

Andy looked nonplussed. "But why...?"

Neil cut him off. "Until I tell you otherwise..." he brandished the photo... "we keep this one under wraps – got it?" He pinned his DC with a steely stare. "It's for your own good."

Andy looked horribly confused. "Look," continued Neil while holding up the other pictures. "You've done really well with these but you've got even more important work to do now."

They heard voices at the door and Neil quickly put the photo back in the drawer.

During the next half hour, the four officers engaged in intense conversation. They now had several strong leads covering both ends of the farm theft cases but it involved three separate forces. Effective organisation and communication was going to be top priority and he needed officers he could count on to make sure everything went according to plan. As far as *he* was concerned, those officers were now sitting in front of him and he was determined to make it clear how much he was relying on them.

"The reason I'm briefing you like this," he began, "is because there's another pressing matter I've got to deal with." He eyeballed the two detectives. "So, it's high time you two showed me what you can do."

This was totally new ground for Nick and Andy. They'd never been put on the spot like this before.

Neil continued. "Steve and I will be pretty much tied up with the Butler case so in both our absences Trudie, as the senior officer here, will be heading things up."

This wasn't news to Trudie: she and the DI had already talked it through. Neil saw her as a reliable lieutenant and had no qualms about leaving her in charge. As they were dismissed from the briefing she was the only one who really knew what Neil's "pressing matter" was. When Nick asked about it, she told him not to concern himself and just to concentrate on the business at hand.

Back in the office, Webster checked his watch again. Just time for a phone call. It was to a Manchester number.

"Is that you Joe?" he said covertly when the phone was picked up. The recipient was equally covert but proceeded to tell Neil something that brought a smile of satisfaction to the DI's face. "Yes," he replied. "I would say it was the *perfect* amount of persuasion Joe. I don't think he'll be troubling anybody on the Moor View Estate again any time soon." He listened again. "Yeah, I'll buy you a pint when I'm next on the wrong side of Manchester." He clearly got a response in kind and laughed before signing off.

CHAPTER FOURTEEN

Up on Kinder, two dogs were hard at it. Conditions weren't brilliant but not bad enough to prevent the search from taking place as had happened the previous day. The handlers had been pessimistic about the outcome because of the scale of the area that might need covering, but these dogs were trained to find human bodies, even in a snow-covered wilderness. The fact that the remains might be well below ground and badly decomposed wasn't an issue. They just needed to be in the right vicinity.

One way or another, Steve Milner had managed to make his way up there, although Neil had contacted Brian Parker in advance to advise him of his DS's potential hiking limitations. Accordingly, the mountain rescue man had advised Steve to stick to the track and go at his own pace so as not to slow the others down, while remaining in radio contact. He'd assured DS Milner that there was no need for him to have any involvement with the physical side of the search but to be around in case there were any developments or to keep any inquisitive walkers from taking too close an interest in what was going on'.

The main group had reached the site by ten o'clock – Milner about half an hour later – but as the day wore on he was beginning to wish the bracelet had never been found in the first place. Totally brassed off, he was stuck on his own in a boggy wilderness with the faint hope that someone would eventually announce that they'd found something. He also felt as though he had the weight of the world on his shoulders and, for a few brief moments, he understood why someone might want to disappear from the face of the earth just like Barbara Butler had apparently done. Then again, she might not have wanted to disappear at all! In fairness, Brian Parker made a point of coming back to Steve to update him at regular intervals but, eventually, even *he* realised it was ridiculous that Milner should be waiting around in obvious discomfort to receive information that could be relayed to him by radio, maybe in his car or somewhere back down in Edale. When that suggestion was put to the detective sergeant, he wasted no time in agreeing and quickly set off back down the trail.

As he plodded and sometimes stumbled along, Milner's mind was preoccupied with his problems – so much so that he failed to appreciate any of the natural grandeur that surrounded him. He also failed to notice a figure steadily drawing closer to him on the trail. But that figure recognised *him,* albeit more from his physical shape and ungainliness than anything else.

"Hello Steve," hailed the figure as they closed in on one another. Milner looked up from his feet, which he'd constantly been checking to avoid taking a tumble, to find his boss in front of him. The realisation nearly *did* make him slip.

DI Webster walked closer and looked at him full square in the eyes. "We need to talk, don't we Steve." Milner knew this was it. He had nothing left.

The spot where they'd met was just above the old packhorse bridge. Neil took the lead and the two men headed down towards it. The path gradually became easier and eventually they drew to a halt. Neil took a few steps on to the bridge, placed both hands on the wall and gazed down into the valley below while he collected his thoughts. This was going to be hard – incredibly hard. Milner wandered over.

"Peaceful isn't it," commented Webster. "Your troubles seem far away when you look at that." He turned to Milner. "But yours are right on your doorstep, aren't they Steve? And any minute now they're going to come crashing through your front door!"

Milner shut his eyes. He was totally at sea. His head dropped. Neil let him be for a minute. Eventually his sergeant gathered himself. "What are you going to do sir?"

Neil considered the question for a second or two before answering. "Believe it or not, nothing for the present, other than to have, *with you... right here,* the most important conversation you've probably ever had since you joined the force." He gestured towards the hills. "Where absolutely no one else can hear us." He cast his eyes over the landscape. It oozed isolation. A distant curlew call seemed to emphasise that fact, prompting a wry smile from Neil. "Just you... me... and the curlews." That raised a philosophical glimmer from his detective sergeant.

DI Webster continued. "Even you must know the net's closing Steve – and the only chance you've got of not getting caught in it is to come clean... to me... now. I'm probably the only hope you've got of not ending up inside with the same scum you've been associating with." He gave Milner a cold stare. "Think about it: a bent copper... doing time."

A respected fellow officer calling him a "bent copper" to his face hit Steve as hard as it possibly could. He realised the only hope he had was to put his case as best he could – his day in the court of Kinder Scout. Milner began his opening argument.

"You know as well as I do, sir, that in our game things aren't always what they seem." He paused for a second to allow Neil to dwell on that remark. "Let's face it. If they were, you and me would be out of a job."

His words succeeded in making Neil think. Had Milner got something up his sleeve? He let Steve continue.

"And just so as you know from the outset, sir, I've never *ever* taken a bung from anyone. Quite the opposite in fact. All I was asked to do was to look the other way or at least not dig too deep."

As the officers leant against the ancient stonework of the bridge, DS Milner slowly revealed the facts about his relationship with the criminal world.

As Steve unloaded his dark secrets, Neil increasingly wondered what hold these guys had over his detective sergeant. A hold that was sufficient to make him betray the good name of the force and his own colleagues. The answer to that question wasn't far away as Milner's emotions began to get the better of him. It was a poignant moment and certainly not the time for a group of jolly walkers to cross the bridge and engage them in pleasantries about how kind the weather had been. Such innocents.

When the hikers moved on, Milner resumed his confession and the reason for his fall from grace was made crystal clear. "I'm a gambling addict sir."

And there it was. Those toxic words hung in the air. An ugly affront to all the natural beauty that surrounded the little packhorse bridge.

Over the next half hour Milner described how he had got into debt with a bookie in Stockport but did what so many compulsive gamblers do and chased the next win in the hope that he'd get lucky. But those bets weren't on the horses any more: they were on the card tables and roulette wheels at a downmarket casino in Manchester that had connections to the bookie. When the people behind the gambling operation found they had a relatively senior member of the CID in their debt, they held off pressing for the money back and instead took it in kind, the tentacles of their activities spreading all the way to Buxton... and further. When they realised that "their man" could no longer shield them from investigation and was therefore of no more use, they wasted no time in calling in the debt... plus interest.

When John Mellor had stuck his oar in that day at the Old Grouse Inn, he had no idea what a nasty piece of work he'd thrown into the stream; one who had just issued threats in the back room not only against Milner but also his nearest and dearest if he didn't pay up or blabbed to his superiors. As the thought of anything happening to his wife and children exploded back into the forefront of his mind, Steve Milner folded and slumped against the bridge wall. "What have I done?" he exclaimed in anguish. "What *have* I done?"

Neil looked feverishly around to make sure no one was approaching. He put his hand on Milner's shoulder, giving him time to regain his composure. He'd seen first-hand in his old job the misery that low-lifes in the gambling world could cause when they got their hooks into someone. That train of thought was broken when a young couple came into view, walking up from the direction of the dale. The officers left the bridge and made their way back up the stream to a spot next to a small waterfall, where they sat down on some bank-side stones.

"What happens now?" asked Milner morosely.

Before his boss could answer, the radio attached to Steve's coat crackled into life. Neil nodded to him.

"Better take that." It was Brian Parker.

"Hello, is that you Steve?" enquired Brian.

"Yes... I can hear you Brian. What is it?"

"We've *got* something." Milner looked at Webster, who nodded for him to continue.

"Anything interesting Brian?"

"You could say that. How about human remains!"

CHAPTER FIFTEEN

Back in Buxton that afternoon, Jane Briggs altered the route of her beat to take in the secondary school. She'd phoned the headmaster's office in advance to see if Mr Cousins would be available because she wanted to update him on the McDonald case. When she arrived Mrs Sheldon, the secretary, was her usual polite self. She noticed that PC Briggs was in a particularly buoyant mood while she waited. Was there some good news she wondered? Eventually the head teacher's door opened.

"Ah, Constable Briggs!" boomed Mr Cousins, his arm extended at the ready, his imposing form filling most of the door frame.

Jane rose rapidly from her seat and shook his hand with an extra firmness of her own. Mr Cousins looked down with surprise. "My... that was a good one! I certainly wouldn't like to feel your hand on *my* collar WPC Briggs"

They both laughed. The headmaster straightened to his full height. "So constable, what have you come to tell me?"

Jane looked full of purpose. "I've got some good news Mr Cousins."

"Well that's excellent. In that case... step this way."

Jane happily accepted the invitation and went in, followed by the head, who moved to one side and then closed the door. It wasn't long before a roar of approval came from within his office that made the secretary sit up. Things gradually calmed down, no doubt as Jane went into more detail, but in no more than five minutes the door opened again.

"Did you hear that, Mrs Sheldon?" Cousins hailed his secretary as he stepped out.

"I certainly heard something," she replied.

"The case is solved," he enthused. "And there's more! I'll explain in a minute but I'm going to see Constable Briggs out myself."

Jane thanked Mrs Sheldon before she and Cousins headed off down the main corridor. As they chatted along the way his tone became more conspiratorial. "I was never going to press charges, you know."

Jane stopped in her tracks. "Pardon?"

"You surely don't think I would be *that* vindictive do you?"

"Well I did think you were being a bit harsh. After all, he had just got his first job, which I thought you'd be pleased about."

"I am, but I couldn't ignore the fact that he appeared to have committed a crime and I was determined to at least make him sweat a bit."

"You certainly did that... *and* his mother... and me as well."

Cousins looked a bit shame-faced. "Well, I'm sorry about the last two." He shook his head. "I just hope young McDonald has learnt his lesson."

They reached the main exit. Jane was just about to leave when the headmaster suddenly had a thought. "Erm... we're having a careers day later this term." He looked quizzically at her. "Would you be interested in coming in to talk to some of the older ones about your job?"

Her meeting with Mr Cousins epitomised the reason why Jane had wanted to join the police force. Not only for the satisfaction of solving a crime but to put a smile back on the face of previously injured parties. Today, she was going to make the absolute most of it.

About 20 minutes later she entered Maskell Road on the Moor View Estate. This time there was no sign of Lewis Bates – not surprising really. It was peaceful, the gardens were coming into bloom and devoid of the odious yob and his motley crew that had been blighting the neighbourhood. It was just after five o'clock when she knocked on the McDonalds' door. She *so* hoped that there was someone home and was just about to knock again when she heard the catch being turned on the inside. The door opened. Two smiles met.

"Hello, Mrs McDonald."

"Oh, hello luv. D'you want to come in?" She stepped aside to let Jane through. "And it's Marion, remember."

"Sorry. Yes, of course."

"Actually, I'm really glad you've called."

"Why's that?" replied Jane.

Mrs McDonald shut the door. "Are you in a rush?"

"No, I'm fine."

"Well in that case I've got something to tell you." She nodded towards the sitting room. "Now you go on in there and sit down. I'll put the kettle on. It's the talk of the estate!"

Marion had a real spring in her step. WPC Briggs gazed out of the window. These visits were becoming a bit of a habit... but so what! It wasn't glamorous, it wasn't exciting, it was just having a cuppa on an ordinary Wednesday afternoon with someone on the local council estate. But it was so real – and it was actually making a difference. She liked it... she liked it very much.

Marion entered the room, carrying a tray with tea and biscuits. "Help yourself luv," she said, putting the tray down.

"Well that's lovely," replied Jane. She gave Marion a sideways glance. "I hope you're not trying to bribe a police officer, Mrs McDonald?"

Her host grinned. "Fat chance when tea and biscuits is all I've got to offer."

Jane eyed the biscuits. "I wouldn't be too sure. I'm anybody's for a Jammy Dodger. Got hooked on them at the school tuck shop." She edged her hand towards the biscuits. "May I?"

"Course you can." Mrs McDonald sat down and took a sip of tea. "Oh, that's better," she said as she put the cup and saucer back on the tray. "Right then. You'll never guess what?"

"What?"

"Somebody's worked Lewis Bates over – good and proper." Jane said nothing. Marion continued: "I saw him, and so did some others round here, only the once mind but that was enough." She winced. "Ooooh, he was a mess." She looked enquiringly at her visitor. "Do *you* know anything?"

Jane remembered DI Webster telling her to play things down. "Actually I have seen him. He and his mother came into the station earlier today."

"Did he say who did it?" pressed Marion.

"Well I couldn't tell you that, even if I knew, but that's not what he came in for."

Mrs McDonald looked baffled. "Well? What *did* he come in for then?"

Jane had so been looking forward to this moment. "To confess to stealing the sports stuff from the school and to say that your Terry had absolutely nothing to do with it."

Marion flopped back into her chair in disbelief. "I need another drink of my tea!"

"Are you sure you don't want something stronger?"

"Maybe later but this'll do for starters." Marion took several sips of her tea before putting the cup down again. She still looked bewildered. "I don't understand?"

"Yes, it's a strange one isn't it?" continued Jane. "Anyway, Terry's off the hook and that's all that matters."

Marion gave her such a look of gratitude. "I could kiss you luv. I've been so worried."

At that moment the door latch went and Terry breezed into the hall. He caught sight of PC Briggs and stopped in his tracks. His mum rose from her chair. "It's all right, Terry,' she blurted out.

Jane got up too. "Hello Terry. How's the job going?"

"Okay," came the guarded response. Terry's expression was one of suspicion. You couldn't blame him – every day he had feared the police would knock on his door to formally charge him with the school break-in. Jane decided to put him out of his misery without further delay.

"Your mum's right, Terry. There won't be any charges."

Terry once more demonstrated that he wasn't the hard case he would have people believe. His knees sagged as he took a deep breath and closed his eyes. His relief was palpable.

"Anyway," added Jane, "now I've delivered that bit of good news I'll be on my way. Your mum can tell you all about it."

She got up from her chair and made her way towards the door, giving Terry a gentle squeeze on his shoulder. Marion followed her. "I'll come and see you out luv. I'll be back in a minute Terry."

With that she opened the door for Jane, followed her out and closed it behind her. It was apparent Marion had something else she wanted to tell her while they were on their own. "Terry doesn't know it yet – I only heard today – but his dad's going to be released on licence at the end of the month."

"Oh Marion, that's wonderful."

"I know. It's crazy when you think about it."

"What d'you mean?"

"Well, for over a year now it seems that everything that could go against us has done, yet in a single day we've had one piece of good news after another."

"Don't knock it Marion. You enjoy it."

Mrs McDonald stood back, folded her arms and smiled

amiably at WPC Briggs. "I think you must be my lucky charm."
Marion hugged Jane and looked up and down the road. "And I don't care if anyone round here *does* see me hugging a copper!" Tears sprang up in her eyes. "Sorry," she said, wiping her eyes. "I'm being silly. Anyway, I'd better go in and tell Terry everything." She gathered herself and glanced up at the heavens. "D'you know what? I know it's not Friday but I think we'll push the boat out and have fish and chips tonight!"

The following morning there was a buzz about the whole station. Everyone had been summoned to the canteen, a tactic DI Webster was increasingly employing for meetings. It made sure CID and uniform rubbed shoulders more often along with a cup of tea or coffee to help things along. The meeting had been called in light of developments in the Barbara Butler case. The only absentee was PC Richard Lowe, who'd been tasked with holding the fort at the front desk. One of the CID contingent lit a cigarette but Neil summarily told him to put it out until he got back to his own office, a general rule the DI was using to discourage smoking in the canteen. He was running the meeting along with Detective Sergeant Milner.

"Okay everyone," he began. "As you probably know, Steve here was up on Kinder with the search party yesterday so I'm going to hand things over to him straight away to bring us all up to speed."

Neil stepped aside, leaving the floor to DS Milner. "Thank you, sir." Milner turned to face the seated officers. "Right, well it was the second day of the search and naturally it's been taking place in the vicinity of where the bracelet was found. They've been using specialist dogs. The terrain is extremely rough, full of bogs, boulders and peat hollows, and it's difficult to access, even though it's not that far from the main footpath. At about 3.30pm yesterday, I received a radio call from Brian Parker, the mountain rescue leader, to say that they'd found some human remains."

The news triggered a stir among the officers. "Do they think it's her, sarge?" asked one of them.

"Just let me finish."

All went quiet again.

"At this stage they don't have much to go on but the search *is* continuing. They could be up there some time. Any identification will depend on what else they find."

Another outbreak of muttering caused Steve to up the decibels. "But I must emphasise... it's *very* early days and the location is extremely challenging."

"So what happens now, sarge?" asked Bob.

Milner was ready. "A specialist forensic team will be going up there as soon as it's physically possible but it can't be rushed if they're to do their job properly. It may well be the body of Barbara Butler but until that is confirmed I don't want any loose talk. It could prejudice the investigation, especially if we suspect foul play. The less speculation out there the better and we certainly don't want the press camped on our doorstep. Any more questions?"

"Yes sarge." Nick Fielding's question was more of a statement. "Anyone who goes up on Kinder is bound to wonder what's going on."

Milner nodded. "Fair point. It *will* be difficult keeping a lid on things but I don't want word getting out because someone here couldn't keep their mouth shut." He let that message sink in before he pressed on. "Fortunately, the actual site isn't visible from the main track and the forensic team is going to keep as low a profile as possible.'

"Is anyone going to inform the Butler family what's going on?" asked Trudie.

"Thank you, Trudie," he replied, "but at the moment the

answer has to be not until we *absolutely* have to or it becomes in our interests to do so." He looked around the room. "Anything else?" His query was met with silence. "Okay. That's it from me."

He stepped to one side to let DI Webster take over again.

"Thanks, Steve. So, it looks like we're going to have to be patient. But that may not be such a bad thing because the farm thefts case we've been dealing with up here looks like it might be the tip of a much bigger iceberg. It's becoming a fast-moving situation so expect to be kept busy." He turned to Milner. "All done, Steve?"

"Yes, I think so."

"Right then everyone, that's it. Off you go."

As the canteen emptied, there were a number of low-key exchanges between officers over the demeanour of DS Milner. It was a long time since they'd seen him that motivated about anything.

Steve and Neil remained in the canteen and grabbed a coffee each before sitting at a table well away from the counter. "Well done," began Neil.

Milner now had some real steel in his eye. "I know I can get this guy sir."

"Look Steve. Just hold on." It was almost a reprimand. "You might not be in a position to get *anybody.*" Milner got the message and eased off. So did Neil, who pulled a photo from his pocket and placed it on the table. It was the one from Andy Bowers' collection that no one else had seen – potentially incriminating if the viewer wished to interpret it so. "I'm showing this just so you know what you could be up against."

Neil was fully aware that he was running a risk himself. He could easily have just hung his DS out to dry. The same thought had increasingly been occurring to Milner and finally out came the question. "Why are you doing this sir?" he asked incredulously. "Nobody here owes me any favours."

"Well you're 100 per cent right there, Steve. But if this doesn't all end in tears for you, it'll be your wife and Trudie you should thank more than anyone."

Milner fell silent as the full impact of his boss's words sank in. Webster hadn't intended to say what he'd just said but it clearly had an effect, and by the look on Steve's face, a profound one.

The net was slowly closing in on those involved in the farm theft cases thanks to good grassroots police work out in the agricultural sticks, but it was a slow process. Neil's *trump* card in all this was still the man sitting in front of him. The guy knew about the set-up better than anyone, but if the criminals he'd been associating with were going down, they'd do their level best to make sure they took Milner with them.

CHAPTER SIXTEEN

It hadn't seemed two minutes since Neil and Anne had received their surprise invitation from the Radcliffes, but here they were on Saturday evening, 10th May, getting all dressed up. Neil wasn't really one for do's but Anne loved them and she'd bought a new outfit for this one. There had actually been a couple of social get togethers at Buxton since Neil had taken over, which is where Anne had met Janet Milner. She knew Neil's efforts to try to save Janet's husband from disaster were as much to protect *her* as anything else and that it was extremely tricky for him. But at that moment he was having to deal with another tricky matter – trying to get the knot right in his tie. "Are you sure we've got to be this smart?" he whinged.

"Yes we have," she answered back. "I checked with Charlotte to make sure we didn't look out of place."

"Oh... you checked with Charlotte did you?" he replied teasingly.

Anne couldn't help smiling. "She really is a poppet – and if you told me she was to be my future daughter-in-law you wouldn't hear any complaints from me."

Her husband stopped fiddling with his tie. "Well, well, well. She has made an impression, hasn't she?"

"Yes she has," Anne replied without hesitation. "But when you think about it, Paul must have made a pretty good impression on *her* mother for us to get an invitation like *this*."

Neil realised she had a good point. The venue for this get together was a small hotel on the outskirts of Alderley Edge, deep in the money belt of Cheshire, where the Radcliffes had hired a room for the occasion. The sign at the entrance to the driveway was classy: stylish gold script set on a navy blue background. Neil scowled.

"What's wrong now?" Anne asked in frustration as they drove through the gates.

"This is Frank Radcliffe all over isn't it? Always out to show off his financial status."

Anne wasn't having any of it. "I hope this isn't a touch of the green-eyed monster on your part dear?"

"No it is not!" snorted her husband. "It's how he came by it – *that's* what gets me."

"Well you'll just have to put up with it for the next few hours. It won't kill you."

'Huh. I s'pose not," he replied grudgingly.

They followed the signs that took them to "guest parking" at the side of the building, a short walk from the main entrance. Once in the foyer, a member of staff pointed them in the direction of the function room, where Frank and Diane Radcliffe were welcoming their guests. Frank was keeping a particular eye out for the Websters – but he wasn't the only one.

Charlotte had been watching with Paul from the sidelines and, when she spotted them, wasted no time in going over to introduce them to her mum and dad. Charlotte was a smart cookie and was determined to make sure things went as smoothly as possible between the parents.

"I'm *so* glad you could come," said Diane after her daughter had done the honours. She gave Anne a knowing glance. "He's a real charmer, that son of yours."

More guests were arriving so the welcome was brief. Charlotte took the opportunity to whisk the Websters away to join

Paul. Neil and Anne soon found themselves with a glass of champagne and being charmed by the equally bubbly personality of their son's girlfriend. There was no doubt that it was *she* who had engineered their being given the invitation. That said, Charlotte couldn't understand why her father had been more than a little reluctant. Her mother, on the other hand, had needed no persuading at all, and that was that! She'd clearly taken to Paul as a potential suitor for her daughter and she had a very good reason...

As the champers went to work, Neil began to relax and enjoy himself. If he was going to be in the company of Frank Radcliffe for the evening he intended to take the maximum satisfaction from eating his food and drinking his booze without having to worry about driving home the same evening. When Anne expressed concern at the amount of booze he was knocking back, Neil broke the news that he'd booked them a room for the night at the same hotel. It was extortionate but he looked forward to mentioning his accommodation arrangements should their host enquire.

As the evening progressed, Anne mingled effortlessly with the other guests, while even Neil managed to find palatable company. When asked what he did for work, he only spoke of his time at Buxton police station before manoeuvring the conversation to another topic. Presumably, Charlotte had made her mother aware that Neil was a police officer so he adopted the same approach when he and Anne chatted to her during the evening.

Neil and Paul hadn't had much chance to talk on their own so they took the opportunity to sneak off to a quiet corner of the hotel bar and take stock of the evening so far. As they sat in comfortable chairs with a pint each of Boddingtons Best it was impossible to deny that they were having a good time.

"Is this what you're going to have to get used to then?" enquired his dad.

"Well, not *every* week. I mean, we'll be at their villa in the Algarve a lot." Neil scoffed – he knew when his son was winding him up. Well he hoped he did.

Paul proceeded to dispel any doubts. "Don't worry, it's not going to be like that. Charlotte and I want to stand on our own two feet."

Neil tilted his head in approval. "You're serious then?"

It turned out to be a silly question. "Yeah... it is Dad."

"I take it *she* is?"

"Oh Charlotte would get married tomorrow if we could afford it. But we can't."

"Well maybe that's no bad thing. Let's face it, you haven't really known each other that long."

"Yeah... that's what *her* dad said, too."

"*I bet he did,*" thought Neil but, before he could expand on that thought, they were interrupted.

The figure in the doorway gave a wry smile. "So this is where you're hiding. Men only, is it?"

"Oh hello, Mr Radcliffe,' Paul replied. "Care to join us?"

Frank took a quick look behind as if to check no one had spotted him. "That all right with you, Mr Webster?" he asked.

Neil and Radcliffe's expressions belied what they were both really thinking. "It's your party!" replied Neil.

This apparent bonhomie was doubtless because they'd both consumed a significant amount of alcohol.

Frank, who had arrived with a pint in his hand, pulled up a chair. "Well I hope you're enjoying yourselves. It's nice to see people having a good time, including this chap..." he nodded at Paul... "and my daughter. By the way, it better be Frank the way these two are going."

"In that case, I'm Neil."

"Okay Neil."

This was all so phoney – but then again... perhaps not entirely?

"I had to escape," resumed Radcliffe. "There's only so much smiling I can do." Both Websters laughed. Frank looked behind again, then back at the other two. "Fancy a small wager?"

"What on?" enquired Neil warily.

"Which one of the women finds us first. A pound says it's Diane."

The others couldn't help but grin conspiratorially. "Come off it Frank," said Neil. "You're the host, she's *bound* to come looking for you." He turned to his son. "Don't have a bet with this chap – you'll never win." The words were out before he could stop himself. He could almost feel Frank twitch. A quick sidestep was required. "Only joking Frank," continued Neil. "It's just that Charlotte mentioned you own a casino."

Frank confirmed the fact and relaxed again – but he would have lost the bet anyway because the next face through the door was his daughter's. They all laughed.

"What's so funny?" she asked accusingly.

"Oh nothing darling," replied her dad soothingly.

She looked at the three pint pots. "I can see what's happening here." She looked at Paul. "I think you'd better come with me. They're obviously a bad influence."

Frank and Neil laughed again. They were beginning to laugh at most things now.

"Go on lad," said his dad.

"But don't tell them where we are," added Frank as they left.

"D'you know," said Neil when they'd gone. "I don't think I've ever been told off so charmingly."

"That's what five thousand quid a year at private school does for you so your lad definitely owes me – and *you* will... assuming they get hitched."

The two of them had entered rambling mode. Frank continued. "Hey, what was that film? '*Of all the gin joints in all the...*' you know."

"You mean *Casablanca*?"

"Yeah... that's the one. But in my case it's '*Of all the boyfriends' fathers in all the towns in all the world he had to have **you**!*'"

"Well *snap* there!" responded Neil.

"Okay... point taken." There followed another few sips of beer before Frank piped up again. "I just thanked my lucky stars you weren't involved when they raided the house that time. She would have remembered."

"C'est la vie, eh?" responded Neil philosophically. With that they clinked glasses and downed the last of their beer. It was timely because an indignant-looking Diane and Anne suddenly appeared.

"Just coming," the two husbands said in virtual unison.

As they set off, they continued chatting covertly as they followed their wives.

"How hard did you have your nuts squeezed to make you play nicely tonight then Neil?" enquired Frank.

"A lot!" came the pained reply.

"Yeah... me too."

They walked a little further. Now it was Neil's turn. "You know what they used to call you at Manchester nick? Well, that's repeatable."

"Go on."

"The dry cleaner!"

"Oh yeah...why's that?"

"Because of all the laundering that went on in that casino of yours... ha ha!" It was a sign of the détente that was developing between them that his host took the remark in good part. In fact he almost looked proud of the tag. After all, they never did catch him.

CHAPTER SEVENTEEN

Despite the best efforts of the police to keep the investigation quiet, it did not take long for word to get out that something was happening up on the moors in north Derbyshire. As Nick Fielding had pointed out at the briefing, the presence of officers and search dogs operating up there was bound to get people asking questions, particularly the press. Enquiries were coming in not only from local reporters but from Derby, Manchester and Sheffield. They could only be fobbed off for so long and it was clear that some sort of statement needed to be made to prevent the emergence of wild and unhelpful speculation. And so, on the Monday after the weekend of Frank Radcliffe's party, Neil found himself heading up a hastily arranged press conference. As far as he was concerned, at this stage of the investigation he just wanted to know if it was Barbara Butler or not. Cause of death could come later.

At the press conference the more diligent reporters had done their homework and the name of the local woman who'd mysteriously disappeared five years ago soon came up – Barbara Butler. Webster refused to be drawn but the journalists were pressing hard and Neil knew they'd start digging, so he issued a blunt warning to them to leave matters to the police. But he also knew it was only a matter of time before they misbehaved.

As soon as the press conference had finished, he was on the phone to the coroner's office and, after some heavy duty persuasion, he managed to secure an appointment at the mortuary in Chesterfield. The bodily remains were still the best part of 2,000 feet up on Kinder Scout and, because foul play could not be ruled out, the search of the area needed to be meticulous. The remains could not be removed until the forensic people were satisfied that everything that could be found had been. The fact that those remains were not at the mortuary that Monday afternoon was of no consequence to Webster, but Andrew Pritchard, the investigating pathologist, *was,* and that's what mattered to Neil.

Pritchard was a tall, slim chap in his fifties, with grey wavy hair. He cut a distinguished figure but had a persona that would make you think twice before trifling with him. He was bespectacled, grouchy and didn't take kindly to being hassled by impatient police officers. He did, however, tolerate DI Webster more than most, having dealt with him a number of times before. For his part, Neil understood a post-mortem could not be rushed if it was to be performed properly and that attitude had earned him some points in Pritchard's eyes. A few preliminary observations might be divulged certainly, but anything else... *well you just had to wait.* That's why he was surprised by the pathologist's opening offering when they met up that afternoon.

"Well, detective inspector," he began. "I can halve the possibilities as to who your body might be straight away. It is female."

"Most helpful Andrew," Neil replied sardonically, although in fairness, Pritchard was technically correct.

"But we have by no means found all of her. At the moment she is minus quite a few bits, particularly a radius and ulna and everything below that on her left side."

Neil was savvy enough about the human skeleton to know he was referring to her arm below the elbow. That got him thinking. "You know that a bracelet was found lying some distance from the body?"

"I do."

"Well could that have been a result of the arm getting detached and dragged off?"

Pritchard's expression suggested that wasn't an unreasonable question. "Yes, that's possible I suppose – but theories like that must be treated as mere conjecture at this stage as I'm sure you realise."

His expression became grave. "You and I have been in this game long enough not to try to make the facts fit the case rather than the other way round.

Neil took his point and moved on. "And there's nothing at all to even hint as to who she might be?"

The pathologist shook his head. "I'm sorry." It all sounded negative but Pritchard hadn't finished. "You think this is the Butler woman, don't you?"

"Yes… I do."

"Well Neil, whoever it turns out to be, I think the question at the root of your enquiries should be how on earth she ended up where she did. I have been up there twice now. It is most inhospitable and the ingress of peat into the skeletal remains is not at all helpful."

"You've seen the case notes I take it?"

"I have." He looked at Webster as though that was an impertinent question.

Neil rubbed his forehead in frustration with himself. "Sorry, Andrew. I'm just trying to keep on top of this before it gets messy."

Pritchard moved on. "Your Detective Sergeant Milner seemed convinced that the husband was somehow involved?"

"He still does," said Webster, "and now he's got a body!"

"Yesss," mused Pritchard thoughtfully. "Well if foul play has taken place he would be a suspect of course – nearest and dearest and all that." He paused while he considered the matter further. "Be that as it may, Mr Butler is also by far our best chance of ascertaining whether the remains are indeed those of his wife: dental records, medical history, X-ray material etc." The pathologist looked hard at Neil again. "But I can understand why you've been reticent about contacting him. It *is* tricky."

"Yes," said Neil. "I could have simply shown him the bracelet right at the outset – and any of her friends and relatives for that matter – and asked if it was hers. But I thought that would just stir everything up before I even knew if we had a body."

"*And* provide time for anybody with something to hide to get their story straight," added Pritchard with a satisfied look.

Neil liked working with Andrew – they were bang on the same wavelength.

"It's a chicken and egg situation," continued the pathologist, "but, now the egg has hatched, I don't think you've much to lose." He peered at Webster over his glasses. "I heard about the press conference."

Neil smiled and shook his head. "You don't miss much, do you?"

"Oh you'd be surprised what filters down to me here in my bunker. So, if I were you inspector, I'd pay Mr Butler a visit before one of our journalist friends does and makes things even more tricky for you."

Webster couldn't get back to the station fast enough and headed straight for Sergeant Barker's office. Trudie blustered a bit at being asked to drop everything but he wanted that bracelet – and *now* – *and* Malcolm Butler's address. But he needed to speak to Steve Milner as well. Fortunately he found him exactly where he should have been, in the CID office beneath a plume of cigarette smoke, wading through the statements given by those interviewed in the original investigation.

It was only right that Webster let his DS know what he'd

discussed with the pathologist but, once that was done, he turned his attention to what Milner was actually *doing.* He nodded towards the case file. "How are you going on with that lot?"

"Not bad sir. I've made a list of anyone who might conceivably recognise the bracelet and I've taken photographs of the outside and inside of it to show them. They're already being processed."

"Good. We need to get on the road with those. Anyway, I thought I'd let you know I'm off to try to catch Malcolm Butler at home in Derby before anybody else does." He expected that bit of news to produce a reaction – and it did.

"You mean *you? Now?*"

"Yep... sorry Steve. I need to meet this guy myself and I need *you*" – he pointed at the file – "to deal with *that* stuff. I'm going to take the bracelet with me."

Milner's knee-jerk reaction was to be annoyed but it only took him a few seconds to compare this relatively minor issue with his other woes. He took it on the chin.

Neil had one further question. "This woman who's registered as living at the same address as Butler – Celia."

"Knowles," replied Steve.

"Yes, that's the one. Do we know anything about her?"

"Not a lot. She didn't figure much in the original investigation but one or two of the other women in their hiking group mentioned her with a touch of innuendo."

"Really?"

"Yes, but nothing more than that. Barbara Butler's sister, however, had *plenty* to say on the matter. I don't think there was much love lost between her and Malcolm."

"Hmmm...okay. Well, make her your first call. See if she's still as vocal. I'll let you know how I get on down in Derby." He took a quick look at his watch. "Right... I must go."

He left the station via the front desk to pick up the bracelet, a piece of paper with Malcolm Butler's address on it and to thank Trudie, his "Miss Reliable".

The station was now as busy as anyone there could remember. The days when CID officers spent hours encloseted with their fags and coffee in the sanctum of their office were long gone. In fact it was now rare that there were two of them in there at the same time. That suited young Andy Bowers just fine but, that Monday afternoon, he walked in unaware that Steve Milner was already there working on the Butler file. He was about to do a U-turn when Steve called his name. Andy reluctantly stopped in his tracks. Ever since Milner had threatened him, he'd kept out of his way and said nothing to anyone other than DI Webster. He stood frozen.

"It's all right, Andy," Steve finally said. "You sit at your desk and I'll go somewhere else."

Andy's desk was nearest the door and he did as his boss told him. Steve gathered up his file and headed for the exit. He didn't intend to say anything further to Bowers, but he did. "I'm sorry." That's all. He put his hand briefly on Andy's shoulder and then carried on walking.

It was about 5.30pm when Neil arrived at Malcom Butler's address. He parked the car a little further down the road from the house and walked back. It was typical middle-class suburbia with pleasant-looking postwar houses, most with tidy front gardens, a short driveway and a garage. There was a shiny Austin Cambridge parked on the drive. That was a good sign. After the frantic day he'd had, it would have been a massive anticlimax if Neil had come all this way to find no one home. He walked purposefully up to the front door, knocked firmly three times and didn't have long to wait before it was opened.

The lady who answered it was probably in her late forties and neatly dressed. She looked at Neil enquiringly. "Can I help you?"

"Yes, I'm sorry to call on you out of the blue," Neil replied, "but I was hoping to speak to Malcolm Butler. It is quite urgent. My name's Webster – *Detective Inspector* Webster – from Buxton."

The woman looked uncertain what to do. "Do you have any identification?"

"Yes... of course," replied Neil, producing his ID from an inside pocket.

The woman looked at it far more closely than he expected then handed it back. "Right... erm... if you'll just wait here a moment."

That at least confirmed Neil was at the right house and that Butler was in. She partially closed the door, leaving him in limbo for what turned out to be a lot more than a moment – certainly long enough for a conversation to have taken place behind the scenes. Eventually the door opened fully to reveal a man of similar age to the woman. He looked equally neat and tidy. Neil assumed that she must have been Celia Knowles.

"Mr Butler?" he enquired.

Neil went through the same introduction process he'd just been through with Celia – the man in front of him was just as wary. "Could you tell me what it's about please?" he asked.

"Yes, of course, but d'you think we might go inside?"

The man had no option but to let Neil step into the hallway. Although he was calm and polite, there was definitely a reticence about his demeanour. "We'll go in here," he said, pointing to the open living room door. Neil followed him in, noting the pleasant decor and furnishings. The woman was nowhere to be seen.

"Sit down inspector," Butler said. "You did say it was inspector, didn't you?"

"Yes." Webster chose a single chair by a little table near the window. Butler sat down in a small armchair.

"So, what can I do for you?" he enquired.

Neil thought the man's reaction to what he was about to say might be telling. "Right, Mr Butler. There's been a development in the case of your missing wife and I hoped you might be able to help us again."

Butler remained calm. He'd already worked out that this officer was a different kettle of fish from the one who'd interviewed him five years previously. "Well of course I'll try to help," he replied. "I did my best last time but, if you don't mind my saying so, your predecessor wasn't a very good listener." Butler seemed to take some small pleasure from getting that off his chest. "Anyway, what else would you like to know?"

Webster delved into his coat pocket and pulled out the little plastic bag, extracting the bracelet. "Can you tell me if you recognise this please?" He handed it to Butler, who gave it a cursory once-over. "If you tilt it," Neil added, "you can see something written inside."

"I'm sorry," Butler replied. "I'll have to get my glasses."

"That's all right. Take your time." Webster was having trouble weighing this man up. His behaviour certainly didn't appear to be that of someone with something to hide.

Butler returned with his glasses on, examined the inside of the bracelet and held it aloft. "So this is your development is it?" This time there was a hint of frustration in his voice.

"Do you recognise it?" pressed Neil.

Butler exhaled slowly. "No I don't. But that doesn't mean it *wasn't* hers. She had all sorts of trinkets and bangles and things that she picked up on her various travels." He looked at Webster again. "D'you think it's linked to Barbara's disappearance?"

Now who was being questioned! "Well that's what we're trying to find out. A hiker picked it up near Kinder Scout and handed it in. We knew your wife enjoyed walking up there and it got us thinking, so we decided to investigate further."

But the momentum was now with Butler. "Did you find anything else?"

Webster sensed that this was the question of a man who thought he already knew the answer. "Yes, as a matter of fact we did... a dead body!" He waited for the reaction.

Butler looked back at him coldly. "It's her, isn't it?"

"We don't know. There was absolutely *nothing* to identify her and that's the other reason I'm here."

"It *is* a woman then?"

"Yes. The investigation has already established that." Neil looked grim faced. "I'm afraid we're going to need your wife's medical history to help determine whether it's her. Dental records would be the most helpful."

"That bad is it?" asked Butler.

Neil's expression said as much. Malcolm lowered his head. "Yes... yes... of course. I'll speak to her dentist and medical practice tomorrow and tell them to expect a call from you."

Webster passed him his notebook, opened at a blank page, and a pen. "If you wouldn't mind jotting their names down we'll get in touch with them."

Butler took the book and did as he had been asked. But Neil hadn't quite finished. "Just a couple of other things before I go."

"Yes... of course," replied Malcolm without a hint of guile. "Our records show that it was you who reported your wife missing.

"Yes, it was, at least as far as I know."

"But according to those same records, that was a full five days after she supposedly went to visit her sister in Sheffield. Why so long?'

This was the first time Butler had shown any sign of losing his cool. "I went all through this with Sergeant Whatsisname. As I said to him at the time, I just thought she was still with Alison. They were thick as thieves those two, even more so after Barbara and I got married. I can't say I cared for it much. If anyone had to disappear, I wish it had been my sister-in-law."

He rethought his words for a moment. "But I wouldn't have wished her dead!" He gave a rueful half-smile. "But I bet *she* wished *I* was."

His outburst came out of the blue. A more complicated picture was starting to emerge but Neil decided enough was enough – for the moment. "Okay, Mr Butler. I think we'll leave it at that. I appreciate your help."

Neil reached into his coat pocket. "I'll give you my card so you can contact me at Buxton police station. I can't stress enough the importance of those dental records. The sooner we have them the sooner we'll know where we all stand. It'll also prevent any unhelpful speculation in the press."

He got up and began heading for the hallway, but suddenly stopped and turned around. "Oh... one other thing. The lady who answered the door to me. Who was she if you don't mind my asking?"

Butler gave him a knowing look. "Come on inspector – you know exactly who she is."

Webster returned a wry smile. "Celia Knowles I take it? From your old walking group."

Butler's expression darkened. "Huh... I'll bet Barbara's sister has had plenty to say about Celia. It won't come as any surprise to you then inspector to learn that Barbara and I were not getting on well at the time of her disappearance – but Celia had absolutely nothing to do with that."

He showed the first sign of real emotion. "But she did prove to be a genuinely good friend when I needed one."

Neil didn't comment further but gave Butler a final instruction as he made his way to the door. "I'm sure you realise this is now a very serious investigation, Mr Butler, so if journalists do come knocking on your door, please don't say *anything*. Just send them on their way." And with that, he went on his own way.

The moment the door clicked shut, Celia Knowles emerged from the kitchen. She must have been listening intently just waiting for that moment. Malcolm was in the hall and she made straight for him, clearly stressed. She put her arms round him and squeezed him tightly. He reciprocated. Eventually she looked up at him tearfully. "What are we going to do?"

He squeezed her again. "Absolutely nothing. There's no reason to worry."

On his way back to Buxton, Webster's mind was like a swirling mass of eels. This whole thing made no sense at all and he was beginning to wonder whether, among those eels, there was a herring – a big red one in the form of the bracelet.

Neil was no stranger to suspects trying to pull the wool over his eyes... but *these two*! If they *were* involved, they were keeping incredibly cool, at least on the surface. He tried to put himself in their shoes. How far would they go to be together if that was their intention? Would they actually commit murder by luring Barbara under the pretext of a good walk on the moors, up to the desolate location where the body was found, and there do away with her? *Really*!! He also recalled a case where a wife had disappeared but then resurfaced several years later only to find her husband had remarried.

In the end he put those thoughts to one side because it was all academic until it could be proved that the body was actually that of Barbara Butler. One thing he was pretty sure about now was that Malcolm wasn't the womaniser Alison Edwards had made him out to be. In Neil's mind, the sister was becoming just as much a person of interest as the husband.

When he finally got back home, he headed for the kitchen, where he apologised to Anne for being so late. He flopped down on one of the chairs and threw his head back. "What a day. *What ...a ...day!*"

"So much for the quiet life," Anne replied, giving him a sideways look.

Neil hadn't got much of a response left in him. "Yeah... sorry..." and for a split second he had the same thought that had gone through Steve Milner's mind that day up on Kinder, albeit for different reasons – the one that wished the bracelet had never been found in the first place.

The following day Steve Milner put the instructions issued to him by Webster into action – getting officers to show the pictures of the bracelet to anyone else they had on record as knowing Barbara Butler. He'd painstakingly gone through all the original statements about the case and recalled interviewing her sister Alison Edwards himself the first time round – *vividly*. She really did have something against Malcolm, encouraging anyone who cared to listen, to believe that he was a philanderer.

When Barbara first disappeared, Alison was more than happy to point the finger in Malcolm's direction. But she had no concrete evidence, just a lot of circumstantial bluster stemming from the walking group that Barbara and her husband were part of.

"Malcolm paid far too much attention to that Knowles woman," she'd spewed to DS Milner when he first interviewed her. "The woman was on her own and, from what I heard, she did nothing to discourage him. I never did know what happened to *her* husband."

Most of what Alison had heard was second hand from two other ladies in the group who she knew well. She wasn't a walker herself.

"Tramping mile after mile uphill and down-dale, even when it's rotten weather, isn't my idea of an enjoyable pastime," she'd told Milner. "Fancied himself as a bit of a charmer did Malcolm and he'd managed to ingratiate his way into a sort of leadership position."

Eventually she'd gone on to describe a deterioration she'd witnessed in her sister's mental state. "I was really worried about Barbara," she'd said. "She started to come to see me more and more. I asked her point blank if she thought Malcolm was carrying on. I think she wanted to tell me he was, but was too loyal and perhaps a bit embarrassed to admit her marriage was in trouble."

So, five years on, it was DS Milner's job to visit her again at the same house in Totley, and even though it had been a long time since their last encounter, he found that her animosity towards Malcolm Butler had not diminished one little bit.

Once he had gone inside and was seated, she wasted no time in resuming where she'd left off. "You know he's slunk off down to Derby don't you? And guess who's with him?'

It was as if she'd never drawn breath – but Steve was better prepared this time. "Yes, we are aware that he's moved, Mrs Edwards, but that's not the main reason I've come to see you. I want you to take a look at this."

He opened the envelope he was holding, took out the photographs and placed them on the table in front of her. "Can you tell me – do you recognise this… and take a close look at the writing on the inside."

If nothing else it halted Alison's diatribe. She looked closely at the lettering; the moment she made out the name "Barbara" she was off again. "Where did you get this?"

"I'll explain in a minute but I need to know – *do you recognise it*?" From her furrowed expression, he couldn't tell whether she was trying to remember if she'd actually seen it on her sister or thinking this might be a way to incriminate Malcolm further. "You need to think very carefully about this, Mrs Edwards," Milner stressed. "If you don't know, just say so."

She looked up from the photographs. "Why is it so important?"

She was fishing; and Milner was beginning to lose patience.

"Please, Mrs Edwards, will you just answer the question."

She took another long look at the bracelet before giving it back to him and sitting up straight in her chair with her arms folded. "Yes, I'm sure I saw her wearing it... more than once in fact."

Her wheedling for information apparently over, Milner realised there was no point in beating about the bush any longer. "Okay. Thank you, Mrs Edwards. I can now disclose to you that a body has been discovered..."

While the rest of CID were out and about interviewing any other people they thought might recognise the bracelet, back at the station Neil was looking at a message that had been left the previous afternoon to "ring someone called Frank". Assuming it was of the "Radcliffe" variety, he couldn't help being suspicious. What did *he* want?

Neil returned the call and, as a result, found himself that Wednesday afternoon in the company of his son's potential father-in-law for the second time in five days. Nothing much had been said on the phone but Radcliffe instigating a meeting at short notice suggested matters had arisen since the party at the weekend. The location he'd put forward for the rendezvous was also a bit of a surprise.

At 2pm, Neil pulled alongside the turquoise Ford Cortina he'd been told to look out for in the pub car park in the village of Hayfield, about ten miles south east of Stockport. He and Frank wound their respective windows down almost in unison. Neil was on his guard when he opened the conversation. "What's all this about then Frank?" He perused the Cortina warily. "And what's with the car? Not your usual style."

"I'll explain in a minute," replied Frank. "Come on, we can talk as we walk." With that he wound the window back up and got out of his car. Neil had little option but to do likewise.

Radcliffe pointed ahead of them. "There's a bit of a park just up here – nice and private. We can have a proper chat there."

He set off at quite a pace, leaving a grumbling Neil Webster to trudge along behind. As they approached a park bench Frank paused to check that there was no one else around, but Neil was fed up with the cloak and dagger stuff. "All right, Frank. What's going on?"

Radcliffe at last appeared ready to talk. "Righty ho, Neil," he replied. "I think this'll do." He pointed to the bench. "Let's have a seat."

When they were both sitting comfortably, Frank began. "Well you'll gather I don't want anyone seeing we're having this meeting."

Neil laughed sardonically. "Well I'd never have guessed. What a pantomime!"

"Yeah, I'm sorry if it seems a bit over the top, but what I'm about to tell you needs to be strictly between us, as you'll soon see."

Neil's interest was now pricked and he started to mellow a little. "Go on."

Frank hesitated for a moment, as though he was unsure how to broach matters. Eventually he began. "Well... it looks like my *daughter* and your *son* are perhaps wanting to move things along more quickly than either of us thought – or so my wife informed me after the do last Saturday."

"Oh!" responded Neil. He hadn't anticipated this at all.

Radcliffe took note. "Quite!" he replied. "So I think you and I need to consider the ramifications of all this."

Neil looked baffled. Radcliffe took further note. "Well let me spell it out." He paused again briefly while looking Webster firmly in the eye. "Quite simply, Neil, I need to be sure that you won't say anything about my past that might upset the marital applecart – and I'm not just talking about the kids, I'm talking about me and *my* missus as well."

This felt completely surreal to Neil. Never in his wildest dreams did he expect to be having a conversation like this with the likes of Frank Radcliffe!

"My wife really likes Paul," continued Frank, "so I think he and Charlotte getting together would make her very happy and, as they say, a happy wife is a happy life." For a moment he looked emotional. "Diane and Charlotte mean the world to me, and I don't want anything upsetting them. I know a cynical copper like you might find that hard to believe but I genuinely have put my former life behind me – *well* behind me." He continued, as if by way of a throwaway. "Huh... the truth is, I tried really hard not to like Paul when I first realised he was yours... but I couldn't manage it."

"Oh, nice of you to say so," Neil replied to the backhanded compliment.

But Radcliffe had a postscript. "It's his dad *I'm* worried about!"

The comment shouldn't have taken Neil aback but it did, leading him to mull the whole situation over for a moment. Now it was *his* turn to do the eyeballing. "Do you seriously think I'm going to mess things up for everyone just for a bit of job satisfaction over something that far in the past?"

Frank became animated. "That's my whole point, Neil. It's in the past! Those days are gone – and it's Diane I've got to thank for sorting me out."

"And I think that's great," concurred Neil, "but come on, she must have had her suspicions when she married you?"

Radcliffe looked guilty. "Well yeah, she did, to some degree – but she didn't ask too many questions. Let's face it, with the lifestyle I was giving her, why would she?"

Suddenly his expression changed dramatically. "That was

until the evening when the casino and the house were raided by your lot and they carted me off."

Even though Neil wasn't personally involved with the raid he remembered the frustration among his colleagues when they couldn't find enough evidence to make a charge stick. "And a fat lot of good *that* did us," he remarked.

Frank couldn't resist a taunt. "Well, come on! You must have been a bit naive to think I'd leave anything incriminating where your crew might find it. But that was the *only* good bit. The whole thing so upset Diane she threatened to leave... with Charlotte, unless I changed my ways."

He gave a philosophical shrug. "The fact was, with my other businesses – the car dealership and the apartments – I didn't need to be involved in anything shady anyway."

He leant back, hands clasped behind his head. "So here I am now, a *pillar* of the community. I even support a couple of local charities."

"And I don't suppose they're going to look a gift horse in the mouth *are* they?" Neil replied.

Frank nodded. "Okay – fair comment."

Neil was feeling pretty philosophical himself now. "Naaaa, I'm a bit long in the tooth to look for unnecessary trouble, Frank. I'll behave myself if you do."

They exchanged genuine smiles and sat in silence, taking in the pleasant surroundings. Neil piped up first. "I hope they go through with it after all this. I don't think I can stand the stress!"

He failed to hide a self-satisfied grin. "Okay... what is it?" Frank asked.

"It's just that Anne would be furious if she found out I knew about what I presume is a pending engagement before *she* did."

Now that did make them laugh.

"Married life eh Neil?"

"Married life Frank."

They both lolled back on the bench, Neil thinking they'd about done but still unsure why so much subterfuge had been necessary for what appeared to be a personal rather than a police matter. He was about to find out.

"Before we go," Frank said, "there *is* something else."

Neil was jolted from his relaxed state. "And what's that?"

"Ermmm… well let's call it a goodwill gesture."

Neil became wary again. It was a reflex action when it came to Radcliffe.

Frank continued. "You know I told you that I'm totally legit these days?"

"Yes, so you keep saying."

"Well it doesn't mean I don't keep my ear to the ground, and a little bird has told me that you've got a bit of a problem up at Buxton."

"And you know this how?" enquired Neil, not happy that Frank appeared to be sticking his nose in where it wasn't wanted.

Radcliffe raised a friendly hand. "Just hear me out."

Neil reluctantly obliged.

"Does the name Billy Lennox ring any bells?" It did – a real clanger of a bell as far as Webster was concerned. Lennox was the guy who was blackmailing Steve Milner over his casino debt and almost certainly involved with the farm thefts.

Frank could tell he'd touched a nerve. "Small world eh Neil," he remarked. "And so is the casino business. Small enough for me to know that Billy Lennox is giving our game a bad name. He got slung out of Glasgow a few years back – extortion, GBH etc – and now he's big enough in Manchester to start making waves we don't want. Bet he couldn't believe his luck when he found he'd got a copper by the short and curlies. Get him to look the other way while he made hay, if you'll pardon the pun."

Neil's heart was sinking. He gave Radcliffe a look of disgust. "And there was me nearly believing you really had changed.

Well, if you're thinking of pulling my strings for your own ends, you've got the wrong man." Neil rose from the bench.

"Oi!" protested Frank. "Just hold on. It's nothing like that – well not much anyway."

"Well what is it like then, Frank?" Webster was seething.

"Look Neil," pressed Radcliffe. "This could be a win-win. All *we* want is to see the back of Lennox – that's it. But if you do it right, you could put this guy away for a long time and get your man off the hook as well."

Silence followed while Neil weighed up Frank's last comment. He looked skywards while he agonised about what to do. Eventually, he sighed deeply. "Okay... but this better be good!"

"Oh it is... *really* good." Frank couldn't have sounded more conspiratorial if he'd tried. "We'll set him up, just like he'll have set up your detective sergeant. Come on Neil, you know how they work it – find the weakness, let them have some beginners luck and eventually let them dig their own hole. Then comes interest on the debt, threats or payment in kind. It's nothing you haven't seen before."

Neil had seen it before all right!

Radcliffe continued: "I'm sure your old chums in central Manchester would be happy to lend you a hand. My little bird, who happens to be a thoroughly disgruntled ex-employee of Billy's, says they might want to check the books. They keep 'em in the back office."

"Really?" replied Neil sceptically.

Frank watched this sink in. "I told you Lennox wasn't very bright." The description of this "master plan" ended with a grin on Radcliffe's face. "You could put in a good word for me with your old mates at the same time."

That irritated Neil no end. "So you'd just sit back and watch it all happen eh Frank?"

"Well yes, I suppose I would. But then again it's the result that matters, and don't give me that 'Mr Clean' number. I know how dirty you could play when you wanted to."

Neil hated being ambushed like this but the more he thought about the proposition, the more he realised it had its merits. In fact, if it could be made to work, it might solve an awful lot of problems. Until then he'd been limited to his own plan 'A' to get Steve Milner out of the mire but this sounded a good plan 'B' or perhaps even a *better* plan than his, although he certainly wasn't going to admit it. But the appeal of a two-pronged set-up was very tempting. "All right, Frank. Just say I went along with this, how would you play it?"

CHAPTER EIGHTEEN

From Steve Milner's "confession" to him that day on Kinder, Neil knew that Lennox was heavily involved in the farm theft cases, partly as the main investor and partly by his efforts to keep the police at bay through the hold he had over his detective sergeant. The distribution and "retail" side of the operation had pretty much been snuffed out thanks to the interception of several of the delivery vehicles and their drivers and also the abandonment of the depot in the backwoods on the other side of Rudyard Lake. The thefts had dried up accordingly and to all intents the model had been broken. But that hadn't unearthed who had been co-ordinating and carrying out the thefts themselves – that was until the following morning when Trudie greeted Neil with some interesting news from Matlock.

"Nice to see you back in the station again sir," she said as she entered his office, notebook in hand. "We almost forgot what you looked like."

"Well you know what they say, Trudie. Crime won't crack itself!"

"Absolutely sir," she responded, tongue in cheek.

"So... what have you got for me?" he asked.

She looked at her notebook. "Just the one thing really. Detective Sergeant Redfern at Matlock station wants you to give him a call. It's regarding Eddie Slater."

"Oh right. Hmmm... I wonder what Eddie's had to say for

himself? Okay, thanks Trudie. I'll give them a call now."

Mick Redfern had been at Matlock station for several years and had crossed paths with Eddie Slater a number of times. He saw him for exactly what he was: an obnoxious petty criminal with no concern for anyone but himself. This low-life had somehow always managed to slither out of doing a spell inside but, after the search of his property, the seizure of the damaged Bedford van and DC Bowers' photographic evidence of the trailer being loaded at his property that day, Slater knew he was on a sticky wicket this time.

On the other side of the fence, Redfern also saw in Slater all the qualities of an archetypal "grass", the sort who would dob in his own grandmother if he thought it might save his skin. So the experienced DS had gone to work on him – after all, why not use a sprat to catch a mackerel. Slater clearly knew who was further up the farm thefts chain and the incentive for him to name names was that he'd probably be treated more leniently, perhaps avoiding a prison sentence altogether, if he "co-operated". That was the bait Redfern was dangling. The question was, would Slater take it?

The phone call to Matlock brought Neil up to speed on that score and, after he'd put the receiver down, he thought how ironic it would be if the thief that had set the investigation off in the first place that night at John Mellor's farm ended up being instrumental in bringing the whole gang to justice.

By early afternoon, Webster began receiving feedback from the interviews being conducted by his fellow CID officers armed with their photos of Barbara Butler's bracelet. Milner's encounter with Alison Edwards was undoubtedly the most revealing and, coupled with his own report from his trip to see Malcolm Butler in Derby, he was more than aware it was possible that this ramblers' soap opera might have nothing to do with the remains found on the windswept slopes of the High

Peak. The whole thing might just be one huge co-incidence.

The responses from the people shown the photos of the bracelet were inconclusive. *Maybe... maybe not...* was the consistent theme coming through but, just to add to the uncertainty, there was an unwelcome development that afternoon concerning the dental records. Barbara's practice couldn't find them. It was extremely embarrassing for the partners and they found themselves under huge pressure from the police. It certainly wasn't the sort of publicity they needed and the staff were having the drains up trying to discover where they'd disappeared to. The worry was that having not seen the patient for so long, the practice had inadvertently disposed of them. Webster went berserk when he heard the news but there was nothing he could do about it. He just had to put this setback to one side while the search for the records continued and get on with other things.

While it had been all hands on deck at the station recently, behind the scenes Neil had been doing his best to manoeuvre things with Steve Milner so that he was in the best place possible to weather the storm that was undoubtedly brewing for him as the farm case investigation reached its climax. The news from Matlock was another indicator that the moment of truth was near and, as soon as his detective sergeant returned from interviewing Alison Edwards, Neil asked Milner to join him in his office. "I take it that you've heard about the dental records debacle?" Webster asked.

Milner shook his head in frustration. "It's like walking in treacle, isn't it sir?"

"Yeah, it sure is. Anyway, that's not the main reason I wanted to see you."

Neil sat back in his chair and set off on another tack. "Were you aware that you were set up when you first started going to Lennox's casino in Manchester?"

Milner looked thoroughly embarrassed. He knew how naive he'd been. Neil continued. "Well if it's any consolation, you're just one of many Steve." He paused momentarily. "You've heard the saying 'knowledge is power'?"

"Yes?" replied Milner tentatively, not sure where the DI was going with this.

"In that case you'll be pleased to know that we now have some knowledge about your tormentor that proves he's not quite as smart as he thinks he is."

The atmosphere between the policemen was subtly changing. Webster leant forward to further his point. "I've been to a lot of trouble to get the lowdown on Billy Lennox, and it could be payback time for you."

Milner was agog and for the next half an hour their intense conversation would take Steve way out of his comfort zone.

Neil felt it was time to sum up. "Look, Steve. I know this is unchartered territory for you... *but it isn't for me.* You'll be fine if you just hold your nerve and stick to the plan." The intensity behind the words was clearly registering with his detective sergeant. "Now go and make that phone call, and remember – everything needs to happen next Friday night!"

During the past few weeks, uniform had been merely hanging on to the coat-tails of the action – well someone had to deal with stolen bicycles, lost dogs and shoplifters! Trudie, as the senior officer, was in the know about most things but DI Webster was conscious that some of those below her might be feeling sidelined. Under Sergeant Barker's eagle eye, they had become a thoroughly reliable team – one that Neil was confident to leave to their own devices while his hands were full with other matters. However, he'd got something far from mundane up his sleeve for them now and he'd arranged with Trudie for her to assemble as many of them as possible in the canteen before the afternoon shift ended. A sign of how relations between uniform and CID had improved was that Detective Constable Nick Fielding had agreed to mind the shop at the front desk while the meeting took place upstairs. Webster didn't intend it to take long.

Even though the farm theft investigation had involved uniform to some degree, the "Body on Kinder" case was far more intriguing. It was beginning to feel like a *whodunit* and they were busily airing opinions when Neil arrived and pulled up a chair to join them. "Right," he began. "First of all, thank you for beavering away while we glory hunters in CID have been... well... glory hunting. The fact is we've reached an impasse – temporary I hope – while we await confirmation that the body we found is that of Barbara Butler."

"How long d'you think it will take, sir?" Constable Briggs asked.

"The simple answer is, I don't know. We're entirely in the hands of the forensic boys and we're still awaiting dental records. In the meantime, we've been interviewing a lot of people in connection with the bracelet, but until we have the pathologist's report we don't know if we're dealing with foul play or not. But I *will* keep you posted."

Neil realised his announcement wasn't terribly informative but it seemed enough to keep them happy so he moved on to the main topic he wanted to discuss.

"So because we're a bit in limbo with that at the moment, we're concentrating our efforts on the person who we now know is behind the farm thefts – a nasty piece of work called Billy Lennox, ex Glasgow – who's causing a lot of misery for a lot of people. Agriculture is a departure for him because his main business is bookmaking and he has a casino in Manchester called the Elite Club. But, believe me, *elite* it ain't. Anything but!"

"So where's the connection, sir?" asked Constable Lowe.

"We think he was offered part of the farm theft action as a

lucrative sideline by one of Manchester's local undesirables and he put the money up."

Neil paused and smiled as he looked at the faces in front of him. "'So what's this all got to do with us?' I hear you say." He looked in Trudie's direction. "It's over to you Sergeant Barker."

"Thanks sir." Her expression suggested she had something novel to say, and she certainly had.

"Okay then… who'd like a night out in the big city next Friday?" They weren't expecting *that*! "On the house," she quickly added.

They looked at one another bemused. Bob went first. "All right, sarge. What's the catch?"

"The catch, Bob, is that *we*, together with central Manchester police, are going to set Billy Lennox up, and some stooges are required for the operation."

There was a moment's silence before an outbreak of laughter.

"Well Bob'll be okay," remarked PC Richard Lowe. "He's been playing at being a copper ever since I've *been* here."

"Oi!" retorted Bob. "You cheeky…"

Trudie raised her hand. "Yes, all right you two." They calmed down. "Actually it's deadly serious. We'll be part of a set up at the casino, and we want two of you to play a seemingly innocent couple who get lured into betting too much. DI Webster knows more about how they trick you into it so I'll let him explain."

"Thanks Trudie." Neil turned to the others. "In a nutshell… they cheat! First they let you win a bit and they'll probably have their own stooge posing as a punter egging you on. They'll then ply you with more drinks so you get overconfident and take bigger risks… and that's when the wheel or the cards, whatever it is you're playing, turn against you."

"That's evil that is," said Bob.

"Yes it is," replied Webster. "But that's the sort of low-life we're dealing with, and this is our big chance to put him away. So who's up for it?"

The response was resounding. He didn't expect anything less. "Manchester will be providing plenty of bodies in case things get a bit feisty. They've had their eye on this guy just waiting for the right moment, so the timing is perfect. They'll take the lead on the night and prep us beforehand."

While Neil had been explaining the scenario, Constable Briggs's brain had gone into overdrive and, once he'd finished, out came the result. "So who's going to be the couple then sir?"

Trudie answered the question instead. "I've been giving that some thought." She could not have looked more serious. "The woman needs to be a real live wire and be able to egg her boyfriend on. I do a bit of amateur dramatics so I think I could manage it. With a bit of judicious make-up I could probably pass for being mid-twenties."

Jane's face was a study. The others didn't know if she was being serious or not and Trudie was really convincing but, in the end, Sergeant Barker couldn't keep a straight face any longer and burst out laughing. "Oh I *so* got you, didn't I?" she crowed. With that they all collapsed into laughter.

"Hey, don't laugh too much," she eventually added. "I'm not *that* old!" She turned to Jane. "All right, PC Briggs. You've got the job. Richard... you're going to be the boyfriend."

DI Webster couldn't resist commenting. "You may laugh, but Sergeant Barker's shown you two how it should be done, so you better get your act together." He turned to Trudie. "I might have to find some other undercover work for you sergeant. I'm impressed!"

Neil was enjoying spending a bit of time in the company of uniform. They didn't take themselves as seriously as CID. Perhaps it was because they were more involved with the day to day trials and tribulations of the general public. However, that didn't mean they weren't at the sharp end of things from time to time as evidenced by Bob's masterclass in how to deal with a wife-beating thug like Eric Smith.

As the minutes ticked by in the canteen, Sergeant Barker began to wonder how Nick Fielding was doing at the front desk. She needn't have worried. When she returned to relieve him, there was no evidence of a crimewave sweeping the town in her absence. As for Constable Briggs, a surprise awaited that day in the form of someone she *certainly* didn't expect to see. He'd called purely on the off-chance that she might be at the station rather than out on the beat.

Jane was in the locker room getting ready to knock off. She had already changed out of her uniform when Trudie popped her head round the door to say she'd got a visitor. "Come and see for yourself," said Sergeant Barker when Jane asked who it was.

Disgruntled about being delayed when she should be heading home, Constable Briggs emerged a minute or so later to find a young man waiting by the front desk. She did a double take. "Hello Terry," she remarked when she realised who it was. "What brings you here?"

He looked a little uncertain so she tried again. "Well?"

This time he managed to produce a reply. "It's just that..."

Jane twigged. "Oh, the uniform! Ha! I don't wear it 24 hours a day you know, despite what you might think."

This was such a far cry from the first conversation she'd had with young McDonald that afternoon in the alleyway by his house. He was cocky then, aggressive and totally disrespectful to someone who wanted to help.

"I just came in to say I'm sorry," he said when he found his voice properly.

"Oh yes?" replied a sceptical Jane. "Did your mum put you up to this?"

Terry looked vaguely hurt. "No she didn't. Like I said... I *am* sorry. I know you've helped us out. And that thing with Lewis Bates."

Jane sniggered. "What – you think I beat him up?"

"No, course not. But I just wondered who *did* do it."

He wasn't the only one. Jane had thought more than once that DI Webster knew more than he was letting on. But as he'd said at the time, "let sleeping dogs lie" – so that's what she did.

"I take it Lewis hasn't been causing any more trouble?"

"No. We hardly see him about these days."

"Well there you go. Anyway, make sure you look after your mum and keep out of trouble. Okay?"

Terry gave her a cheeky grin. "Hey, d'you think they'd let *me* join the police?"

"I don't think we're quite that desperate Terry," she responded with a laugh. She didn't pull her punches. "Now go on with you!" She pointed to the door.

But Terry hesitated. "No... I'm serious. What do I have to do?"

Jane sighed and looked at the front office clock. "Look, I'm going to miss my bus if I'm not careful. Come on." She pointed to the door again. "You can ask me any questions as we're walking. I'll get my coat."

Richard, Trudie and Bob had been observing from behind the front desk, from where they could just about make out the gist of the conversation.

"So what's he got that I haven't?" remarked Richard. "And he only looks about 17."

"What, so you never had a crush at that age then Richard?" Trudie asked.

"Trust me lad," remarked Bob darkly. "You're well out of that. She'd run rings round you, and most other blokes for that matter."

Richard considered the comment for a moment. "I wouldn't mind finding out, though."

CHAPTER NINETEEN

In contrast with Barbara Butler's dentist, the doctor's practice was on the ball and happy to liaise directly with Andrew Pritchard. More than anything, the pathologist wanted to check whether Barbara had suffered any physical damage that would have left tell-tale marks on her skeletal remains. This would at least give him something tangible with which to compare his own findings. He'd already roughly worked out the age, height and stature of the Jane Doe, but nothing you could hang a concrete ID on. In any case, he wasn't in the habit of issuing interim bulletins that might lead an investigation like this up a blind alley. He wanted to produce a comprehensive report of his full findings but only when he was good and ready. So as far as the Barbara Butler case was concerned, CID were treading water.

However, the hiatus gave DI Webster an opportunity to organise a catch up with Phil Morris from Macclesfield and Alan Wright from Leek to take stock of where they were with the farm thefts investigation. All three were agreed that the co-operation between forces had played a big part in shutting the operation down, but they were also in agreement that there was still unfinished business – bringing the ringleaders to justice. It was with this in mind that Neil had made an appointment to visit Jim and Sandra Hargreaves again at the Old Grouse Inn.

It was late afternoon when he got there, a good hour before opening time, and as he knocked on the door he found himself looking forward to a time when he could visit the pub purely to enjoy a pint and a bite to eat with police work firmly off the menu.

His relationship with Jim and Sandra had improved no end since the frosty reception he'd received during their first meeting but it was going to be severely tested during the next half hour or so. Before he could say anything contentious, they sat him down and put the kettle on. They knew there was no point in offering him anything alcoholic when he was on duty but it didn't stop them enjoying some light-hearted banter before Neil got down to the nitty gritty of why he'd come to see them. He knew the next few minutes weren't going to be easy.

"You what!" Sandra shouted in disbelief when Neil put his request to the pair of them. "After the way he treated us!"

Webster had to be at his diplomatic best to pick his way through this one. "Look... you have every reason to say *no* to what I'm asking, but there is a reason Detective Sergeant Milner behaved in the way he did."

Neil hesitated, putting the Hargreaves truly on tenterhooks. He continued warily. "You remember the Scottish guy he came in here with?"

"You mean the one that John Mellor and Bill Ollerenshaw threw out?" asked Jim.

"Yes... him. Well he's a seriously nasty piece of work and those threats that you heard him make to Steve Milner that day also included his wife and family. He's being blackmailed!" Sandra and Jim looked stunned. "The guy's name is Billy Lennox and we can put him away for a long time if we can gather enough evidence against him."

He eyed Sandra and Jim intently. "We're really close but it's very complicated and we need every bit of help we can get.

The Hargreaves looked at each other. They were doing their thing – silent communication. Neil waited for what seemed like an eternity. After a final extra-long stare at each other, the response came... from Jim. "All right. What do you want us to do?"

When Neil arrived home that evening, Anne gave him her customary warm welcome. She seemed in a *particularly* good mood.

"You're very cheerful," Neil remarked as he hung his coat up.

Her reply was unequivocal. "That's because I am."

"And why's that?"

"Well guess who's coming for lunch this Sunday?"

Neil's brow furrowed. "It's not your mother is it?" he answered.

"No, it's *not* my mother!" his wife retorted.

Neil had always got on perfectly well with his mother-in-law. That's why he knew he could joke about the subject. "All right. Who *is* coming for lunch on Sunday?"

She wasted no time in revealing the answer. "Paul and Charlotte... *again*!"

Anne was clearly tickled about the prospect and remained in a buoyant mood all evening. Even Neil's announcement that he would have to work really late on the coming Friday night was met with: "That's a pity." His wife's mind was firmly on Sunday.

Anne was still in a good mood the following morning, and it also started on a positive note for Neil. Not long after entering his office at the police station, he received the phone call he'd been waiting for. It was from the pathologist Andrew Pritchard.

"I have some news for you detective inspector," he announced in his customary formal manner. "The body should be with me here in Chesterfield later today." That was *so* Pritchard, Neil thought: deadpan, no frills and straight to the point.

"Thanks, Andrew. I appreciate your letting me know."

"We've done as much as we can up on the moor but the

removal and transportation of the remains will be a delicate job as I'm sure you'll be aware."

"Understood," replied Neil equally succinctly.

But the pathologist hadn't quite finished. "You'll also be pleased to know that I now have the dental records. I won't bore you with where they were eventually found but I received them late yesterday."

"Hallelulia!" exclaimed Neil. "Those *and* the body. It's like they say about the buses isn't it? You seem to be waiting for ever and then two come along at the same time."

There was silence at the other end then a simple "quite" from Pritchard. "Anyway, I've had a look at them," he continued. "They're actually rather good. There are some x-rays, which is always helpful, and if you were thinking of asking, I expect the full post-mortem findings to be ready towards the end of next week."

"Excellent Andrew," replied Neil, thinking that was that, but, slightly out of character, Pritchard decided to divulge some information he thought DI Webster really should know. It was nothing they'd discovered on the body but it was something that might help to establish the probable cause of death.

Meanwhile Trudie was busy on the phone in *her* office making calls to a number of police houses between Buxton and Glossop. They were all to constables who'd attended the briefing and lunch at the station in April, all of whom had kept in much closer contact with Trudie since. She needed some manpower for Friday night's operation and, once she'd explained the mission, there were no dissenters. It was another testimony to their feeling part of a team once again.

She eventually emerged from her office and returned to the front desk, where Constable Lowe was gazing into space. "Wakey wakey Richard!"

"Oh... sorry sarge."

"I wonder where *your* mind was?" she enquired. He couldn't disguise a grin. "Well next time you think about having a moan about me," she continued, "just remember who gave you boyfriend duties with Constable Briggs on Friday."

"Yes sarge."

Trudie switched into serious mode. "Joking apart, you two need to be really convincing."

"Ha! No need to worry about that," he replied. "She's had us doing role play."

"Ooooh! Sounds nice."

"Hmmm. I don't know. She's really bossy."

Trudie burst out laughing. "There you go. A case of be careful what you wish for, eh Richard? Anyway, all you've got to do is play the innocent couple on the night. The Manchester boys will make their move as soon as the moment's right."

"Yes sarge."

Richard began to look nervous but Trudie gave him a reassuring smile. "Don't worry... you'll be fine. I think you ought to be more scared of Jane than them." The expression on Richard's face suggested she might be right.

It was certainly a morning of planning and Neil had organised a pep talk of his own: to officers Milner, Fielding and Bowers in the main CID office. Recently, Milner and Bowers had hardly spent time in each other's company, but circumstances had forced that to change. The phone call Webster told Steve Milner to make earlier in the week had been to Billy Lennox, and under the guise of the former making a blackmail payment to the Scot, a meet had been arranged at The Quarryman's Arms in Glossop.

Neil's experience in dealing with hard cases like Billy made him wary. If things went wrong, it could have disastrous consequences for Milner, Andy Bowers and even himself. If it went right, Lennox would be nailed and with a bit of luck, Steve Milner could be off the hook.

That morning Neil went over the Glossop strategy again with all three CID officers until he was happy that they knew how to play things on the night. Eventually he sent Andy and Nick Fielding on their way but he wanted a few more minutes with Milner. "I've had a bit of good news this morning Steve," he said to his detective sergeant after the others had gone.

"What's that sir?"

"Barbara Butler's dental records have been found and we should have the full results of the post mortem some time next week."

"It's all happening, isn't it?"

"Yes, it is. But another word about this coming Friday."

"What's that sir?"

Webster's face hardened and he jabbed an accusing finger at his detective sergeant. "Don't be doing this just to save your own neck, Steve. This is for your wife and family and if that isn't enough incentive for you to pull this off, then you deserve to go down!" With that he got up and left his office, leaving a shell-shocked Milner realising for the first time why Neil and Trudie were going to so much trouble to dig him out of the hole he'd made for himself.

Back down in Derby, Malcolm Butler and Celia Knowles had been feeling very uncomfortable since DI Webster's visit. They'd taken the view that they should co-operate fully with whatever the police asked them to do so that any suspicion about their involvement with Barbara's disappearance would be minimised.

Having to deal with providing his wife's dental and medical records had been an unpalatable task and, on top of that, Webster was quite right, the press had indeed started pestering them. They'd felt besieged in their own home. So much for journalistic integrity – and the body hadn't even been identified yet.

That evening the pair of them sat together on the settee in their front room, pondering the situation.

"I blame that sister-in-law of yours for all this," said Celia. "How did you ever see anything in her in the first place?"

Malcolm shook his head stoically. "I don't know... I just don't know."

"I can understand why you liked Barbara – but *Alison*! She never forgave you for finishing with her did she? But why of *all* people did you then have to go and fall for her sister?" A look of sadness and frustration crossed her face. "If only I'd met you first, *none* of this would ever have happened."

They sat in silence with their thoughts. The discovery of the body up on Kinder had brought the possibility neither of them wanted to face to the fore – that Barbara had committed suicide because she believed that Malcolm was being unfaithful... and he never was.

Celia's own bitterness was now beginning to overflow. "I bet Alison is *willing* the body to be Barbara's, just so she can point the finger at us." She finally burst into tears.

Malcolm comforted her. "We did nothing wrong, Celia. This was all Alison's doing. I kept telling Barbara there was nothing going on but she'd been... I don't know... brainwashed by her sister. She just wouldn't believe me." He shook his head dolefully. "I can't tell you how miserable we both were." He looked softly at Celia and squeezed her hand. "I'm not sure what I would have done if I'd not had you to talk to."

She looked up at him and gave his hand a squeeze in return, but she was still fretting. "I'm so mixed up Malcolm. I'm beginning to hate myself as well for thinking that if the body *is* Barbara's, there would be nothing to stop us getting married. What does that say about *me*!"

They sat deep in thought. Neither moved when the phone rang, disturbing the silence.

"I don't want to answer that," said Malcolm acidly. "I bet it's those bloody newspapers again and I'm fed up of them!"

"What if it's someone else?" asked Celia.

Malcolm sighed. The phone kept ringing and he finally went into the hall to answer it. He returned a short time later.

Celia looked at him expectantly. "Well?"

"It was the police station at Buxton. They say the body is now in the mortuary at Chesterfield and it won't be long before they have the full post-mortem results."

Celia shuddered. "Oh this is just horrible!"

"I know," he replied despondently, "but I suppose it has to be done." He put a consoling arm around her and she looked up at him sympathetically. He couldn't think of the right words to say so he kept it simple but sincere. "Shall I go and make us a cup of tea?"

The smile he received in return, albeit weak, suggested that he'd got it right.

CHAPTER TWENTY

Jane Briggs certainly turned heads when she and Richard Lowe entered the Elite Club just off Manchester city centre on the Friday night of the casino set up. She looked good in a police uniform but an absolute knockout dressed for an evening on the town. The casino was up a side street, slightly away from the main bustle. A neon sign and some illuminated gambling chips announced its presence. Once inside the foyer they stopped and spent a few moments taking in the surroundings. The layout of the place had been described to them but they wanted to get their bearings. They'd only been standing there a minute or two when a gritty Scottish voice came from behind them.

"Can I help you?"

They turned around to find a woman whose appearance seemed to match the venue: a tight, short cocktail dress, chandelier earrings and sparklers on her fingers, all a bit brassy. In the background stood two well-built men, suited and smiling, probably at Jane, while still managing to look menacing. This suddenly seemed a far cry from role play back in the sanctuary of the police station.

The couple had entered the casino hand in hand but Jane was holding on to her pretend boyfriend just a little bit tighter now and he found himself taking the lead. "I hope so," he replied. "It's my girlfriend's birthday, so we thought we'd have a night out."

He looked at Jane with a smile. "It's just that we've never been to a casino before and it would be something a bit different." He felt Jane's hand relax.

The Scottish woman's hard face relaxed too. "Well happy birthday dear!" she responded, now full of bonhomie. "Now you two follow me and I'll set you up just fine. We'll go to our best croupier, Maxine, and she can show you how it all works. I'm Carol by the way."

Two minutes later they were sitting at one of the roulette tables with its wheel and colourful number markings.

"Maxine," Carol said. "I want you to look after this lovely young couple." She looked at Jane. "What's your name again, hen?" She immediately offered a mild apology. "Sorry. That's the Glasgow in me!"

"It's Jane," Constable Briggs replied.

Carol turned back to Maxine. "It's Jane here's birthday so we'll give her £5 in chips on the house and see if she can make it grow."

Maxine wasn't that much younger than Carol but wore the casino's uniform: a cut-away waistcoat over a white blouse and black skirt, which was also pretty short. She gave the roulette wheel a playful spin. "I'll do my best," she replied.

Jane found her voice at last. "D'you know, I've always fancied a go at roulette." She looked at Richard. "It'll be just like in James Bond." She was getting going now. "You'll have to have a vodka-martini, shaken but not stirred."

She laughed and Carol laughed with her. "Oh, I'm sure that can be arranged."

Jane nudged Richard. "See!"

"I'll leave them in your capable hands then, Maxine," said Carol. She turned to the couple. "Have fun... but not *too* much beginner's luck please. I'll send someone along to get your drinks order." With that, she went on her way.

The casino was getting busier and the atmosphere intensified, with rattles and rings from slot machines located around the room. From one of them, a pair of eyes had been following Carol, who was now chatting to a man near the door. Carol pointed discretely towards Maxine's table. "Those two I've just been with. They're possibilities. Give them their first drink on the house."

The man nodded. "No Billy tonight?" he asked.

Carol's cold, expressionless face gave nothing away. "No… he and Carl have other business to attend to. Now go on."

The man left without further ado.

Back at the table Jane and Richard ordered their drinks, neither of them a vodka-martini. They noticed there was another roulette table on the go. It was busy with players, while there was no one else playing on their table. Still, it gave Maxine an opportunity to explain how the betting worked. Meanwhile, those eyes by the slot machine were now focused on *them.*

Soon after the complimentary drinks arrived, another player joined the group – a worldly looking woman. She made herself comfortable close to Jane and laid her chips on the table. "Not playing?" she asked them, matter of factly.

"We're just about to get started," replied Jane.

"*I* don't play much," continued the woman. "I just come in for a flutter on a Friday and keep it simple. Usually even money bets to start with – black or red. I don't like taking too much risk."

"Should *we* do that?" Jane asked her.

"Well that's up to you. You never know – it might be your lucky night."

Jane turned enthusiastically to Richard. "Did you hear that Rich?"

"All right. Come on then," he replied. "We didn't come here not to have a go."

Jane rubbed her hands together with excitement. "Right then… I'll go forrrr…..black!"

"How much are you betting dear?" Maxine asked.

Jane had the five £1 chips she'd been given. "I'll just start with one." She tentatively placed her chip on a black box.

The lady to her right laughed at Jane's caution. "I did that to start with. Anyway, I'll go for black as well." She placed a £5 chip next to Jane's.

Maxine set the wheel in motion, sending the ball in the opposite direction, while announcing: "No more bets."

Jane and Richard's eyes were glued to the wheel. It seemed to take an eternity for the ball to drop but, when it did, it landed on red. The woman next to the couple aimed a mild rebuke at the wheel.

"I'm glad I only put £1 on," said Jane.

"I'll pick the colour next time," replied Richard.

"I'm sure your luck will change," Maxine commiserated as she readied to spin the wheel again. "Place your bets," she called.

Richard decided to put his chip on black. The lady put hers on red and won. Richard looked decidedly miffed and so did Jane, who looked at the remaining chips. "Oooh dear – only three left," she said. "I'm glad we haven't paid for these." She looked at the lady. "I think I'll follow you this time." She followed the woman's lead – and won. Anyone would think she'd won the pools she was so excited.

"Maybe you should try putting two chips on this time dear," the woman suggested.

"Right then," Jane responded confidently, once more following the woman's lead. Suddenly she found herself £1 to the good. "Look Rich… we're in credit!' she enthused.

Maxine smiled at the couple. "I'm pleased you're enjoying yourselves. That's what we're here for."

While Richard wasn't watching, Jane whispered covertly to

the lady by her side. "Trust me, he can afford to show me a good time." The lady winked at Jane, who smiled back.

And so it went on – a loss here, a gain there – but as the minutes passed the latter began to slowly outweigh the former. Jane and Richard gave the impression they were getting genuinely excited by their winning streak. But they knew their script and, after about three quarters of an hour's play, Jane took another sip from her glass of white wine and excused herself to go to the loo. Richard said he thought it was a good opportunity to have a break and do the same. As Richard stood at the urinal he was joined by a smartly dressed customer, who positioned himself next to him. They were the only two people in there.

"How's it going?" asked Bob

"Okay," replied Richard. "The pattern's about right."

"What about Jane?"

Richard smiled. "Oh she's *really* enjoying it."

"Well as we speak," continued Bob, "Trudie will be impressing on her in the ladies to keep focused. The Manchester guys are just waiting their moment, so we don't want to blow it. You two better be ready for when it all kicks off. I don't actually want a pee so let's go."

Meanwhile, 15 or so miles away at The Quarryman's Arms in Glossop, the pub where Andy Bowers had photographed Lennox and Milner together on his stake-out, Carol's husband Billy was, as she put it, "attending to business". It was a drinker's pub: drab and dingy, no frills, and no food apart from crisps or pork scratchings on a good night. Unlike his relationship with Jim and Sandra Hargreaves at the Old Grouse Inn, Billy was on very friendly terms with the landlord. The latter was more than happy to put a private back room at Lennox's disposal if he made it worth his while. Needless to say, the clientele was mostly men and at ten o'clock on a Friday night there were plenty in there.

But tonight it included a group of five none-regulars occupying a table in a far corner of the bar. In contrast to the hubbub out front, Billy and his henchman, Carl, were in the sombre quietness of the back room... waiting.

Lennox took a sip of the whisky in front of him and looked at his watch. "Let's see what he'll cough up tonight," he drawled in earthy Glaswegian tones. "Nothing like having a copper by the nuts, eh Carl?" He smiled malevolently at the thought. "Pity we can't make some more use of him." Billy checked his watch again. "He's late. You can remind him to be more punctual if you like."

There was a knock on the door. The landlord stuck his head inside. "He's here Billy."

Lennox sniffed disdainfully. "You'd better show him in then."

Back at the Elite Club, Jane and Richard's luck had changed. All the gains they had made from their five free chips had vanished, despite encouragement and advice from the woman by their side. Constable Briggs was on her third white wine. "Look," she remarked almost in annoyance. "We've run out of chips! And I was really enjoying myself."

"Well we've got plenty more if you want to buy some," suggested Maxine.

Jane turned to Richard. "Oh come on Rich. Our luck's bound to return soon." She gave him the sort of look that would loosen any man's wallet. Jane leant forward seductively and whispered in his ear – but it was no sweet nothing. "I'm fine," is all she said.

Richard played along and took a £20 note from his wallet, making sure the croupier saw he still had plenty left. A look passed between the croupier and the woman next to Jane, a look that was spotted by those other eyes, the owner of which now made his way to the gents where a radio call was made. He then returned to Jane and Richard's roulette table and walked up to

Maxine. He produced his Manchester Police ID. "Step away from the table please," he ordered.

Maxine nervously did as she was told and the man positioned himself between her and the wheel, with its secret ball-blocking pins and magnets.

Suddenly a booming voice rang out from near the entrance. "Everyone stay where they are." The doors opened and 20 officers from Manchester CID swarmed in. But their entrance was met with resistance, a nasty skirmish breaking out close to Richard and Jane's table. Fists flew and one of the bouncers pinned Jane against a slot machine. Richard didn't think twice, grabbing the man and forcing him to the floor as other officers joined in to help him.

Richard shepherded a dazed Jane to the entrance, where he spotted Trudie. "Look after Jane, sarge, will you?" he yelled before re-entering the fray.

Meanwhile, at The Quarryman's Arms, the landlord made way for an agitated-looking Steve Milner to enter the smoke-filled back room, closing the door behind him.

"Nice to see you again Steve," Billy said. "Come and make yourself comfortable. I brought Carl here along for company. You don't mind, do you?" Steve said nothing and sat down.

Lennox ruminated for a moment. "Carl and I were just saying it's a real shame about the farming project. Mind you, it was good while it lasted." His reasonable manner was that of a criminal boss who is about to threaten someone. "The thing is, Steve, like I told you the last time, before those two farmers stuck their noses in, you're not a lot of use to me now."

His expression was hardening, any hint of pleasantries now gone. "So, now it's just down to paying your debt." He cocked his head slightly. "I think we said £300 today... plus £50 interest." He glanced at Carl. "Isn't that right Carl?" The heavy nodded, a man of few words.

Lennox extended his hand, palm up, and stared coldly at Milner. The latter was slow to respond. Billy glanced again at Carl. "Didn't you tell me what a nice home Stevie has, Carl? Pity about his greenhouse. It would be a real shame if there were more *accidents* there and anyone got hurt." Lennox pulled his hand back; his jaw clenched. "Have you no brought anythin' with yer Stevie?"

It could not have sounded more intimidating but Milner was determined to make this as prolonged for Lennox as he could. Eventually he put his hand into his jacket pocket and extracted a bundle of banknotes.

Billy cracked a smile and nudged his heavy. "You see, Carl? I was right about Detective Sergeant Milner here. He's a man of integrity." He looked at Steve and grinned. "But I'm still going to check it."

He took the bundle and proceeded to count the notes out on the table. He was about halfway through when the door flew open. Lennox erupted. "What the hell....!" It was the landlord, shaking his head like a madman, but he couldn't get a word out before he was barged unceremoniously out of the way by Milner's boss, who stopped a few feet short and raised his warrant card. Carl stood up poised for action.

"William Lennox!" announced Webster. "I'm arresting you on the charge of aiding and abetting the theft of farm property, extortion, blackmail, intimidation and operating a casino in a manner contrary to rules of the Betting, Gaming and Lotteries Act. Anything you say now may later be used in court against you."

He moved straight on. "Detective Sergeant Stephen Milner, I'm arresting you on the charge of conspiracy to aid and abet the committing of the aforementioned farm thefts."

Milner was first to react. He looked shell-shocked. "But it's not what it looks like sir!" he bleated.

"Just get him out of here!" demanded Webster, who looked thoroughly disgusted. Bowers and Fielding had now joined him. They grabbed Milner, handcuffed him and bundled him out through the door.

Webster stood alone in front of Lennox and his muscle-bound lackey. "So what's it going to be Billy? Are you and your missing link here going to come quietly or are you going to make my day and put up a struggle."

For a moment Lennox wasn't sure which way to jump but decided to play it cool. "You're Webster, aren't you?"

"Detective Inspector Webster to you."

"Ah well *detective inspector*... charges are one thing..." he fixed Neil with a stare.... "but making them stick... now that's quite another isn't it? And *you* havna got enough." He gave a dismissive shrug of the shoulders. "That little transaction you just saw was simply an *amicable* arrangement – and I don't think that sergeant of yours is in a position to say anything different." He sneered at Webster and shook his head. "I'm tellin' yer – you're going to regret this."

What Lennox didn't realise was that he was dealing with someone who'd seen it all before. Neil laughed... as contemptuously as he could. "Well Billy. If I didn't know better, that sounded to me like you were threatening a police officer."

Lennox turned to his sidekick. "Did *you* hear anything Carl?"

Carl shook his head. "No boss."

Webster looked at Lennox enquiringly. "Can he do *yes boss* as well?" Carl looked irritated, but Neil continued. "Trust me, Billy. I've put away low-lifes that make you look like Andy Pandy." He could see Lennox was rising to the bait. "And d'you know what?" he continued. "The lads in Glasgow were right – you really aren't the sharpest tool in the bag, are you?"

He gave Lennox a second to wonder what was coming before dropping his little bombshell. He was right in Billy's face now.

"You see, if you didn't want us getting our hands on incriminating material about your extortion rackets, best not to have kept it at your casino." He checked his watch. "The raid took place about half an hour ago."

Neil got the reaction he wanted. Lennox jumped up and fired a volley of expletives before coming out from behind the table along with Carl. "Get out of my way!" he growled.

Webster stood his ground.

"Okay Carl," ordered Lennox.

With that command, Carl launched into Webster. Big mistake. Before he knew it, five of Derbyshire Constabulary's finest, who'd left their table in the corner of the main bar, piled in and soon had the pair of them subdued and in handcuffs. Neil stood back and wiped a smear of blood from his mouth with the back of his hand.

He looked at the much worse damage on the faces of Billy and Carl. "Huh! You were more stupid than even *I* thought. Assaulting a police officer, eh? That'll go nicely with the signed statements I've got from blackmail witnesses and rat's abandoning your sinking ship. Trust me Billy – you are *so* sunk!"

The disdainful look on Neil's face said it all. "Take them away!"

❋❋❋❋❋

CHAPTER TWENTY ONE

Neil had returned home late that night so it wasn't until they got up on Saturday morning that Anne noticed the mark on her husband's face. It felt like deja vu – and she was not impressed. "I hope it was worth it?" she remarked icily. Memories of what had happened to him in Manchester were not *that* distant. "And how's that going to look at Sunday dinner?"

She was right – by Sunday lunchtime the bruise was coming out and prompted a comment from Paul the moment he and Charlotte walked through the door.

"I see Mum's still got a good right hook then Dad?" he quipped among the pleasantries.

"Yesss," replied his mother darkly.

"Oooh!" winced Charlotte when she saw it.

"Don't worry," replied Neil. "It's not as bad as it looks." Anne didn't want to linger on the subject a moment longer so it helped when Paul proffered a bottle of wine he'd brought with him. That did take her by surprise.

"That's very nice of you."

"Actually it was Charlotte's idea," he confessed.

His mother was so tempted to ask if it was a special occasion but she restrained herself and restricted it to: "Thank you."

"Shall we have it with dinner, Mum?" pressed Paul.

Neil answered on her behalf. "Absolutely. We can celebrate seeing Charlotte again. I'll do the honours." He took the bottle and headed into the kitchen.

The atmosphere over dinner was excellent. The kids were bubbling away, Anne was happy but not yet entirely sure why, and Neil was starting to feel the satisfaction of having wiped up Billy Lennox. It was slightly tempered by not knowing the fate that awaited Steve Milner and possibly himself – but he wasn't going to let that detract from this thoroughly pleasant afternoon.

After the dishes had been cleared away they adjourned to the sitting room for coffee, where Anne wasted no time in moving the conversation along. "Erm... when you rang, Paul... didn't you say there was something you wanted to tell us?"

Paul smiled. "Oh that. Yes. It was just to say that Charlotte and I were thinking of going to London for a few days."

"London? That sounds nice." She couldn't hide the fact that she was underwhelmed.

Paul continued his tease. "What did you think I was going to say, Mum? That we were going to get engaged or something?" He glanced at Charlotte, then back at his parents. "Well... we are."

Anne grabbed a nearby cushion and threw it at him in a mixture of annoyance and delight. "You... you...!" She couldn't actually think of *what* to call him. Paul loved it. "Oh that wasn't fair!" she protested.

"I'm sorry Mum, but we just wanted it to be a surprise."

Anne gave a huge sigh. "Well it was certainly that!"

It *was* a surprise to her, of course, but not to Neil, who sensibly kept his mouth shut, rose to his feet and went across to Paul who was sitting next to Charlotte on the sofa. He held his hand out. "Congratulations son." His hand duly shaken. Neil turned to Charlotte. "Come here." She got to her feet and he gave her a quick hug. "I hope you know what you're doing?"

"Oh I do, Mr Webster," came the sincere reply.

Paul stood up. "Come on Mum – forgiven?" Anne sighed

again. "I suppose so." It sounded grudging but the smile on her face gave away just how delighted she really was. It was *their* turn to hug. Anne then turned to Charlotte and they did likewise.

When Monday morning came around, the atmosphere at the station was surreal – almost an anticlimax after all the action of Friday night. Was this *really* Buxton? Everyone reported for duty with the exception of Detective Sergeant Milner. His whereabouts was not being disclosed.

An edict had been issued by DI Webster that, without exception, all officers were to be on parade at ten o'clock in the canteen. He'd left the front desk in the hands of one of the office staff so the meeting had to be lightning quick – just long enough for a tea or coffee!

"Okay everyone," he began. "I just wanted to say a big thank you for the hard work you've done to bring the farm thefts case to a satisfactory conclusion and particularly for your commitment in Friday night's joint operation in Manchester and Glossop. It was a top job. And we also owe a big thank you to a contingent from... let me see... Chapel-en-le-Frith, Hayfield, New Mills and Glossop itself." He turned to Trudie. "Have I got that right, Sergeant Barker?"

"And Whaley Bridge, sir."

"Oh yes... and Whaley Bridge. Anyway, they did us proud. Our appreciation will be shown accordingly – namely with an invitation to come here and sample some more of Mary's toad in th' ole." That brought a round of approval.

"What happened to you then, sir?" enquired Bob, referring to Webster's face.

"Oh that... well the wife wasn't happy with me being back so late." That did raise a laugh. "And that's it. Now get back to your duties the lot of you and nick someone for parking their car where they shouldn't have."

With that, they all drained their cups and headed off to their respective posts; all except Constable Briggs, who asked Richard Lowe to stay behind for a minute. She seemed rather subdued, well for Jane anyway, and he noticed. "You all right?"

"Yes, I'm fine. I just wanted to thank you for looking out for me on Friday. I was a bit woozy and I wasn't sure what happened."

"I'm not surprised you were woozy – you took a right bang from that idiot."

"I mean it Rich. You could easily have got a thumping yourself."

"Well I didn't, did I? But thanks anyway. Shall we go?"

Jane wasn't finished. "Do you fancy going for a coffee some time?" Her words came so out of the blue it took Constable Lowe a second or two to grasp what he'd just heard.

"What... me and you?"

"Yes... *me and you.*"

Because it was quiet in the station for once, DI Webster saw an opportunity to deal with a little unfinished business, and the afternoon saw him heading in his car on to the tops again. He was getting even more adept at avoiding the ruts on John Mellor's farm track, although his mission this time was very different from the one when they'd first met. As he pulled the car into the yard it didn't take long for Tegg to make an appearance. He followed Neil up to the kitchen door, tail wagging away.

After a couple of knocks, Mrs Mellor pulled the door open. She was clearly surprised when she saw who it was. "Oh...hello!"

"Sorry to call unannounced, Mrs Mellor. I just wondered if John was about?"

"You're lucky – he's not long since returned from Bakewell Market. Bought a couple of new'uns." She noticed the blank look on Neil's face. "Bullocks."

He couldn't help but laugh. He was at the Mellors wasn't he.

"Oh, right."

Once inside, Jean gave her husband a shout and it wasn't long before he appeared. He too was surprised to see Neil. "Ay up! Not in trouble again am I?"

"No – you're perfectly safe today John. Anyway, how are you?"

"Fair to middlin'."

"Jean tells me you've been out shopping."

"Oh aye. I've just put 'em away. They're all right." He was clearly happy with his morning's work and he was even happier – well as much as he ever was – when Neil told him they'd arrested the man who'd broken into his farm in April. The news warranted a cup of tea and, as they sat there that afternoon, chatting away, with Tegg at John's feet and a couple of new beasts in the byre, Neil started to understand why Mellor had opted for the life he had. The DI would have been very happy to stay longer but he'd got a couple more calls to make so, when he'd finished his cuppa, he got to his feet. John and Jean did likewise. There was, however, one more thing Neil wanted to do before he left.

He'd been holding a small brown parcel all the while he was there and he handed it to John.

"What's this?"

"Well take a look."

The farmer opened it warily and what started as a look of curiosity gradually turned into a smile, something you didn't often see from John. He looked up at Neil as the smile grew bigger.

"What is it John?" asked an inquisitive Jean. He removed the rest of the paper to reveal the cash tin. He opened it slowly and extracted the photo of Beth. He was visibly moved.

Neil decided to help him out. "Our lads at Matlock gathered it in a search they carried out that way." He was purposely vague about the location. "It was pure luck that I spotted it at the station when I was down there."

John was very quiet and Jean put her arm through his. He gathered himself and looked at Neil, still clasping the picture in both hands. "Thank you." He gave a big bucolic sniff and turned to his wife. "Happen we'll make a country copper of him yet Jean."

It was just after five o'clock when Neil pulled into the car park at the Old Grouse Inn, yet it was clear that some "early doors" customers had already arrived. One or two were even sitting on the outside picnic tables that had looked so forlorn the first time he'd visited. Once inside, he made his way to the bar.

"Hello Sandra," he said as he approached.

She looked up, then glanced at the clock. "Off duty are you, Mr Webster?"

"No... not yet I'm afraid. I just wondered if I could have a word with you and Jim. It won't take long."

"Yes, of course. He's round the back. Hang on." Neil smiled to himself. Jim did seem to spend a lot of time "round the back". Anyway, she soon flushed him out.

"All right, Jim?' enquired Neil.

"Oh, not bad," he replied while he finished dusting his hands off from whatever he'd been doing.

Neil checked to make sure there was no one else within earshot. "I just wanted to let you know that Billy Lennox won't be darkening your doors again any time soon."

"Have you got him then?" asked Sandra enthusiastically.

"Yep. I think he'll be taking his ablutions in Strangeways in the future and not in that stream over the road."

"Fantastic!" Jim cried.

Sandra glanced in her husband's direction then back at Neil. "What about Milner?' she asked bluntly.

Webster knew this would be coming and thought for a second or two before he gave his answer. "Well it's up to you how you take this, but the whole thing, including that statement you gave about witnessing the blackmail threats, has had a profound effect on him. Trust me – he's a changed and chastened man."

"And so he should be!" said Jim coldly, "the way he treated us!"

Sandra hadn't finished on the matter either. "We didn't do it for *him*, you know, we felt sorry for his wife and wanted to help you get that horrible Scottish bloke."

"Well one way or another we've ended up with a good result," said Neil. "I just wanted to thank you."

A customer approached the bar and, as Neil had said all he wanted to, it was a good time to finish. He thanked them again and went on his way.

His final appointment of the day, if you could call it that, was back in Buxton with Trudie over a drink after work. It was still only about 5.30pm and the pub where they were meeting had plenty of spare tables. She was already there and just about to sit down when he arrived. He walked over.

"Ah... there you are. Thanks for coming."

"That's okay."

"Right then, what can I get you?"

"Oh, I think I'll have a cider please."

"Coming up – and I am personally going to murder a pint."

He soon returned, placing their drinks on the table before sitting down and lifting his glass. "Cheers Sergeant Barker!"

Trudie lifted hers. "Yes... cheers sir."

Neil took several swigs before he put his glass down. "My, I was ready for that. Even though I say it myself, I think we've earned this." He glanced briefly around to make sure they couldn't be overheard. "Actually, I wanted to have a chat, away from interruptions at the station – just to take stock of things really."

"That's fine sir, although I have got a tennis match a bit later."

Neil gave her a mischievous look. "Are things going well on court?"

"Oh, you're as bad as Bob and Richard," she tutted. "But in answer to your question, yes... pretty good actually. It works well because neither of us have what you would call nine-to-five jobs and we see each other when we can. There's no pressure."

They both took further sips of their drinks. It was like a dividing line between topics and Neil was soon on to the next one. "Well, we've got the post-mortem results to look forward to next week, haven't we?"

"Of course," said Trudie. "Now *that* should be interesting."

"Actually, Andrew Pritchard gave me a call the other day."

Trudie's ears pricked up. "Oh yes?"

"It seems that during the search up on the moors, one of the dogs unearthed a small bottle, not far from the body. The sort they use for tablets at a chemist – and there were some bits still in it, which they sent off for analysis."

"And?"

"They were barbiturates – sleeping pills."

Trudie leant back in her seat. "So it *was* suicide then."

Webster tilted his head in thought. "Well it would certainly explain how she managed to get to where she did – somewhere off the beaten track she'd visited in better times... but also somewhere she could secretly end it all. With everything going on with that sister of hers, her husband and Celia Knowles – you could easily make the case."

"Anyone else going with you to the PM?"

Neil looked unsure. "I'll have to think about it. I don't want any of the family involved until we're certain it *is* Barbara Butler." He considered the issue for another second or two. "D'you know, it might be an opportune moment to get Steve Milner back in. I've got to do it some time. After all, he has been involved with the case more than anyone else." Neil took another sip of his pint. "Bet it's given them something to think about at Division – a detective sergeant, already on their radar, who gets himself arrested in the takedown of a known Manchester villain."

"Personally, I think they'll hold their noses and swallow the undercover story sir," replied Trudie. She leant forward. "After all, it was partly true and any accusations Billy Lennox might make could be interpreted as the desperation of a drowning man. Heaven knows, there's enough evidence against him."

Neil liked the sound of that. "I couldn't have put it better myself, sergeant. Hey! When I get the call to account for all this, I think I'll just send you instead."

"Not likely!"

They drank up and headed for the door. Outside on the pavement, Neil had one last word.

"You do, of course, realise that if Steve Milner 'retires early', which I somehow think he will, we'd be looking for a new detective sergeant?" That brought an interesting look to Trudie's face.

And so the day arrived for the Barbara Butler post-mortem results. DI Webster stuck with his idea of including Steve Milner and called at his house on the way to Chesterfield. Janet waved her husband off from the door with a smile. How much she knew about everything, Neil wasn't sure, but he took it as a positive sign when she waved to him too while he was waiting in the car.

It was the perfect day for a trip to the mortuary, dull and drizzly, with low cloud shrouding the tops as they made their way literally uphill and down dale. Conversation between the two was sparse, almost as though everything that could be said, already had been. They hadn't heard a peep out of Division. Perhaps no news was good news, Neil surmised.

Andrew Pritchard received them in the special examination

room at the hospital, where the remains of the body were laid out. His greeting was friendly but brief. "Detective Inspector Webster... Detective Sergeant Milner. Let's get straight down to it, shall we?"

Without waiting for a response, the pathologist turned and headed for the table on which the remains lay. The officers, now sporting the obligatory white coats, followed, looking on as Pritchard began his summary.

"The first thing I will say is that the examination and analysis of these remains and the surroundings in which they were found has been extremely challenging."

"I can imagine," replied Neil as he pictured the inhospitable terrain up on Kinder Scout.

"Anyway, my conclusions are in two parts. First: cause of death." He turned to cast his eye over the remains. "I've examined the skeleton thoroughly and any unusual marks *that* I have found only suggest passive injury, probably from pulling or gnawing, most likely by foxes but certainly not violent enough to kill anyone. Any evidence of non-skeletal injury, perhaps from strangulation, asphyxiation etc, is of course long gone."

Neil realised Pritchard had to go through this stuff even though he'd already been tipped off by him as to what the probable cause of death was. Milner, however, was hanging on his every word. The pathologist moved over to another smaller table where he picked up a glass jar which contained a pharmaceutical bottle.

"Our answer, I think, is in here." He tapped the jar. "*Phenobarbital*, more commonly known as *Nembutal*."

Milner turned to Webster. "Sleeping pills then sir?"

But it was Pritchard who answered. "Yes, detective sergeant – and if taken in quantity, more than enough to dispatch someone... and I don't mean just to the land of nod!"

To all three men, suicide had always seemed to be the most

likely cause of death, the only *feasible* one really, and now they had their evidence. Both officers immediately pictured more interviews ahead with Barbara's sister Alison, Malcolm Butler and Celia Knowles. The pathologist moved on.

"And so to the identification of the body."

Andrew Pritchard was in his element now and Webster could so easily imagine him in front of a class of rapt students studying for their pathology exams. There was sometimes an element of drama during such revelations but this post-mortem now appeared to be heading just one way. The pathologist wasted no time.

"Due to its degraded condition, the main skeleton provides few clues as to its owner. Therefore, I sought my answers in the dental records... and they were absolutely conclusive." The sighs of relief from Webster and Milner were almost audible. Pritchard continued.

"Quite simply... this is *not* Barbara Butler!"

There was stunned silence in the room... verging on disbelief. Neil eventually found his voice.

"Well if it isn't her Andrew ......who the hell is it?"

CHAPTER TWENTY TWO

As the following week unfolded the atmosphere in the station was difficult to define. The excitement of the casino raid and the wrapping up of the farm thefts had taken everyone involved to a high they'd never experienced before at Buxton, but it was counterbalanced by the non-resolution of the Barbara Butler investigation. Neil had been in the job long enough to accept such disappointments – the nature of the beast as it were – but this one felt particularly untidy. It didn't help that the press were having a field day now that they'd got hold of the pathologist's report. As he sat in his office with not one but two newspapers on the desk in front of him, Webster winced as he saw their respective headlines.

The Gazette

THE BODY ON KINDER

Police Investigation Draws A Blank

The Post

NO ANSWERS TO THE MYSTERY ON THE MOOR

While he sat there considering whether to actually read the articles, a knock came at the door.

"Come in."

It was Bob Lomas. "Sorry to trouble you sir. Just to let you know there was a call from Division while you were out earlier."

"What about?"

"They didn't say, but would you give them a ring back please. It was a Mrs Kennedy, Superintendent Jackson's secretary."

Webster gave a perfunctory grunt.

"Well that didn't take them long."

"Trouble?" enquired Bob, having become increasingly aware just how far the DI had stuck his neck out to save Steve Milner.

"Who knows Bob, who knows." His face looked sour as he gestured towards the newspapers on his desk. "Seen those?"

PC Lomas rolled his eyes.

"Yes, I have sir. Pity they don't show as much interest in the good stuff we do, like putting the likes of Billy Lennox away. I just wish I'd been there when you nabbed him. He took some er... *subduing* I understand?"

"Yeah, he put up a terrible fight," replied Webster, looking a picture of innocence. "Our lads had it all on to get him under control." Bob chipped in again. "I heard down the grapevine he's not been able to give a statement yet. Got a bit of an issue with his jaw I understand."

Neil glanced up at Bob sagely.

"Who says there's no such thing as job satisfaction?"

But the grin on the DI's face soon disappeared as he grabbed the two newspapers. "Take those away will you please Bob. It won't be long before nuisances start crawling out of the woodwork with their conspiracy theories when they've read that stuff."

When Lomas had gone, Neil picked up the phone and pressed the button for the switchboard.

"Can you get me Division please – Mrs Kennedy..."

As the day wore on, the DI found himself at a bit of a loose end so he took the opportunity to poke his nose round the door of the CID office. It was a nice change to go in there and not have thick cigarette smoke assaulting the lungs. Andy Bowers had only started smoking under Steve Milner's influence and in the latter's absence appeared to have cut down at least.

"All right lads?" Webster enquired blandly. There was an equally bland "Yes thanks sir," in reply.

"Much happening?"

There clearly wasn't, judging by the difficulty Nick Fielding and Andy Bowers had of coming up with a coherent reply. Fielding scuffled about in some paperwork on his desk, eventually selecting a note of some sort.

"I've had a call from a place called Brampton Hall. It's a small country house a few miles east of here. Apparently it has got stables and pheasants and stuff and they're concerned about some damage to a boundary fence. They're not exactly jumping about but I've arranged to go up there this afternoon and take a look."

"And you Andy?"

"Actually, I'm off down to the Pavilion Gardens in a minute sir."

"Oh yes, fancy an ice cream do you?"

Andy half-smiled at the boss's remark.

"No. It's just some toe-rags have been riding their bikes and scooters over the flowerbeds. Made a right mess apparently. I'm going with Jane in a few minutes. She spoke to the head gardener when she was down there earlier."

Neil nodded in approval.

"Okay then. I'll leave you to it." It really did seem eerily quiet.

His next stop was Trudie's office. As was often the case, she was sitting at her desk beavering away with some paperwork. He popped his head round the door.

"I take it Bob's told you I've been summoned to Division tomorrow afternoon?"

"Yes he has."

"Yeah, I thought he might have. So if you wouldn't mind holding the fort while I'm away?"

Sergeant Barker was well aware what a crucial meeting this was so her reply came without hesitation.

"Of course, sir. I hope it all goes well."

"So do I. It'll certainly be interesting."

She checked that the door was closed. "Actually, before you go – I've had a phone call from Janet Milner."

"Oh yes?"

"It wasn't very long. She was really quite emotional."

"And?"

"She just said 'thank you' and that was pretty much it. I think it was all she could muster."

The pair of them said nothing for a moment. It was Neil who broke the silence.

"Life can get very complicated for some people, Trudie. Take the Barbara Butler case. It was like trying to stick jelly on a fork, almost as if it was playing with us – and I'm annoyed with *myself*."

"Why's that sir?"

"Because it was my call. I could have left it alone but instead I decided to pursue it, and one way or another we've gone all round the houses and ended up with more questions than we started with. Certainly no answers. I'm not sure we ever *will* know who the poor woman is that Andrew Pritchard's got at the mortuary."

"Yes, but if it *had* been Barbara Butler's body up there...?"

"I know... I know..." he replied acceptingly. With that he decided enough was enough on the topic and so did his sergeant, who felt the mood needed brightening.

"Twiddling your thumbs a bit now are you sir?"

"Is it that obvious?"

"Afraid so – in which case why don't you just nip off and twiddle them with Mrs Webster. I think I should be able to *hold the fort* for the rest of the day."

At that moment it wasn't DI and sergeant – it was two friends and, quite simply, he couldn't think of any reason not to do as she suggested. The place was dead.

But Neil didn't go straight home. Instead, he took a detour to one of the residential estates on the outskirts of town. He parked his car on the road outside a very respectable 1930s-style house with a mature garden, its trees and shrubs providing a nice degree of privacy. He walked up to the front door and knocked. There was no answer so he tried again. Still no response. He stood there mulling over what to do and eventually walked around the side of the house where there was a gate leading into the rear garden. Perhaps if he tried the back door? He wasn't too comfortable about the idea but it didn't actually come to that in the end. He spotted the person he wanted at the bottom of the garden, working on the frame of a greenhouse. He headed in that direction and shouted as he got closer.

"Steve!" The figure looked up. Webster kept going and after a double take, a look of recognition appeared on DS Milner's face.

"Oh, hello sir. I wasn't expecting *you*."

"No, I don't suppose you were and I'm sorry to drop in out of the blue. I did knock on the front door but there was no reply."

"No, Janet's out this afternoon."

"Well it's just that I thought I'd let you know I'm going to Division tomorrow."

"To face the music?"

"To be honest, I don't know what I'm going to face – but at least we'll hopefully get some idea of where we all stand." He took a breath. "And that's it really." He cast his eyes around the greenhouse plot and grinned. "You know Steve, you didn't have to take it literally when you were put on *gardening* leave."

"Yes, very good sir. Actually, I really wanted to get on with repairing the damage. It feels like one in the eye for Lennox from me to show him he didn't win." Neil liked that.

"Yours might be a metaphorical 'one in the eye' Steve, but if it makes you feel even better, you'll be pleased to know Billy received quite a few non-metaphorical 'ones in the eye' while resisting arrest." Webster was right – it did make Milner feel better.

"Huh... couldn't have happened to a nicer chap!"

With that Neil left Steve to it, promising to let him know how things went. Twenty minutes later he was walking through his own front door, taking his wife completely by surprise. She looked at him twice to make sure she wasn't seeing things. She wasn't.

"What are *you* doing here?" She glanced at her watch. "It's only half past three!" She looked at him with feigned suspicion. "You are my husband, aren't you?"

"All right... all right. Yes it *is* me and, if you've quite done, *me* would like a hug *and* a kiss." He pretended to look past her. "That is unless I've caught you with your fancy man in the kitchen."

She scoffed.

"Just shut up and come here."

The following morning, DI Webster had a definite spring in his step as he entered the station.

"Hello Bob. Hello Jane. Hello Trudie," he hailed as he passed them at the front desk on the way through to his office.

Bob and Jane looked at one another.

"What was all that about?" asked Bob.

"And he never calls me Jane," added Constable Briggs.

"And quite right too," interjected Trudie. "It doesn't pay for senior officers to be too familiar with junior ones." She carried on with what she was doing. Jane pulled a face but Bob wouldn't leave it alone.

"Well he must have got out of the right side of the bed this morning." He didn't see Trudie's smirk and carried on. "He was as miserable as sin yesterday when he heard Division wanted to see him... and it's this afternoon!"

Sergeant Barker finally did stop what she was doing and turned to him.

"Bob – just accept there are some things that you'll never understand." With that she returned to her office leaving PC Lomas looking mystified.

"What was all that about?"

This time it was Jane's turn to lose patience with him.

"Is that the only thing you can say today Bob... 'what's all that about?'" Before he could respond they were interrupted by the arrival of a woman at the front desk.

"It's okay Jane, I'll deal with this," said Bob. "It's time you were off anyway." He turned to the lady as Jane went to get ready for her morning beat.

"Yes madam, what can I do for you?"

"I'd like to see Detective Inspector Webster please if he's available."

"And you are...?"

"My name's Barbara Hastings... Mrs."

"And what is it concerning, Mrs Hastings?"

"The bracelet – the one in the case of that missing woman. I think it's mine." Talk about being stopped in your tracks – Bob thought he'd misheard!

"I'd totally given up ever finding it," she continued, "and then I saw the recent newspaper reports about the case. Your Mr Webster was mentioned, so I thought I'd better come and see him."

Bob had now gathered himself a bit.

"Err right, Mrs Hastings. Well, if you wouldn't mind taking a seat over there, I'll be back in just a minute."

He was straight into Trudie's office.

"A knock might have been nice, Bob," she commented.

"Sorry sarge but I've got a lady here says she thinks Barbara Butler's bracelet is hers!" Trudie's reaction was scepticism personified. She frowned. Bob continued. "She's asked to see the boss."

"Well she's going to see me first. What's her name?"

"Mrs Barbara Hastings." Trudie left her seat.

"Okay Bob – come on."

PC Lomas returned to the counter while Trudie made her way over to the seated lady.

"Mrs Hastings?"

"Yes."

"Hello – I'm Sergeant Barker. If you'd like to follow me we can discuss what you've come about in one of the offices. Detective Inspector Webster's tied up at the moment."

The lady got to her feet and the two of them were soon ensconced in an interview room. Before Trudie could get started, Mrs Hastings opened the handbag she'd been carrying and placed a photo on the desk. She pointed to the picture.

"There – you can see the bracelet on my left wrist," and for the second time in ten minutes she'd stopped a police officer in their tracks. "My husband bought it for me quite a while ago. I really liked it and we had it inscribed. I was a bit stupid really because the clip had gone wonky. I'd meant to get it seen to. Anyway, it wasn't until I got home after a day's walking with friends up in the High Peak one weekend that I noticed it missing."

At that point Trudie felt she needed to stop her. The person in front of her was clearly not a crank.

"If you can just hold on there, Mrs Hastings, I'll check again to see if Detective Inspector Webster is available yet."

She thought for a second. "Actually, would you like a drink while you're waiting? I might be a few minutes."

"Yes... that would be nice thank you. A cup of tea please. Milk and no sugar." Trudie exited the interview room tasking Bob with tea duties on her route to the DI's office.

The conversation in there was quite surreal. They'd been put right on the spot hadn't they. Bluntly, if this lady could prove the bracelet *was* hers and had genuine identification – against all their instincts to the contrary they couldn't think of a good reason why they shouldn't hand it over. On the face of it, Barbara Butler had simply returned to the status she was before the bracelet had ever been found – a missing person, no longer the subject of a possible murder enquiry. Eventually they came to a decision and Trudie rejoined Mrs Hastings in the interview room, giving Bob another little job on her way.

"Sorry to keep you Mrs Hastings – DI Webster will be along in a minute. Was the tea all right?"

"Oh yes, fine thanks."

"Well I'm sure you'll understand, there are some formalities we'll need to go through before we can release the bracelet."

"Yes, of course. You'll want some identification for a start won't you." She opened her handbag and delicately extracted another envelope which she pushed across the table. "That's my passport and marriage certificate. I've also got a copy of this year's council rates demand showing my address. You can also check with the school where I teach if you want. One or two of my colleagues are bound to remember the bracelet."

Feeling as though she was still playing "catch-up" with this woman, Trudie examined the documents carefully. She'd just about finished when the door opened and Neil walked in.

"Mrs Hastings?" he enquired.

"Yes, that's me."

"Hello, I'm Detective Inspector Webster. I understand you've come about the bracelet."

"That's right."

He took note of the items on the table.

"You won't mind if I examine these will you?"

"No, that's why I've brought them."

He went straight to the photo and squinted as he tried to focus on the bracelet.

"Have we got a magnifying glass somewhere Trudie?"

"Yes, I'll fetch it."

He knew she'd have one somewhere. On her return he scrutinised the photograph closely. Eventually he put the glass down and thrummed his fingers on the table.

"It looks very like it but it's hard to be certain."

Mrs Hastings didn't appreciate the scepticism and responded immediately.

"Have you actually got the bracelet here?"

"Yes we have." There was no point in denying it.

"Well if you get it... *now,* and use that magnifying glass again, you'll see the fault on the clasp. It's wobbly. And the final stroke down on the last 'A' in 'BARBARA' is longer than the other one. Not by much, but they don't match. We told the engraver about it and he knocked something off."

Trudie was having difficulty suppressing a smirk so it was an opportune moment for her to leave the room to fetch the bracelet. Hopefully Bob had brought it to the front desk. She just knew it was going to be game, set and match to Mrs Hastings and she was proved right. After some administrative formalities, a receipt was signed and the bracelet went on its way with its rightful and very happy owner.

That morning's turn up for the book certainly had the station buzzing, but Neil had to put that to one side as he refocused his mind on the grilling he expected to get at Division that afternoon. How was he going to spin things concerning the Milner affair to the top brass without insulting their intelligence? As he pondered this, he made his way up to the canteen so he could at least have a decent meal before he went.

"Off down to Matlock are we this afternoon, Mr Webster?" said Mary as the DI waited at the counter for her dish of the day. "The weather's nice."

"Now how did you know I was going there Mary?" he enquired more in hope than expectation. She continued about her business nonchalantly. He did, however, catch a quiet "good luck" from her as he was heading off to his table.

Mary was absolutely right about the weather and it did at least make for a picturesque drive down to Division, but as Neil entered Police HQ in the old spa town, he was unaware of the political machinations that had been going on behind the scenes between two neighbouring forces leading up to the meeting. In the end the Manchester and Salford top brass had managed to "persuade" their equivalents in Matlock to see the bigger picture – one where both forces could jointly bask in the success of bringing to justice one of Manchester's most infamous villains. What Manchester did *not* want was some nasty little scandal out of Buxton raining on their parade. So, in a nutshell, Milner was to be quietly pensioned off and the less said about anything else the better.

There were two other senior officers present alongside Superintendent Jackson at the meeting, one of whom had been instrumental in getting Webster the job at Buxton in the first place. He made a point of taking Neil to one side after proceedings.

"Relieved eh Neil?" was his opening remark.

Neil puffed out his cheeks.

"Yes, I suppose I am really."

"Well I just thought you should know – we're not going to let Buxton nick get away *completely* untouched..." Neil's heart began to sink. Was this the sting in the tail?

Earlier in the day, in those few minutes before the DI had joined Trudie to interview Barbara Hastings, he'd managed to speak to Andrew Pritchard. He'd wanted his advice before releasing the bracelet but he'd also taken the opportunity to arrange a quick drink with him on his way back to Buxton from HQ.

Andrew was lucky enough to live in the pretty little village of Baslow, the route to which took Neil past Chatsworth House. On this peerless evening he slowed right down to marvel at the magnificence of it all – the herds of deer, the Emperor Fountain in full pomp – it could not have been choreographed better. Geographically he was 35 miles or so from the hurly burly of Manchester city centre but at that moment it felt *a million* miles and he liked it – he liked it a lot! But he knew he couldn't dawdle too long – he had an appointment to keep.

In the surrounds of a friendly rural pub, Andrew Pritchard was a different man from the one people were used to seeing in his job as a police pathologist: relaxed, charming and with a mischievous sense of humour. All that said, when they'd gone through the pleasantries and settled down with their drinks, Neil still had the Kinder case on his mind.

"There really ought to be a national record base for missing persons Andrew," he bemoaned. "Information that police forces across the whole country can access. All *we've* got is details relating to Derbyshire."

Pritchard was happy to indulge Neil, at least for a few minutes.

"Well that might not actually suit everyone," he responded. "Some people just plain don't want to be found and I think your

Barbara Butler was probably one of them. Okay, we don't know what happened to her but think of the upset it would cause in that tangled web of hers if she suddenly reappeared."

That definitely made Neil think.

"Umm... yes... I see your point."

"Still, science did its job as far as it could," added Pritchard. "And I think we'll see huge advances in the years to come regarding human ID. You never know, eventually it might reveal the identity of our mystery body."

"D'you know what Andrew," responded Neil. I wish I'd never clapped eyes on that bloody bracelet."

His colleague put a friendly hand on his shoulder.

"Well, we always keep learning and unlikely coincidences are one of the biggest traps of all. Adding two and two together and making five. This case caught us all out. At least you solved one mystery – you reunited the bracelet with its owner. Anyway, come on now, that's enough shop."

The following morning, Neil arrived at the station a little later than usual. Quite simply, having got the trip to Division behind him, he'd decided to take his foot off the pedal – for the moment anyway –and the first manifestation of this was to have a very leisurely breakfast with Anne. He finally exited the house at about ten before taking a stroll to work through the park. He was the boss after all, so why shouldn't he. His relaxed mood was interrupted by a message that had been left on his office desk the previous afternoon. "Please ring Mr Radcliffe" – followed by the number.

Webster shook his head. "I know what *he* wants," and he was absolutely right. Frank took great pleasure in reminding him of the role his information had played in the demise of Billy Lennox – a win-win – co-operation for the greater good etc, etc. Neil found it hard to bear but he let Frank have his moment.

The conversation appeared to be coming to an end, mercifully as far as Neil was concerned, but Radcliffe did have a postscript.

"Oh, by the way, thank Anne for inviting me and Diane for dinner at yours on Sunday!" There was silence from Neil's end but a laugh from the other. "You didn't know that did you?"

After digesting the call, Neil realised it was time to let Trudie know how things had gone at Division, so he arranged two cups of coffee and called her into his office. During the conversation he acknowledged how accurate she'd been that day at the pub when she gave her opinion that it wasn't in the top brass's interests to make a fuss. Perhaps Sergeant Barker had the makings of top brass herself. The first female chief constable perhaps?

"Is that it then sir?" she enquired as they wound things up.

Neil hesitated for a moment.

"Erm, not quite. There is one other thing." He was finding it hard to restrain a smile. "How do you like the sound of *Detective* Sergeant Barker?

Acknowledgments:

A big thank you to friends, family and the team at Spiral Books for helping me bring my first novel to fruition and publication.